JACOB'S
Faith

NEW YORK TIMES AND USA TODAY BESTSELLING AUTHOR
LORA LEIGH

ELLORA'S CAVE
ROMANTICA PUBLISHING

An Ellora's Cave Romantica Publication

www.ellorascave.com

Jacob's Faith

ISBN 1843607484, 9781843607489
ALL RIGHTS RESERVED.
Jacob's Faith Copyright © 2003 Lora Leigh
Cover art by Syneca

Trade paperback Publication 2003

Also by Lora Leigh

❧

Wolf Breeds 3: Aiden's Charity
Wolf Breeds 4: Elizabeth's Wolf

About the Author

ဆာ

Lora Leigh is a wife and mother living in Kentucky. She dreams in bright, vivid images of the characters intent on taking over her writing life, and fights a constant battle to put them on the hard drive of her computer before they can disappear as fast as they appeared.

Lora's family, and her writing life co-exist, if not in harmony, in relative peace with each other. An understanding husband is the key to late nights with difficult scenes, and stubborn characters. His insights into human nature, and the workings of the male psyche provide her hours of laughter, and innumerable romantic ideas that she works tirelessly to put into effect.

Publisher Note: Lora Leigh is currently revising her Legacy series books. The previous versions are no longer for sale; the new versions will be available soon.

Lora Leigh welcomes comments from readers. You can find her website and email address on her author bio page at www.ellorascave.com.

Tell Us What You Think

We appreciate hearing reader opinions about our books. You can email us at Comments@EllorasCave.com.

JACOB'S FAITH

Dedication

Dedicated to my critique group, yeah, you know who you are. You guys ROCK! And to Terri, proofreader second to none. Thank you for all you do.

Prologue
Somewhere in the near future
Experimental Breed Labs, Mexico

ಐ

Jacob exited the small shower attached to his cell, a towel wrapped around his waist as he dried the long strands of his hair with another. The hot shower had eased the strained muscles that came with daily training, but did little to ease the tense premonition that had filled him for the last days.

It throbbed in his gut, and tightened his chest. The chill of warning seemed to infuse his being. He couldn't shake it. It was unusual for his sixth sense to kick in so hard and heavy when not involved with one of the Council's bloody missions. While incarcerated at the Labs, the highly developed ability to sense danger was normally quiet. Now though, it tightened his chest and sent a prickle

of warning escalating up his spine.

The advanced sixth sense was something he kept carefully hidden. The premonitions became stronger each month, the development of once latent talents peeking from the edges of his mind in a way that kept him off balance. It wouldn't do to let his creators know. The advancement of any of their extra senses could well be the final nail in the coffins of the Wolf Breeds. Life was hard enough as a genetic experiment; he would prefer it didn't get any harder.

At the rate they were going they would be disposed of before the year was out anyway. Despite the years of bloody training and cruel conditions, the Breeds still hadn't developed the sense of hatred and bloodthirsty savagery their creators were looking for. Except for their creators. Given a chance, every Breed within the cells would take out the throats of the

Council members and scientists and soldiers who wielded their perverted powers.

A silent, hidden snarl echoed in his mind at the thought of his captors as he entered the main area of his small cell. He stopped the moment he crossed the threshold from the bathroom. His head lifted, nostrils flaring as his gaze went immediately to the furious young woman who sat on the thick mattress in the corner of his cell. A woman that should not be there.

For a moment, desire sharp and sudden flared within him. An instinct to possess that he was hard pressed to keep hidden beneath a shield of unconcern. The animal instincts that fought for supremacy each time he was in her presence were becoming harder to hide as each day went by.

His chest immediately tightened in fury as knowledge seared his brain. The day he had feared would come, had hoped to avoid, was now here. He glanced through the glass partition that separated his cell from his Pack Leader. Wolfe stared back at him, and in his furious eyes, Jacob saw concern and anger as the other man watched him.

Wolfe, the Pack Leader of the small group of Wolf Breeds sent him a silent warning, his look shuttered and brooding. Jacob glanced to his left then, seeing Aiden propped against the far wall of his own cell, his expression stoic, his gray eyes furious. The woman in Jacob's cell was born of the same female that Aiden had been. They were more than just Packmates, they were blood siblings. It was a relationship Aiden took seriously. He carried more than one scar on his back from protecting his sister from the cruelties of the soldiers in the Labs.

Jacob's gaze went back to the woman. Her fists were clenched, and her eyes swam with tears. He inhaled carefully and almost staggered at the scent of her lust. It was hot and sweet, tempting. In his life he had never known such a potent, though faint scent of need. As though her flesh was rioting with it, despite the anger that poured off her body in waves. It swirled about his senses, stroking them, heating his body. The animal within roared out in demand as he fought to still its ravenous call.

He was shocked, confused. The scent had lust surging through his body. Only with extreme control did he keep his cock from coming to instant attention, the effect was so instantaneous. The blood thundered through his veins, pumping a heady message to sensitive nerve endings and primitive desires. His woman. The thought seared his brain. She was his, and despite his fears for her, for the Pack should he openly acknowledge that claim, he could not stem the rising need to do just that.

She was dressed in the regulation cotton shirt and white pants and beneath the shirt her breasts rose and fell harshly, the full mounds swollen and tipped with hard little nipples. His cock twitched beneath the towel, intrigued with the scent of rising need that infused his nostrils. His mouth watered at the sudden thought of tasting her, burying his head between those smooth thighs that his hidden money paid to keep lotioned and silky. He wanted to thrust his tongue down the cleft of her cunt and lap at the moisture, thick and sweet, that he knew he would find there. His tongue literally throbbed with the need.

He shook his head. He knew her too well, knew she was not ready for his desires. Faith was a Packmate, and trained with him regularly. She was a bit immature for her eighteen years of age and filled with anger, but she was pretty enough with her big black eyes, and thick, shoulder length auburn hair. Her body was delicate, small and graceful, with slender bones and a fragile appearance. She was sleek and conditioned, and stronger than she appeared he knew, but he could not stem his fears that she would be easily broken with the hungers that swept through him.

Jacob turned carefully from her, his gaze going to the outside of the steel bars that made up the door and the front portion of the cell. There stood Bainesmith, the scientist in charge of the Labs, her beady little black eyes glittering with satisfaction, her arms crossed over her miniscule breasts as she watched him. Her harsh, Asian features were pulled into an expression of avid pleasure.

He had fucked her often enough that he could see the rising excitement in her fiendish expression. If Faith's lusts weren't so overwhelming, Jacob knew he would smell the stench of the other woman's perversions.

Delia Bainesmith was the most hated of all the scientists who worked the Breed Labs. Her hunger for power would destroy them all, Jacob often thought. She considered the Breeds her own personal death squad, and her fury in their refusal to kill with bloodthirsty abandon would soon see them all dead. And Jacob knew if he wasn't extremely careful, then he and Faith could become the first casualties to fall to her demonic punishments.

He lifted a brow. "Is she here for a reason, Bainesmith?"

The scientist's thin lips quirked in amusement. The Bitch, they called her. Her sadistic pleasures had been known to make their lives hell. They all carried the scars of the whip she applied herself when they displeased her. They had all known the sickening smell of her lust for them. The stench of her depravity.

"She's a gift, Jacob," she told him mockingly. "All prepared for you. I expect you to breed her tonight."

Jacob glanced back at Faith. She didn't seem so willing for breeding, despite the scent from her body. She looked furious, violent. He scratched at his chest absently, noting the greedy hunger in Bainesmith's eyes when he turned back to her.

"Thought I was your personal toy." He gave her the hooded half angry look that he knew turned her on.

He couldn't afford to reveal his needs yet, and he sure as hell didn't want to give the scientist reason to turn on Faith. Manipulating the calculating woman who ruled their lives was hell enough. He knew if he showed any attachment, any preference for Faith, then her life wouldn't be worth living. The thought of the many ways Bainesmith could hurt her terrified him. He couldn't risk her, she was becoming too important to his own survival.

"I've decided to share you a bit." Bainesmith shrugged, but he could see the anger in her eyes. Damn, what the hell had he done to displease her now? "And don't pretend, my savage wolf; I've seen how you watch our little Faith. I'm sure you'll have a wonderful time with her."

He fought to keep his expression clear, only mild amusement reflecting in his eyes. He hadn't been careful enough; it appeared he had somehow revealed his attraction for the younger woman.

"I'm pretty tired, Delia," he sighed, grasping frantically at a means of preventing what he knew would come. "How 'bout tomorrow? She's pretty enough, but your training maneuvers are getting harder every day."

Bainesmith shrugged her thin shoulders, but her eyes gleamed in malicious amusement. "Whenever, Jacob." He worried about that smug little smile that shaped her lips. "I'll just leave her there with you, though. Do as you will."

He narrowed his eyes when she turned away as though unconcerned. The soldiers flanking her smirked but followed in her wake like the trained mongrels they were. The lights were extinguished, leaving only the dim lighting that each cell had for its personal use.

"Someone want to tell me what's going on?" He glanced at Faith, then to the two men on each side of his cell.

Wolfe snorted in disgust, but the look he gave Faith was filled with compassionate fury. "They drugged her."

Jacob's heart thumped hard in his chest.

"Drugged her?" He glanced at her again, watching as she bit her lip, pulled her knees closer to her chest and wrapped her arms around her legs defensively.

Jacob bit off a rough, violent curse. They gave the women they brought to him and the others an aphrodisiac to ensure their arousal and their ability to accommodate the width of a Breed's cock, which was thicker than normal. But never had they dared to bring one so young.

Their sexual training had begun at an early age, as part of their education in defeating whatever enemy they came up against. Faith was the oldest female, but they hadn't begun such lessons with her yet. He had dreaded the day they began. And he feared he was to be the first in a line of lovers for Faith. Fury rose inside him. He would die now before allowing another to touch her. He knew his rage would be like the bloodthirsty beast Bainesmith lusted for if another dared to touch her after he took her as his own.

"What is the point behind this?" he questioned Wolfe furiously. "Why would they begin her training in such a way?"

The Pack leader growled in irritation. His lips lifted, displaying sharp canines as his anger rose as well.

"It's not training, Jacob," he bit out. "Bainesmith is convinced she can force Faith to conceive. That all it will take is the aphrodisiac to force her ovaries to produce, and in turn she believes the minute amount of normal sperm we possess will fertilize it."

Jacob watched Faith's expression as Wolfe spoke. Pure terror glittered in her black eyes as her body shuddered.

"They want me to rape a child and impregnate her?" He laughed mockingly. "What do they think will force me into this?"

The scent of Faith's arousal was thick in his head, and his body responded to it, but he controlled who he fucked, not the malicious doctor whose schemes for grandeur drove her. And he sure as hell wasn't going to give her a child of his to torture.

Wolfe snarled. "The aphrodisiac was potent, Jacob. Would you see her suffer? And it's not as though we both

14

don't know that Faith would have been willing had you approached her."

Faith's face flamed. Jacob shot his Leader a disgruntled look but received only a resigned shrug in return. They were all aware of Faith's fondness for him, she had made no secret over it in the past months as her body matured. She had flirted and teased him openly several times, as she tested his attraction to her. An attraction he would not have acted upon until she was older, and the danger of Bainesmith's fury did not exist.

Fury arced through him. She was a virgin, and despite her flirtatiousness lately, she was shy and timid in her interactions with others. There would be no way to hide his taking of her. No way to protect her modesty. He knew the soldiers, knew Bainesmith, and he knew this night would be used to torment the girl in every way possible.

"I do not want this," she bit out, finally speaking as Jacob watched her in compassion. "I did not want you out of pity, Jacob."

Violence throbbed in her voice, along with the unwanted heat of arousal. Tears sparkled in her eyes, on her lashes. He could see the tormented desires, the ache of emotion in her eyes. He grimaced, fighting the need to howl out in fury. What demon could have spawned something as evil as Bainesmith? God help them all, but he was being forced to destroy Faith's innocence, and her last measure of kindness. She would know nothing but shame and fury from this night after the scientist was finished tormenting her with it.

Jacob glanced at Wolfe again. What was he supposed to do? How was he supposed to protect her now? Wolfe knew his softness for her, knew his worries. What in the hell was he supposed to do?

Wolfe turned from him, shaking his head in resignation as he disappeared into the only private sector of his cell. Jacob turned then to Faith's brother, seeing his fury in the dark swirls of thunderclouds that were his eyes.

"Jacob," Aiden's voice was a hard, warning growl. "You hurt her, and I'll kill you."

Jacob raked his fingers through his hair in frustration.

"Dammit Aiden, do you think I would willingly hurt her?" he asked him angrily. "What would you have me to do?"

Aiden's gaze went to his sister, and in it, Jacob glimpsed a helpless rage, an impotent need to protect that surged through the other man's emotions and his body. Jacob knew the brother's fury because it was similar to the cold, hard core that lodged in his own chest. Faith would suffer for this night with him, and he knew this.

Jacob felt his jaw knot as he fought a particularly vile curse. His hands were nearly trembling with his need to touch her, but his heart ached, shredded at the thoughts of what would come tomorrow.

"I would have you protect her, however you must," he said furiously before turning and disappearing into the private bathroom.

There would be no way to muffle her cries, but at least she would be assured that those who cared for her would not witness the act. They gave her only the appearance of privacy to ease her though, knowing the shame that would fill her come the next morning.

And Wolfe knew how he was feeling. Only hours before, Bainesmith had dragged her own daughter from Wolfe's cell after trying to force him into breeding her. Her own daughter. She was a demon, spawned from hell itself.

Jacob sighed wearily. His cock was thick and hard, engorged from the scent of Faith's arousal as it never had been before with the other women brought to him. But Faith had attracted him for months. He knew her, desired her anyway. She was a part of his Pack, and a part of who he was. He would have eventually taken her. Jacob had known for nearly a year that the time would come when Faith would lie beneath him. He would have preferred to give her the choice, to have allowed her an arousal she could attempt to control. He would have eased her into the mindless needs, not have her thrown into it.

Damn Bainesmith, he cursed silently. How was he to protect the gentleness of this woman through the savagery of the world she had been born into?

"Faith." He moved closer to her, kneeling on the mattress as he stared into the overly bright eyes that watched him with such vulnerability. "I am sorry."

She bit her lip, staring up at him, and Jacob felt his heart clench at the emotion in her gaze. He laid his finger to her lips before she would have spoken, expressing those emotions. She likely believed in love, in happily ever after, despite the reality of her life. He could see the dreams in her eyes, her belief that he would make it come out all right. What was he to do when he could not protect her, could not save her from the misery he knew was coming to her?

"No weakness, Faith," he mouthed, reminding her of the microphones within the cells, and wishing he hadn't had to. He wouldn't speak of the cameras that he knew watched them. She knew. There was no help for it. Even the bathrooms were similarly equipped.

A tear slipped from her eye. He felt her body tremble, felt her inner pain begin, and howled silently in misery.

"Trust me, Faith. Relax, I don't want to hurt you," he told her, his hands moving to her legs, drawing them away from her chest as he helped her to lie back on the mattress.

She was still, almost unyielding as he practically forced her to uncurl her body and lay back. He was furious with Bainesmith, with himself, and with Faith. The scientist for her cruelty, himself for his weakness, and Faith for her belief in him.

She stretched out slowly, tears sliding from the corners of her eyes, dampening her flesh, the dark fire of her hair at her temples. He hated the tears, hated himself because he knew there would be more where those came from.

Jacob lowered himself beside her, burying his mouth at her ear as he pulled her body into his embrace. She was small and delicate, fragile in his arms. His hands caressed her back, her hips as he tried to soothe her past her fears.

He couldn't reassure her. He couldn't show her kindness, or it would be used against her later. Bainesmith enjoyed exploiting their weaknesses. She enjoyed playing them off against each other. He couldn't allow Faith to be a weakness, or else her life would count for nothing.

She shuddered, whimpering as his lips pressed to the delicate skin of her neck. Her body trembled, and he felt the heat of her skin as her arousal grew.

"I'm frightened," she whispered, her voice trembling, thick with her tears. "What have they done to me, Jacob?"

"No need for fear, Faith," he promised her, wanting to growl at the incredible pleasure that the feel of her body brought to his. "Just relax. It will be over soon enough. Trust me in this."

Her breath hitched as she fought to swallow her tears. "I do trust you, Jacob," she promised him.

He turned her head, groaned at the trust and the depth of emotion in her eyes before he covered her lips with his own. Her lashes fluttered against her cheeks as she moaned hungrily. Her lips opened for him, her tongue twining with his immediately. Jacob flinched at the incredible pleasure that washed over him. Her tongue shyly mated with his own, causing the glands at the side of his tongue to pulse, to ache.

He clasped her hip, rolling her to her back as he came over her. His lips closed on her tongue and created a gentle suckling motion as she bucked against him. He speared his tongue into her mouth, encouraging her to do the same. Sweet mercy. He shuddered, his grip tightening on her as his body shook with a sudden lust he couldn't explain. All he knew was that the taste and the touch of her was driving him higher in his need, something no other woman had done in his sexual lifetime.

His hand moved from her hip, desperately loosening the large buttons of her shirt so his hand could cup her breast. It was warm and swollen, the nipple a hard little pinpoint of need against his palm. She cried out his name, trying to muffle the sound against his shoulder as his fingers tweaked the little point. She was fire in his arms, and suddenly his control was desperately weak.

Jacob had never known a time when he could not contain his sexual impulses. It had never mattered before how needy the woman was, how desperately she cried out for him, his control had never been tested. Now, with this small virgin, her body quaking beneath him, Jacob felt his own body trembling.

His lips slid from hers, over the delicate, stubborn chin, along a throat so soft he felt an incredible need to nip at the skin, to mark it. To mark her. His lips paused at the area where neck and shoulder met, and he could no longer contain that need. His canines nipped at her roughly, scratching the skin as she arched violently in his arms, crying out his name again. He covered the wound with his lips, stroked it with his tongue and drew it into his mouth to allow his saliva to ease whatever pain would have occurred.

With the urge to mark her satisfied, he moved to the swollen curves of her breasts. Tipped with light pink, engorged nipples, his hand curved around one pale mound, plumping the flesh further.

"Jacob," her cry was desperate as he lowered his head and covered the hot tip.

She arched to him, aiding him as he jerked the shirt from her, nearly ripping it in his need to uncover her. His hands went to the drawstring of her pants, loosening them, pushing them past her hips, desperate to sink his fingers into the soft flesh of her cunt.

The smell of her was intoxicating. He could feel his blood thundering through his veins, his cock throbbing. Damn her, what was she doing to him?

His tongue laved one nipple as she kicked her pants free of her body, then laved the next as he pushed her legs apart. He could barely breathe for the exquisite pleasure he found in touching her. Her nipples hardened further beneath his tongue, flushing, reddening from the suckling motions of his mouth.

"Easy," he groaned as her hands speared through his hair, her body trying to arch closer.

There was no *easy* with her though. Arousal, both natural and drug induced was pouring through her body. He felt her tremble against him, heard her desperate cries in his ears. Jacob fought the need and rushing desperation of his own instincts. He wanted this time to be one of pleasure for her, not one of rushed release. If he gave her nothing else, he wanted to give her the memory of his desire for her, his need to bring her the greatest pleasure possible.

His hand smoothed over her abdomen, his fingers shook, amazing him, as he drew closer to the bare flesh of her pussy. Breeds had no hair on their genitals, male or female. There was no explanation of this, but as his fingers touched the petal smooth perfection of her cunt, his blood pressure sharply increased. He could feel his blood boiling in his veins, rushing through his body as though he had been drugged as well.

Her juices coated the silken lips like soft warm syrup. His fingers slid through the narrow slit, drawing the wet silk in its wake as his lips slid from breasts to abdomen, moving unerringly to the fragrant heat of her cunt.

"Jacob?" Confused passion filled her voice as he moved, drawing her thighs further apart, determined to taste the liquid perfection of her rising need for him.

"It's okay, Faith." He fought not to pant, to keep his voice even, comforting. "Easy, baby. I just want to taste you. Just taste, Faith."

As he settled between her splayed thighs, he looked into her rounded, dark gaze. She was flying on lust. Her body was pumped with the rising heat of her need and the desperate pleasure assailing her. Needs he was determined to ease soon. Because there was no way in hell he could hold off for long. But first, first he had to taste her.

His head lowered, his tongue swiped through the sweet syrup and he couldn't halt the sound of appreciation that he allowed to rumble against her flesh. Her cunt trembled; he could see the throb of her clit. She tasted sweet, earthy, like the scent of the mountains after a summer rain. And he was desperate for more.

Jacob allowed his lust to rule as he ate at her tender flesh with hungry lips, and a seeking tongue. He slurped at the fountain of her vagina, his tongue spearing into the hot, tight channel as she climaxed violently. Her body shuddered and wept more of the silken fluids into his mouth. The more he consumed of her, the more he needed. She was addictive, hot, and he had been a man starving and unaware of it.

As his tongue drove inside her cunt furiously, sliding and thrusting inside her, the hand holding the sweet nether lips apart from below slid in her slick juices, halting at the velvet opening of her anus. He groaned as he pressed against it. He pushed his tongue harder inside her vagina, and heard her cry as his thumb slid into the tight, hot passage.

There was no control left. Instinct and lust ruled him, and though he fought the incredible depths of his need, the pleasure overcame any thought of gentle considerations. He reared up on his knees. His hands went to her hips, and though he fought for gentleness, he was terrified he was bruising her all the same.

"Turn over," he growled, gripping her hips and flipping her on her stomach. "On your knees." There was no time, no control left.

She came to her knees, crying out in her arousal, begging him now. Her hips pushed closer to him, the firm mounds of her buttocks tightening, releasing, the small entrance of her ass peeking out at him. Below that, the smooth, glistening lips of her sex tempted his most carnal desires.

She was his. The thought seared his brain. His woman and his body, and her complete submission was suddenly paramount. Complete submission. No matter his desires, no matter his needs. His finger went to the small hole. It was well lubricated from the thick fluids of her body. His finger sank in, pushing the syrup into the tight hole, lubricating the area further. He pulled back, jerked a tube of lubricant from a shelf at his side and proceeded to prepare her. He had to master her, dominate her body, then he would take the tight channel below, and plant his seed inside her womb. But first. First, she would know who controlled her lusts.

His movements were jerky, his needs ravenous. It was all he could do to ease the preparation of her body, to stretch the delicate flesh with first one, then two broad fingers. He watched as she took him, the tiny hole stretching, the muscles clenching hotly on him as he thrust in and out of the tight channel.

"Jacob," she cried out in desperation as his cock lodged at the entrance to her ass.

Jacob fought himself now as he looked at the thickness of his cock and the small hole he was preparing to invade. It was possible. He had done it many times before with other women. But not a virgin. Never women unaware of what was coming. She pressed against the thick blunt tip of his erection, her head tossing, her body trembling in his grasp. He fought the need. He fought the desperation clawing at his loins until she backed into him further.

The head of his cock disappeared inside the tiny hole as she screamed out. Pain or pleasure? He couldn't be certain which, and no longer had the control to question it. He pressed further, feeling the hot bite of her muscles closing in on him, milking his cock. He was aware, only fleetingly of a hot jet of thick fluid shooting into the small channel. He wasn't coming.

He knew he wasn't coming, but it happened again, then again, further lubricating the area as he sank in to the hilt.

His body, so much larger than hers, came over her then, blanketing her, his lips went to her neck, unerringly locating the mark he had made earlier. He heard the growl that rumbled in his throat, fought, then gave in to a need so violent it tore him apart.

His mouth opened, his canines piercing her silken skin as she screamed out beneath him, her body arching to him, her pleas shattering him. She was chanting his name now. Begging him. Her cries echoed around him until he felt everything around him explode. The room shook, brilliant light exploded around them as pipes burst exploding with a hiss of steam. The earth rocked as walls crumbled in a cascade of steam, shattering glass and screams.

Chapter One
Six years later

સ

She could feel Jacob watching her. She could always feel him watching her. As long as Faith had memories, she had memories of Jacob and those light blue eyes as they followed her wherever she went. Or they had, until their escape from the Labs. Until he left six years before.

Since his return several weeks ago, he was never far from her though. He hovered over her now, making her feel self-conscious, on edge. She was a Liaison of Pack Security, not an Enforcer. She negotiated peace between the Packs, and carried information from the various informants within the secret Genetics Council members that still existed within America. She wasn't a killer. She wasn't a soldier. Not that she couldn't do her job now. She could do what she had to do. But Jacob's obvious concern that she couldn't do it rankled.

They were Wolf Breeds. Created in a Lab, raised beneath the cold, unfeeling regard of the scientists, doctors and soldiers assigned there. Their DNA had been re-engineered at conception, their sex determined, their strength enhanced, their senses altered. She wondered if even the scientists who created them had known what to expect. She knew the soldiers that hunted them now could have no idea what they were walking into.

Faith watched the soldiers move silently along the mountain face. She held the automatic rifle close. She watched them with narrow-eyed intent, remembering so many more like them. The soldiers at the Labs. Those who held her down as Bainesmith injected her with the drugs that tortured her body, drove her insane with need. The same soldiers who had viciously whipped her brother Aiden weeks before that for halting their attempt to rape her. Soldiers who had in every way made the Pack members' lives hell. They all deserved to die.

For the moment, the soldiers weren't moving in her direction, thankfully. There were two teams, six men in each, scouring the lower point of the mountain. She was reasonably confident they wouldn't find her, but one never knew. She fingered the trigger. They would be so damned easy to take out. She could blow their heads off with one bullet and no one would miss them. They were evil. Black hearted, inhuman, more animal than they claimed she was.

She could feel the adrenaline pumping through her system, the rage and anger filling her. They were there to destroy her, to destroy her Pack, and she was supposed to have mercy. Have mercy to ensure the approval of a government that had secretly backed the horror of the Genetics Labs. Have mercy to ensure her own survival. She was rapidly running out of mercy.

"You okay, Faith?" Jacob's voice was a soft intrusion in the headset she wore.

She breathed in deeply. She fought to still the raging beat of her heart, the hatred that made her want to cover the forest in bullets. Screams resounded in her ears, memories, dark and brutal, threatened to rise up to swamp her.

"Aidan, take her position—"

"Leave off," she hissed into the mic. "I'm in control, Jacob."

Her voice was hard and cold. For a second she imagined the flare of heat and anger her tone would bring to his eyes. Another hard breath. This wasn't the time to allow the anger to take control of her, to let her emotions surge so dangerously.

"Three are breaking off, heading up the mountain," she reported, watching the camouflaged figures closely as they moved through the forest. "Looks like advanced scouts."

They couldn't afford to let them get too far up the mountain. The cabins, though well hidden, were not impossible to find. They were out of Pack territory though, so that made it harder to secure their location, and their safety.

"I have them." Aidan's voice had her lips twisting in anger. Of course, he was closer, but it was the need for violence that spurred her disappointment.

"Let's see if we can't find a way to push them back without a confrontation, or giving ourselves away," Jacob told them quietly. "I don't relish the thought of finding another mountain to hide in. We don't strike unless they break the perimeters of the cabins. Remember that."

The reminder was directed at her, Faith knew, it was also an order to move.

Staying low, she began a slow path parallel to that of the soldiers moving in a canvassing motion through the forest. As though they expected to find one of them hiding behind a tree. Or up a tree, or in a bush. They were morons.

She kept her eyes on them, the rifle ready, her finger on the trigger. She bit her lip, wishing this mission were over, that Wolfe and his mate were safe so she could return home, return to the comforts she had surrounded herself with. They were cold comforts. Replacements for the man who had never returned, but for now, they were all she had.

The mark on her shoulder throbbed in reminder. Jacob's mark. Her blood thundered, her cunt clenched. Faith fought to breathe. She had done that before. When the merciless bastards injected her with their drugs, making her body and her mind betray her. Her pulse thundered, rioted as arousal, stark and all consuming, filled her once again at the memory.

Her breath hitched.

"Faith." His voice was soft, gentle, but she could hear the command beneath the tone. "Fall behind me, Faith."

"I'm fine," she whispered, almost stumbling as the dark memories poured over her.

Was it reality or a dream? How often had she questioned her memories of that evening? Jacob, his voice hard and dark, thick from his need as he touched her. His hands hadn't been rough, yet neither had they been gentle. His mouth had been ravenous, his tongue destructive, sweeping over her cunt, plunging into her vagina.

Then his hands, harder, rougher as he turned her, positioning her before him, preparing her, not for the invasion she had expected, but one more primal, and much more dominate than she had ever expected.

A sound to her right, faint but warning, had her turning in alarm. The heavy male body tackled her. For a moment, Faith didn't know if it was reality or memories that had her falling beneath the heavy weight as hard hands groped at her breasts. She could hear Jacob screaming in her ear, the retort of gunfire, the screams of wounded.

She dropped the rifle, twisting away from the heavy weight as she came to her feet, her dagger falling into her hand from the sheath at her thigh. She grinned as she faced the bastard who aimed his rifle at her face.

Fury, thick and hot surged through her veins as she snarled, giving him a clear view of her healthy canines. She almost terrified herself with her daring as she growled low and threatening. Death didn't frighten her now, not anymore. All the wasted years that stretched ahead of her, deprived of her mate, did though.

"Do it," she whispered. "You die either way."

His finger tightened on the trigger. Faith flinched as a shot broke the sudden silence, and blood sprayed around her. Not her blood. The soldier's blood. She stood still, silent as he fell to her feet, his eyes wide in surprise.

Breathing heavily, she looked up. Jacob stood tall and fierce thirty feet from her. His eyes were narrowed in fury; his face chiseled from cold hard marble as he took in the blood that she knew marred her face and neck. He inhaled deeply, growling with a low, primal sound that echoed in her womb. His light blue eyes glittered in his dark face, his expression so taut it was savage.

She backed up.

"Go." His voice carried a ring of fury, lust, and pain. "We have to get to the cabins. These are Bainesmith's soldiers. I'll deal with you later."

Chapter Two

ဆ

Dr. Delia Bainesmith was dead. That was all that mattered now. The evil she spread with her human DNA re-engineering was over. The cruel, malicious pleasure she found in their pain had been put to an end. And now, with Hope curled on his lap, Wolfe was finally reunited with the mate he had given up six years before.

His second in command and Enforcer of Pack Security, Jacob, turned from them, fighting the alternating joy and envy he felt for his leader. Wolfe had nearly waited too long to claim the woman he had been forced to leave. Now, they would be able to make up for those years they had lost.

Jacob refused to look back at the couple as he left the cabin. Anger and need rode him hard, arousal was a steady beat of blood in his cock to torment and torture him. But it wasn't the woman Wolfe held that kept Jacob's body in a constant state of readiness. It was the one who awaited him outside.

As he closed the door behind him, Faith moved from her position at the end of the house, her black eyes watching him warily as he stalked toward her. She was a Wolf Breed, the slender, compact lines of her body were lightly muscular, her breasts high and firm beneath the black T-shirt she wore with black jeans. Her reddish brown hair was a raggedly cut cap of silk and framed her slender face in a way that gave her a vulnerable, untouchable look.

"They're all right?" she asked as he neared her.

Jacob growled, baring his teeth in warning as she stepped back from him. She was always stepping back, never forward.

"Were they not, you would have known," he bit out, furious with her once again.

"Well, bite me, why don't you," she snapped, her brows lowering in a frown. "It was a reasonable question."

"From a most unreasonable female," he accused her harshly. "Return to the cabin and rest. You have not slept in days and I'm tired of the shadows under your eyes."

The shadows, and the light of fear that haunted her gaze ate into his soul. She was still small, delicate, the sight of her made him tremble in hunger. The thought of how he must have hurt her before made him shudder in fear.

"You rest." Her body came to attention immediately, anger pulsing through her, scenting the air. "Do I tell you how often to sleep?"

He turned to her more fully, fighting the need to reach out to her, to drag her to him.

"Do as I said," he snapped.

"Fuck you, Jake, you go to sleep…"

"Do not worry, the day will come when you will do just that, Faith. Until you can handle it, I suggest you run now and run fast, or you may learn what it feels like to have your mate mount you without your permission." Fury snapped in his body. Her continued defiance roused the beast and made it howl.

He watched her pale. Terror flashed in her eyes a second before she ran. He cursed violently, dragging his hands through his hair as he tamped down the beast that demanded he run her down. He couldn't. He never could. She was his mate, and yet he would be forever denied her touch. His ravenous, grieving howl echoed through the mountains now, as it echoed through his soul.

Damn Bainesmith, the Labs and Faith. For those three reasons he had stayed away from his Pack, and the woman who tempted and tormented him. For two of those reasons he would leave again.

He couldn't trust himself, couldn't trust the lack of control that had raged through his body the first time he had taken her. And he couldn't face her fear of him now. He saw it in her eyes each time he came near her, heard it in her voice when she spoke to him, and he hated it. Hated hearing it, and hated himself for causing it.

He stalked to the jeep awaiting him several feet away. It was already packed and ready to go. Wolfe wouldn't need him any longer. The others could clean up the mess, and Wolfe would have them all packing up and heading out soon. There wasn't much left for him to do. He started the ignition, stared toward the cabin Faith had stayed in and shook his head. Damn, if only she was a little older, a little more experienced. If only they had been born, rather than created, raised rather than trained. If only he could have stayed —

* * * * *

Faith watched the jeep pull out of the cabin yard, her eyes narrowing in anger and pain as Jacob drove away. He wouldn't be back. She knew he wouldn't be. Her mate. The thought was a silent sneer.

She hadn't seen him in six years. Had waited each day with bated breath, thinking that would be the day he would return to claim her. That he would realize he needed her. Realize she needed him.

Her teeth clenched as anger seared her insides, as hot and devastating as the arousal that often plagued her as well. She didn't need him. She ignored the little voice inside her that assured her she did. She could live without him easily. She tamped down the protest from her heart and from her body that she couldn't. She had her vibrators; she had her home, her coffee and her freedom. Who needed a mate? She did of course, sarcastic and mocking, her inner voice jumped to the fore.

She sighed wearily, sadly. It would be time to return home soon. They would get Wolfe and Hope back to the Pack compound outside New Mexico, and then she would return to

New York. Back to her life. Back to her job. Back to her loneliness.

Chapter Three
Six months later

ဆာ

He knew that ass. Jacob watched the woman as she shifted her hips, looked around the bar, then turned back to the bartender. Her short auburn hair was cut close, framing her irregular face and giving her an almost pixie look. She was barely five feet five inches, dressed in soft black jeans, a black leather jacket and hiking boots. And she had the prettiest rear he had ever seen on a woman. She was tempting seduction, hot lust and a warning he didn't need. He groaned silently.

She shifted again. Her buttocks flexed and his dick throbbed. Hell, he didn't need this. It had taken more years than he wanted to remember before he stopped waking in a sweat, the feel of that tight ass gripping his cock, driving him crazy. Hell of a time for a rescue, he had always thought. And here she was, six months after he was forced to walk away from her again, somewhere she shouldn't be, tempting him and the fragile control that kept him away from her. And this was the wrong damned place and the wrong damned time to be tempting his control.

The dirty little South American bar was filled with thieves, cutthroats, mercenaries and whores. He was here to buy information, get laid and get out, in that order. And she walks in. He sighed wearily. His internal trouble barometer was going off the scales, and the six yahoos at the table nearest her looked much too interested in that cute butt to suit him. That was his ass. Didn't matter that he had never finished fucking it, or the tempting little cunt beneath it. He still considered it his if it was anywhere in his vicinity. And what the hell was that man doing with her? She wasn't supposed to be with a man.

Every possessive instinct he possessed roared out in protest. The soft, feral growl that rumbled in his chest was no surprise. It was all he could do to keep it to a soft warning rather than the vicious snarl he wanted to release.

"Jake, what the hell's wrong with you?" His companion, a gunrunner and general badass, hissed from beside him.

"Problems," Jacob grimaced then tossed back the rest of his whisky. "We'll have to fight our way out."

"Why?" Confusion filled Danson's voice.

Jacob glanced at the other man, seeing the calculation in the hazel eyes that watched him. He nodded at Faith.

"See that tight ass?"

There was a moment's silence. Jacob glanced at the other man only long enough to get more pissed than he already was. Danson's quiet, intense perusal of those tempting curves was an insult to Jacob's possessive instincts.

"Nice ass," Danson's voice was too appreciative to suit Jacob.

"That's my ass, Danson, twisting around at that bar. My ass, my woman, and she's about to get herself and me in a hell of a mess."

He stood to his feet, grimacing at the sudden tight fit at the crotch of his jeans. His eyes narrowed as the six bastards ahead of him geared themselves to confront the pretty little ass flexing as the woman looked around the room again. Damned fine ass, he sighed. He was gonna wallop it first chance he got for being so damned stupid as to walk into this bar.

* * * * *

"It's gonna turn into a fight," her friend and adopted Pack mate, Hawke drawled lazily as he leaned back against the bar and watched the small group of men who had been calling out obscenities and impossible suggestions for the past few minutes.

There were six of them, and Faith could smell the rancid scent of unwashed bodies and violent lust. They were men looking for a fight and a woman they could hurt. Evidently, the whores in this place were too damned easy if they actually thought picking on her right now was a good idea. She shifted uncomfortably. She didn't need this. She was here to find Jacob, that was all. Despite the pulse of adrenaline that sped through her veins, she fought for enough common sense not to push the bastards further.

Damn him, she thought, and damn Wolfe for sending her here. She was doing just fine where she was. A nice little apartment, a job she could work at as needed, and no problems. Four years was a long time out of training, and six years out of the Pack was even longer. Her last dismal failure as an Enforcer, after Hope's kidnapping six months ago, should have shown him that. She doubted his decision in this little mission he had given her. Didn't they all have cell phones for a damned reason?

And to top it all off, he sent Hawke with her. Not that Hawke wasn't a damned fine fighter and a hell of a guide when she needed one. But he was a man, and a male Breed at that. Dominating, bossy, particular, and one problem right after the other. Regular human men were hard enough for her to deal with nowadays, but a Breed male was an insult to the independence she had established over the years.

"Faith, I say we come back later," Hawke muttered as the men behind her became a bit more restless. "I don't want to be fightin' for your virtue, hon."

So much for his willingness to fight, she sighed. Any other time he would be pitching head long into the fray. They had been searching for Jacob for two months now, and she was tired of being bruised and bloody from the fights he instigated.

She glanced over her shoulder, restraining the urge to roll her eyes. It wouldn't be her first fight or her last, she was sure. But she definitely wasn't in the mood tonight. She just wanted to find Jacob, give him the information and the message she had, then return home and sleep for a month.

Why she had to go traipsing after his ass, she didn't know. Orders. She was Liaison, she mocked Wolfe's words silently. It was her job. Like Jacob wanted her running around after him. He had shown how important she was to him when he walked away from her, again, six months ago.

"Don't worry about my virtue, Hawke, it's been in doubt for years," she replied mockingly.

She pushed her hand impatiently through her short hair. She wasn't going to think about it, she promised herself. She had more important things to deal with than the memory of her lost virtue or the man who had taken it. Or if it even counted as lost virtue.

She shifted impatiently, her hand falling to the revolver strapped to her thigh, thankful that she had checked it before entering the seedy little bar. If things got out of hand too much, it was there, but she sure as hell didn't want to have to deal with the problems that would come with using it.

"Faith, this could be a bad thing," Hawke drawled lazily. "We draw too much attention and we're screwed. We'll never find your man then. "

"He's not my man," she muttered as she sipped impatiently at her beer. "And he's supposed to be here tonight. He better be, I sure as hell paid enough money for the information." Damned good thing it was Wolfe's money and not hers, she thought. She got testy where her money was involved.

"Uh oh, they're getting up from the table. Gang rape time, baby. We better get the hell out of here," Hawke warned her with a hard edge of amusement. Damn him, he sounded like he was enjoying the thought of the coming fight. Energy pulsed through her own veins, the restless, charged anticipation inside her longing to escalate into the hard driving fury the fight would produce.

"Shit!" She slapped her beer on the bar and turned to leave, furious that male morons were going to foul this up for her. She didn't need another fight. Didn't need the all consuming arousal it produced later. No vibrator, no mate. She would be in hell.

As she turned around, she came face to face with the first of the morons in question. Suddenly, a large area cleared around the bar, the two dozen or so patrons now watching with interest, but little intervention as the six goons faced her.

The biggest, a broad, football player sized behemoth stared down at Faith with lustful, dull brown eyes.

"You readee to play, leetle gurl?" He asked her in halting English.

Faith barely managed to keep from rolling her eyes. Oh yeah, she really wanted to play, her life's ambition was to play with a King Kong wannabe with the brains of a gnat.

"With you?" She arched a slender, auburn brow with curious amusement. "Sorry, babe, but I already have a date tonight." She moved back carefully, aware of the other three men lining along the other side of the bar.

If he didn't understand the words completely, he definitely understood the sneer in her voice. One hand gripped the flesh between his legs as he smiled, displaying the rotten teeth he seemed so proud of.

"I say you play, leettle girl," he grunted in rough English.

"I say you fuck off," she said easily, her body tensing for the fight to come.

"Faith, your manners," Hawke reminded her sarcastically. "Not every women gets such a gentle proposition."

"Manners be damned." She grimaced. *"I'm going to kick Jacob's ass for getting me into this."*

* * * * *

Hawke grinned. He needed her mad. Faith's antipathy was beginning to worry Wolfe and the rest of the Pack. She lived, and that was all. She did her job as required, collected her pay, and the rest of the time she stayed holed up in that kick ass apartment she had managed to con someone out of. She was one of the few Pack members who didn't live within the perimeters Wolfe had set out for them. She was their messenger, informer, and a general spy among spies from what he could figure out. But he liked her. Get her mad enough and she could kick ass with the best of them.

Her training was rusty though, as Wolfe had warned him it would be. He had spent two months getting her back into shape before steering her to Jacob's true location. Not that she seemed too impressed with his efforts to get her back to peak ability. All she did was bitch about her bruises and scratches. Anytime he expected her to light into him over a broken nail. Damned woman, this was what he got for bringing her back to her mate? He controlled his snort. He would be smarter and mate with a much less stubborn female.

Hawke sighed, his attention momentarily diverted as a shadow moved along the end of the bar. His eyes widened, a shiver danced over his spine as his acute sense of smell picked up the animal that had moved closer. Perhaps not an animal, no more than he was himself, Hawke knew, but this was a prime male. His dark brown hair lay thick and heavy along his shoulders, pale blue eyes watched the scene with interest.

He lounged against the bar, clearly determined to be of no help at all despite his obvious link with Faith. And there was a link. The male across the room carried the same scent that Hawke often caught when he came too close to Faith. The smell was dark and elusive, a warning. A mark that Faith belonged to another, to the man making no move at all to save her. Hawke had finally led Faith to her mate, and he had a feeling Jacob wasn't too pleased with his efforts either.

* * * * *

Jacob grimaced as Faith's body tensed for the coming fight, her attention focused on the six men who were determined to rape her. Her body, lean and fit, lightly muscled and honed to peak condition was still small, fragile looking. The male with her was prepared as well, casting Jacob another look, this one filled with a message. Jacob smiled and shook his head, grunting at the fury that washed over the other man's expression.

This new Faith was an enigma. He tilted his head, watching her, seeing irritation and impatience reflecting in her face. The savage pleasure of the coming fight was absent, but it was still something she was looking forward to. She was testing herself, he thought. Pitting some inner anger, a desperate surge of emotion against the bastards who dared to get in her way. It was—arousing—to watch. Her companion on the other hand, seemed more than worried.

Jacob had no intentions of letting Faith get hurt. If it even looked as though she was about to break a nail on the bastards she was fighting, he would rip their throats out. That was his woman. His blood mate. His teeth had marked her skin, her blood had filled his mouth as she screamed out beneath him. That was no small thing. The time in between then and now didn't matter. Whether her scream was of pleasure or pain, was beside the point. Fact was fact. She was his. And as he watched her, he realized he was tired of waiting for her. Tired of needing her. Damn her to hell, it was time to rid her gaze of the fear it held each time she looked at him. If he could keep his control long enough to show her the tenderness he wanted so deeply to give her.

Getting past her fears may prove to be difficult. He had hurt her that night in the Labs, he knew he had. The effects of the drugs they had given her, and the overpowering scent of her lust had driven him past any thought of control. Any thought of tenderness. But he was tired of waiting. He had realized that after he left the Pack again, six months before. He was growing tired of waiting, of hoping she would forgive him and cease to fear him. He had slowly given up. But now, she was here and he would claim what was his. That is, after he got her away from that damned male shadowing her.

Hawke. That was all he went by. The Pack he had been born to was now under Wolfe's control after Wolfe, Aiden and Jacob had destroyed the Labs where they were being held before extermination.

His few conversations with Wolfe assured him that ·Hawke was an able enough fighter, and a hell of a manipulator. As an Enforcer, one of the elite members of the Pack and charged with the security and protection of the growing numbers of Wolf Breeds, Hawke was known for his savagery and loyalty to the Pack.

Jacob sighed. He hoped to hell Hawke wasn't fucking pretty little Faith. He would hate to have to kill the other man, but that tempting bit of woman was his now. She had dared to come looking for him, and now she had found him. He figured it was as good a time as any to finish what had tormented him for six long years. He couldn't forget her, couldn't let her go, and he was damned tired of waking deep in the night, hot and hungry for her.

"Do you need help, Faith darlin'?" he called out, wondering if she was aware he was there.

For a moment, silence filled the room. A sense of waiting as all eyes turned to him.

"You finally decide to show up, asshole?" she asked him, the tense amusement in her voice almost hiding her nervousness.

"Your language has deteriorated, I can see," he told her as he lifted a bottle of whisky from the bar and motioned to the bartender for a glass. "Should I await your pleasure, baby, or help you along here?"

He heard her snort at his choice of words. A defiant sexy sound that made his erection throb in anticipation.

"They're worms. Give me five minutes and I'll be right with you." He almost winced at the thread of excitement that wove through her voice.

That little throb of expectation hadn't been there before she learned he was watching the game displayed before him. She was a woman now, confident; she thought she was in control. That knowledge filled her voice and the loose-limbed, prepared stance of her body. Had he somehow been wrong all these years? Had Faith grown up, had she gotten past that long ago night and the pain he had dealt her?

He poured a double shot of the whisky. He had a feeling he was going to need it. For all the interest he had in the changes that had overtaken her, it was still a battle not to wade in and kill the stupid humans who thought they could mark what was his.

"You stay out of this, gringo," one of the men warned him tightly, his scarred face twisted into a sneer. "This one, she is ours."

The guttural, rough English of the Romeo wannabe had Jacob grimacing. He downed the liquid in his glass, wincing at the burn as it hit his throat.

"Go for it." He waved the glass towards them. "If you can take it."

As though his permission was all that was required, the six attacked. Jacob forgot the glass and tilted the bottle to his mouth as Faith and Hawke met the surge of sweaty, dirty bodies that converged on them. If he didn't dull the rage boiling inside him, then there was no way he would manage to let Faith take care of this little problem herself.

He turned, leaning back against the bar, and watched with narrowed eyes. Growls, human and canine filled the room. Surprised cries of male pain followed, as Faith became an animalistic fighting machine. And Hawke was no slouch. With a mix of Asian fighting techniques, dirty grassroots redneck kicks, and snarling teeth, the two Breeds fought the determined lusts of the South America bullies.

It wasn't a pretty fight. Jacob tipped the bottle to his mouth, his fingers clenched, his body filled with the need to kill as one bastard fought to hold Faith down to a table. A knee to the groin, and the flat of her palm to his nose convinced him otherwise. In surprise, Jacob watched as the two hundred plus pounds of male crumpled to the floor. He lifted his brows in amazement as the man then stayed there. One down, five to go. She'd better hurry, the stink of their lust was making him crazy to jump in and destroy them.

"Bastard. That was a new jacket," Faith cursed as Jacob heard the rend of cloth.

A shattered male scream followed. Angling his head to see better, he grimaced at the white knuckled grip she had on one man's crotch. She twisted. The bastard paled and went to his knees as she released him, crumpling over as he began to vomit disgustingly.

Faith was like a wild woman. She ignored the two men Hawke was fighting off, and faced the two who came at her from each side. Pride filled him as a slender leg kicked out at one. Chest shot. Jacob had a feeling, seeing the power behind that kick, that the ole boy just might not survive that one. He went down hard. Hawke's two followed similar fates. The last one, the largest and the instigator of the attack, began to back away from the two slowly, a dawning horror on his face revealing knowledge he shouldn't have had.

"Demons," he muttered before turning and running.

"Well, hell," Jacob drawled as he stood to his feet and moved purposely for the door. "Let's get the hell out of here before the local soldiers get in on the fun." Not to mention before his cock managed to bust his straining zipper. Watching that ass twitch and bunch was going to kill him.

Chapter Four

ఴ

Jacob pushed Faith out the door of the bar, leaving Danson and Hawke to follow. Inside, it sounded as though the whole place was erupting into a fight. Nothing surprising, Faith knew. Too much alcohol, too much testosterone. The combination was sure to cause trouble.

"Took you long enough to show up," Faith bit out as he rushed her to the dirty black SUV parked behind the bar.

His arm was wrapped around her waist, holding her close to his larger body as he pulled her to the parking lot. Now wasn't the time for her damned lust to spark and turn on full force, yet she felt it heating, moistening her, preparing her for him.

"Danson, take Faith's buddy with you. I'll call in the morning. Hide deep. I don't have time to bust your asses out of the local lockup," Jacob called back, his voice dark, violent as the hand riding low on her back pushed her faster to the vehicle

"Hey wait, that's my partner," Faith protested as Hawke followed Danson quickly to a matching vehicle. "Damned traitor."

"Get in." He opened the door and pushed her into the dusty seat quickly before moving to the driver's side and jumping in. "We don't have time to argue over it."

Faith snarled. Bossy.

Jacob started the vehicle up and accelerated quickly from the parking lot. They were on the main road, heading out of town when sirens flashing on a disreputable sedan rushed past them.

Breathing out a hard sigh, she glanced over at her reluctant rescuer. Damn him, he was as handsome as he always had been. His shoulders were broad, clothed in a dark T-shirt that conformed to every line of the lean muscles beneath it. His muscular chest tapered to powerful hips and thighs.

His hair was thick and such a dark brown it was nearly black. It framed the hard contours of his features, fell to his shoulders and raked back from his face with careless fingers. In profile, his features were savage, relentless. With high cheekbones, a straight, arrogant nose, and lips that were just shy of full. He had sinfully kissable lips. They made her mouth water.

"What the hell are you doing here?" he finally bit out, dragging her away from her admiration of his male form as he checked the rearview mirror to be certain that the local police weren't turning back. "Were you looking to get raped, Faith?"

He flashed her a brooding look. He looked sulky and sexy all at once. A prime male, irritated and put out, and just a little aroused. Or a lot aroused if the bulge she had glimpsed in those jeans earlier meant anything.

"Looking for you." She leaned back in the seat, crossing her arms over her breasts as he maneuvered through the narrow back streets of the small town. "What the hell are you doing here? You know I've been looking for you for over two months now? Every time I was certain I had found you, you were gone again. And no, Jacob, I wasn't looking to get gang raped, as you should well know."

He shot her a hooded look. Faith decided she didn't care much for that look. The way his eyes glittered from beneath his lowered lashes affected her too much. For a moment, she remembered the Labs, the lust, white hot and violent as the pleasure tore through her body.

She took a deep breath. The mark at her neck, the wound that never healed, throbbed at the remembrance. There was a corresponding pulse in her vagina, and the smooth slide of slick readiness. She didn't need this. She had fought to forget him for six years. To forget the memory of his touch, the hunger and lust that rose like an inferno as his cock pushed deep inside her anal entrance. The memory of the sheer dominance of the act, the incredible sensuality of it, left her shaking in reaction.

"Are you fucking Hawke?" His voice was a rough rumble as he asked the question.

Shock and surprise flared in her at the abrupt question. She felt more than a little insulted at the rough accusation she heard in his voice.

"What business is that of yours?" she bit out. "You have no rights over me, Jacob. Even Wolfe doesn't ask me anything that personal."

"Wolfe hasn't fucked you, so it's no business of his," he bit out. "All I want is an answer."

"Why? And it's not like you've actually fucked me either, Jacob," she reminded him as she wondered if the act they had shared so long ago had actually constituted sex.

"So I know if I need to kill him or not."

Faith blinked, not entirely certain that she had heard him right. Not certain if the throb of violence and arousal in his voice was real or a figment of her imagination. Not that she imagined things often, but surely she couldn't have heard him right.

"Kill him?" she asked for clarification. "For what exactly?"

She watched his hands tighten on the steering wheel, then glanced up to see the muscles at his jaw bunching in anger.

"For fucking you." That was definitely a cold edge of violence in his voice, she decided.

Faith shook her head in amazement.

"You gonna break my vibrators too?" she asked him with false innocence.

Silence filled the vehicle. Arousal, hot and pulsing, wrapped around her. Hers and his. She could feel the heat radiating from him now.

"Do you have a vibrator?" His voice lowered, thickened. Faith narrowed her eyes, watching him carefully.

"Several," she assured him mockingly. "Tucked away nice and safe at home. So let's conclude our business so I can return to them, or I might be forced to fuck Hawke. You know how it is, Jacob, a woman needs her fix."

His lips thinned. Faith turned away from him. She didn't want to look at his lips, didn't want to remember the feel of them. But the flesh between her thighs remembered. Clearly. It pulsed and throbbed and the slide of her moisture already had her panties damp. Damn, she wished she hadn't lost her backpack the week before in that frigging hell hole Hawke had dragged her into the last time. Some stupid broad was likely enjoying her little BOB right now. Life just wasn't fair.

"You didn't answer me," he reminded her.

"I resent the question." Faith shrugged, fighting for nonchalance. "Rephrase it."

His growl was dark and deep. A primitive, savage sound. He was Alpha, and the demand for an answer had just been voiced.

"No, I'm not fucking Hawke," she bit out, resentful that he would make a command. "But it's still none of your business, Jacob."

He shot her a hooded look, his pale eyes glittering with naked lust. Faith felt her body responding with a surge of moisture that pulsed from her cunt, and a hard ache in her nipples. He had never looked at her like that before. Like he was hungry, starved for her, and didn't care if she saw.

Then just as quickly the look was gone. His gaze became shuttered, considering.

"Everything okay with Wolfe and Hope then?" he finally asked her broodingly, turning his eyes back to the road.

"They fuck and they fight, then they fuck some more, from what I hear." She shrugged her shoulders negligently. "I haven't seen either of them since the day he killed Bainesmith. Thanks for sticking around to help clean up the mess, by the way."

He slanted her another of those hot looks that went straight to her loins. The ache between her thighs was a warning, a prelude to the hot lusts that occasionally tortured her body. Rather than deal with the sickening displays of male lust she had encountered so far though, she used the cold comfort of her vibrators. She was going to buy stock in Duracell soon.

Silence filled the vehicle as he navigated the narrow alleys and rough roadways until he turned on a rough path that led into the jungle surrounding the town.

"Where are we going?" she finally asked him impatiently. "I need to get back home as soon as I give you the papers Wolfe sent. I do have a life, as I keep reminding our renowned leader."

"We're going to a house I've borrowed. I'll read Wolfe's papers then." His voice was dark, deep and sexy. Surrounded by the jungle, the sultry heat and the wild sounds of the night, Faith felt an uncomfortable mix of lust and primitive needs. Needs she knew she no longer had the strength to fight.

Within minutes, they pulled into a small clearing, surrounded by a high stone fence. Flipping open the dash he pulled out a remote, flipped a switch and the heavy iron gates swung open.

"Nice little place," she mocked him as he drove into the circle stone driveway and pulled up to a two-story hacienda complete with a wraparound balcony.

"Come on." He opened the door, sliding smoothly from the seat and walking around the vehicle.

Faith followed suit, tucking her hands in the light leather jacket, feeling the press of heat on her skin soaking into her body. Her womb fluttered, her flesh felt sensitized, her breasts swelling beneath the light cotton of her shirt. The reaction was similar to the drugs they had pumped her full of at the Labs. The drugs that raged through her body and lost Jacob to her forever.

She entered the house, staring around at the wide foyer, the curving staircase and large open rooms. The interior was cooler than the air outside, but not much. She shed her jacket as they entered, holding it in front of her uncomfortably as she followed Jacob through the long hallway, then into a spacious, well-lit kitchen.

"Beer?" He pulled two from the modern refrigerator and set it on the counter for her.

Faith picked up the cold can, popped the lid and drank from it gratefully. The beer at the bar had been tepid and bitter. This went down smooth and cool, but did little to stem the heat she felt between her legs.

Holding the beer carefully with one hand, she reached into the inner pocket of her jacket and pulled out the sealed envelope Wolfe had given her months before. It was wrinkled, dusty, but still in fairly good shape. She tossed it on the table and looked at him expectantly as he watched her from the other side of the sink.

"In a hurry?" He arched a brow, his expression mocking.

"I do have a life to return to," she reminded him blandly.

"Not to mention your vibrators," he growled, clearly put out with the thought of her toys.

"Yeah, don't mention my BOBs. I already miss them."

"Bobs?" he asked, frowning, his brows lowering warningly.

"Battery Operated Boyfriends." She smiled tightly. "BOBs."

He grunted. Moving away from the sink, he stalked to the kitchen table as he cast her a brooding look. He pulled out a chair and waved towards it before moving to the other end to take a seat himself. Faith took the offered chair then took another long drink from the beer. The liquid was cool, but more than that, its potency seemed to ease the tight knot of nerves in her chest.

Jacob had always made her nervous. Since she was young, she had looked up to him, idolized him, and then coveted his touch. She had gotten more than she had bargained for in that.

As he tore the envelope open and began reading the letter, Faith finished her beer then laid her head on the table. She was tired. The last two months had left her with little time to sleep as she searched for Jacob. Not that she had slept much before that. And damned if that fight hadn't worn her out. Her body ached all over. Unfortunately all the aches weren't due from the fight.

* * * * *

Jacob looked over at Faith as he read the last page of the letter. He sighed tiredly. He had wondered why Wolfe hadn't just used the damned cell phone to contact him. Now he knew why. Faith. Delicate and as fragile looking as ever.

She had filled out in the past years, her breasts and hips were fuller, her legs more defined and sexy as hell. But she wasn't the girl he had known six years before. The girl he had known would have balked at six goons attempting to rape her. She would not have waded into a fight so eagerly. She was a negotiator, and a damned good one, not a killer.

As Pack Liaison, Faith had coordinated the known Packs, working between the Pack leaders and aiding in bringing peace among them rather than open warfare in some cases, as many of the Packs were eager for bloodshed rather than peace. She was also a courier between Council informants and Wolfe. But Faith wasn't a fighter. Until now.

He wiped his hands over his face with an irritated motion. Damn life, it tried to kick his ass every chance it got, and this time it could be the final blow. What the hell was he supposed to do now? He glanced back at the papers, reading over them once again.

Information I've gathered indicates Faith is in heat, a prelude to the violent sexual frenzy that begins genetic altering in the ovaries. You marked her and as, apparently, she can bear no other touch, it's up to you to breed her. I'm sick of paying the bills on her damned vibrators. Take care of it.

I know from the time I've spent with Hope now, that the mark you left on Faith is the same as the one I left on Hope. She's your mate, bound to you and to your body. We aren't certain how it works yet, or what the mating frenzy means in terms of our Breed, but it's a serious enough condition to be a cause for alarm. Expect a measure of anger, fury. Her mood swings will become wild, and I have no doubt she's as angry over your desertion as Hope was and still is, over mine.

The mark meant much more than we thought it did, six years before. The affects of it are immediate, and remnants of it never entirely leave the system. I'm still gathering information, but in Faith's case, the symptoms appear stronger than they were in Hope's. Faith is becoming impulsive, temperamental and antagonist. This worries me daily, as it seems to grow worse daily.

Caffeine and alcohol appear to make these effects worse, and over stimulate the body. Faith's intake of both is exceedingly high recently. They will make the arousal sharper, the degree of it higher. Trust me, Jacob, you want to limit this as much as possible unless your stamina is equal to that of a rabbit.

It was my intention to steer clear of your relationship with Faith, as you know. I'm more than aware that you feel the mating that occurred in the labs was too close to rape. I've never agreed, but the time to address it never seemed to present itself. I am now forced, as Pack Leader, to address it anyway. Aiden and I are in agreement on this. It is time to make your peace with that night, and with Faith, before she comes to serious harm. I expect a report from you soon.

The letter was much longer, the explanations more in-depth than he was comfortable with, but Jacob clearly understood why his Pack Leader had sent Faith on a fool's mission. Or was it a mission to find a fool? He shook his head in mockery. Could he have been wrong? Was she stronger than she appeared? Able to withstand not just his lifestyle, but also his lusts?

Not the way she looked right now, sleeping like a baby, her head pillowed on her jacket. Part of Wolfe's letter was filled with his worry for her. Her nocturnal habits and lack of sleep. The edge of weariness that lay on her like a cloak, dulling her black eyes, giving her creamy skin a pale appearance. But she was still the most beautiful woman he had ever laid his eyes on. His dick reminded him forcefully just how much a woman she was.

For years he had awakened in a nightly sweat, his cock spurting as he dreamed of being surrounded by the wet heat of her ass, her muscles clenching on him, holding him tight inside her as she took every inch of his cock and backed into him for more. What had always confused Jacob was that it wasn't his cum he was spurting. The fluid was slick, the amount not overly large, but enough to worry him. Unfortunately, there was no explanation for that one in the letter.

He breathed wearily, his eyes falling on the empty beer can as he grimaced. No more alcohol for Faith. The side effects sounded pleasant, though he doubted her system needed the added burden. His cock had twitched in anticipation as he read that part of the letter, but he instantly rejected using such means to control her lusts. The first time he had touched her, taken her, had been due to the potency of the drugs pumping through her system. Next time he took her, he wanted no outside influences, no side affects, and no drugs.

He rose from the table and went to her. Hunching down beside her, he stared into her delicate face. Her lips were parted, damp and tempting. Her auburn lashes lay thick and long on her cheeks. Her high cheekbones and slanted eyes gave her a mysterious, seductive appearance.

"Faith?" He allowed himself the pleasure of gently moving a strand of silken hair from her cheek, letting his finger caress the silk of her skin.

He wondered if she still used the lotion he had started her on when she was barely a teenager. Wolfe had managed to take care of the details of it, but it had been the precious hoard of money Jacob kept hidden that had bought it. Expensive, non-scented, but with enough moisturizers to keep her skin satin smooth.

He had always marveled at the creamy tone of her skin. She wasn't dark skinned as the males of the pack were. She had a perfect peaches and cream complexion, beautiful and so damned seductive she took his breath. Feeling the silken texture now, the warmth and resiliency of her skin made his blood heat at the thought of tasting her, running his lips and tongue over her.

"Faith?" He whispered her name again.

She didn't answer, merely breathed in deeply as though his voice somehow satisfied her.

"Wake up, baby," he whispered. "You make me carry you to bed and I might end up fucking you in your sleep."

She licked her lips and breathed in softly, but didn't wake. He could sense the weariness filling her. She was dead tired. Exhaustion, alcohol and nerves. Jacob shook his head. At least she was too tired for the lusts that Wolfe warned could accompany the alcohol. Evidently, the Felines had been studying the mating anomalies of their Pride while the Wolf Breeds were just fighting for survival.

Damned cats, he growled silently. He had met with their Liaison, Tanner, several years before. A cocky, arrogant feline intent on causing nothing but trouble. His kidnapping of an influential Council member's daughter had nearly caused an international incident. His mating of her had caused trouble for the Feline Pride as well as the Wolf Packs.

Sighing wearily, Jacob rose to his feet then picked her up from the chair. She grumbled a bit, but tucked herself into his chest and sighed again. She was too light, too easy to carry. Wolfe said she had lost weight recently, and it appeared it was weight she could ill afford to lose.

Holding her securely in his arms, he went up the wide staircase and into the bedroom beside his own. The large bed, draped with mosquito netting, was perfectly made in case of company. The servants came in daily and kept everything prepared.

He pulled the light comforter and silk sheets back from the pillows and settled her on the bed. He had intended to let her sleep clothed, to let her undress herself, anything but do what he knew he was going to do.

Jacob had to forcibly still the trembling of his fingers as he finished pulling the shirt from the waistband of her jeans. The small buttons slid easily from their moorings, the soft fabric parting, falling over her stomach, but catching at her breasts as the last button slid free.

The backs of his fingers slid over her skin, flesh as soft as the finest silk with a soft glow of creamy perfection. Lifting her up, he slid the shirt from her body as a muted moan whispered past her lips. She shifted in his arms, causing the hard tips of her nipples to brush against his shirt, burn through to his chest.

He laid her back on the bed, staring down at the full, ripe mounds of her breasts. They were swollen and firm, the nipples peaked and hard. Breathing in carefully, his hands went to her jeans. The snaps slid free easily, the material parting and revealing the tender skin of her abdomen. Taking a deep breath, he moved to her boots and managed to unlace them without tangling the strings too badly. He returned to the jeans then, they slid from her body easily, leaving her clad only in a triangle of damp, peach colored silk. Her legs shifted, and in the dim light he could easily see the plump lips of her cunt, and the moisture that had soaked through the fabric.

Jacob swallowed tightly. He could smell her arousal, just as he had for the last hours. It swelled his cock, made him drunk on his need for her. He knew if he didn't get away from her, if he didn't leave the room, he would touch her. And if he touched her, Jacob knew he would fuck her. Reaching across her, he dragged the comforter over the perfection of her body.

"Damn," he muttered, turning away from her. "Damn it all to hell."

She was worn to the bone and he knew it. So tired that she fell asleep sitting up, her head pillowed on her arms as she tried to rest, and all he could think about was fucking her.

* * * * *

Faith heard his curse, and watched from beneath lowered lashes as he left the room, closing the door softly behind him. A tear slid from the corner of her eye before she managed to blink the others way.

She turned on her side, curling into a ball as she fought the arousal pulsing through her body. She was so hot, she pushed the blanket from her body, and wished for nothing more than an air conditioner, preferably set on the lowest temperature possible.

Damn him. Would it have hurt him to touch her, to have eased the agony that the sight of him created? She sneered at herself. As though she wanted to beg him again, only to have him leave before he could ease the suffering. She had survived without his touch, without his cock for six years now, she would survive the rest of her life without it.

Her hands were still clenched in anger, and the dark, vibrant need still pulsed through her body. Her vagina ached, a physical, almost painful emptiness that haunted her. She needed to get away from Jacob, and get away from him quickly, before she made more of a fool of herself than she already had.

She would leave the next morning, she decided. She had found Jacob and given him whatever Wolfe had sent; now it was time to go.

Faith held back her whimper of longing. She ached now. Her eyes closed tightly as she rolled to her back and stared up at the ceiling. She listened to Jacob in the next room. Drawers closing, a door, the shower. She imagined him stripping, his body hard and muscular, broad and tall. And she knew the sight of his erect cock was more than impressive.

His long, dark brown hair would flow past his shoulders and beneath the spray of the shower would become so dark it would be black. His pale blue eyes would close, the scent of soap and man would mix with the steam, overpowering the senses, making her dazed with the need to taste him.

She whispered his name, a hungry sound that made her chest ache with her need to touch him, to be touched by him. Then the sound of the shower was silent. Long minutes later the door closed and she heard him returning downstairs. She sighed wearily, clenched her teeth and resigned herself to yet another long, sleepless night.

Chapter Five

ॐ

The woman would drive him crazy. There was no doubt about it. Jacob listened to her as she paced the living room floor the next morning, the cell phone headset attached to her ear as she listened to Wolfe. He had known their Pack leader would be calling her, but he hadn't expected the slow anger he saw burning in her.

She was dressed in those damned jeans that she had tried to wash earlier. They were stained with blood. Hers and others, he knew. They were ripped at the knee, but they cupped her ass perfectly. Jacob leaned against the doorframe, watching as she paused in front of the large windows overlooking the side gardens, and listened to Wolfe talk.

Damn, that butt was cute as hell. He couldn't get over it. Nice and round, without sticking out too much. Just a perfect handful. His cock reminded him it was a nice tight fit there, too. He had spent the night tossing and turning, tormented by memories of just how tight.

"That's bullshit!" Jacob winced at the anger in her tone. She wasn't listening to Wolfe anymore. "Dammit, Wolfe, I don't have a week to hang around here and deal with him—"

Jacob lifted a brow as he watched her push her fingers impatiently through her hair. *Deal with him?* A pleasant way to phrase how she could handle his intentions towards her.

"Who cares? I have things going on—"

Things? A unique way of phrasing her affection for her vibrators. He should call Wolfe himself and have the damned things blown to hell for her.

"He's a big boy—" she snarled, and Jacob winced. Damn, she was getting mad.

"Wolfe. No. Wolfe. That's my damned place. Do you have any idea how hard it was to find? To secure at that price? Don't you do it—"

There was definite alarm in her voice now. Jacob could practically feel her sense of fear increasing. Her body tightened with it, her fists clenching at her sides as she fought for control.

She listened for long moments, but Jacob could feel her anger building with each word her Pack Leader spoke.

"I'll leave the Pack, Wolfe."

Jacob frowned at the hardened purpose in her voice, then shock filled him as she continued.

"No. Evidently, you have a problem with the efficiency in which I perform my job. That's fine. I can handle that. But no one, Wolfe, even you, Pack Leader that you are, can tell me when and who to fuck—I'm not arguing it, Wolfe—dirty bastard left me six years ago and you want me to just spread my legs for him," she bit out. "Find him another whore. Better yet, leave him alone, from what I've heard he's good at finding them himself." Her voice rose with each word until it vibrated with rage.

She was angry because he left? Not angry over the night he had taken her, but angry because he had stayed away? It made no sense to him. She should hate him, despise him for the way he took her, for the violence of his lusts, not sound furious because he had left her after hurting her.

Jacob watched her body tremble now, could hear the hurt and pain in her voice and decided enough was enough. When her voice began to thicken with tears, then it was time to step in. Damn Wolfe, after sending Faith to Jacob, he no longer had rights over her. Jacob was her blood mate, her alpha now. Wolfe had no rights over her.

He stalked over to her, surprising her when he jerked the phone from her belt, released the headset and brought the receiver to his ear.

"Fuck off, Wolfe," he bit out.

There was silence over the line.

"Hope thinks she'll hold onto the apartment and the toys, Jacob, rather than give in to you." Wolfe's voice was hard, commanding. "We need the place for another Liaison as well. We don't have time to pamper her feelings."

Jacob frowned. At the moment, he considered nothing more important than pampering her feelings. It was a surprising revelation for him.

"You forget, the pack doesn't own that place. I'll pay the rent for another apartment," he growled, hell he was paying the rent for the one Faith had now. "Take it out of my account, and set it up. But leave her place be. Period."

"I can fight my own battles, Jacob," Faith hissed, her hands propped on her hips, fury radiating through her body. "I don't need your help. Let him put someone else in my place and he'll see just how well I can fight."

"What the fuck is wrong with her?" Confusion filled Wolfe's voice as he heard her furious declaration. "She knows better than to challenge me. I don't understand that woman anymore."

"She can't challenge you, Wolfe, but I can." Jacob kept his voice low, his gaze on Faith as he watched fire glittering in her black eyes. "Let her things alone. You don't have the authority to do this." As Pack Leader, Wolfe's demands were automatically obeyed to a point, but Jacob wasn't about to let him upset Faith like this.

The hierarchy of the Pack was cemented. Wolfe was Alpha of the pack, but Jacob was only a periphery member. He was Alpha Enforcer, the head of all Pack's security, and holding as much authority as Wolfe did himself.

There was another silence. "We could lose her, Jacob." His voice was hard. "I can't afford to lose any of my Pack. Especially a female."

"I'm going to kick your ass, Jacob," Faith raged as he narrowed his eyes, his anger flaring at Wolfe, his impatience rising.

"If you had brains, you'd be a danger to yourself." He then heard Hope's voice in the background. "What does female have to do with this? She's part of the family, Wolfe. Not a damned breeder."

Jacob rolled his eyes. He heard Wolfe growl in exasperation.

"Leave it be, Wolfe," Jacob advised him. "It's not worth the fight. And I won't see Faith upset in this manner. "

"So I need you to fight my battles?" she asked him, furious, her face flushed, her breasts heaving beneath her T-shirt. No bra. Damn her, and her nipples were hard too.

On the other end, Hope was raging as well; evidently unaware of what Wolfe had been doing until the last moment. He wanted to feel sorry for his Pack Leader, but in this case, Wolfe had brought it on himself. Besides, it appeared he had his own furious female to deal with at this point.

"Leave the apartment, Wolfe. Faith can decide for herself what to do with it. And who to fuck, I believe?" He was asking her more than he was Wolfe.

"You're a brave man," Wolfe sighed. "I thought only to make it easier. She seemed pretty angry with you. I thought perhaps if I made it an order—" He could hear Wolfe's shrug in his voice. Then Hope's sarcastic comment behind it. This didn't seem to be the week for mate pleasing. Jacob wondered if it was a mood phase, or some strange PMS.

"Like I need you to tell him that," Faith snorted. "Who went and made you Sir Galahad, asshole? I haven't needed you in six years, and I'll be damned if I need you now. And give me my friggin' phone back." It was jerked out of his hand before he could do more than grunt at her sarcastic comments.

* * * * *

Faith swore she was going to kill Jacob and Wolfe. Damned men. First her Pack leader has the nerve, the unutterable nerve, to order her to fuck Jacob, then he threatens her apartment. Her beautiful, bright home, where all her treasures were stored. Where her vibrators rested on velvet, her coffee grinder ground her coffee beans to perfection, and her refrigerator, the modern dream that it was, reminded her when her stash of beer and cola was getting low. Love his heart, she was going to cut it out.

"Dearest Wolfe?" Her voice was sweet as sugar, but there was murder in her heart. "May I please speak to Hope? Woman stuff, ya know?"

Wolfe hesitated. "Faith, I will leave things as they are for now. There is no sense in angering Hope further."

"Why would I do this to my Pack Leader?" She wanted to sneer but confined the baring of her teeth to Jacob instead as she met his amused gaze. Damned men. Overbearing jackasses.

Wolfe sighed.

"Faith?" Hope's voice was furious.

Faith turned from Jacob, her body shaking with anger, with hurt. She had thought that Wolfe understood all the years she had suffered. Thought he knew the hell she had experienced living without Jacob.

"He ordered me to fuck Jacob, Hope," she growled, keeping her voice low, her pain hidden from everyone but the woman who, during late night phone conversations, had kept her sane in the past months. "Ordered me to let another have my home. Do not let him take my home, Hope." It was all she had that was hers and hers alone. Every inch of it, decorated to suit her taste, lovingly cleaned and cared for by her alone.

"Don't worry, Faith." Hope's voice was trembling in fury as well. "Take care of yourself, and your own needs. I'll take care of my mate." The determined anger in Hope's voice eased the knot of fear that had been steadily growing in Faith since

Wolfe had begun his little private discussion with her. She took a deep, calming breath.

"Thank you," she whispered.

"You're welcome, Faith. I'll talk to you later. I have a mate to deal with at present."

The phone disconnected. Faith stood silently, her back to Jacob, fighting the well of fury and hurt that continued to grow in her.

"Since when did you decide to become my protector?" she asked him, fighting not to scream, to keep her voice calm, even, despite the tremble in it.

She clipped the phone back in its small holder on her belt, then turned to face him, her fists clenched to keep from smacking the bemused expression from his face.

"He was wrong." Jacob shrugged. "I was merely trying to help, Faith."

"I do not need your help." She fought to breathe normally, to still the hard, furious beat of her heart. "I have not needed you in six years, and despite Wolfe's belief to the contrary, I do not need you now."

He crossed his arms over his chest, staring down at her in lofty amusement, his lips curling into that little half smile of superiority that she so hated.

"Your body does," he said with such confidence that she was grinding her teeth together in fury. "But, I don't believe Wolfe has the right to order you to my bed. I want you there because you cannot deny me, not because you are ordered."

Her eyes widened.

"You think I cannot deny you?" She bit out, so furious, so enraged with his patient amusement with her that it was all she could do not to attack him. "You think fucking me is a done deal?"

He chuckled. Bastard. He was laughing at her. "My dearest mate, I have no doubt it is. But it always has been. You're a big girl now, I think you can take me."

Shocked fury filled her system. He stood so tall, so confident before her. As though he knew the ways of all things, supreme in his own knowledge. She wished she could refute his claim, but knew she would choke on such a lie.

"As I remember it, I had no problem taking you before," she reminded him, feeling the need for violence rising strong and steady inside her. "I think your done deal is more like an itch that needs scratched in your case," she sneered. "What, miss out on your weekly piece last night?"

His eyes narrowed on her. The amusement in his expression dropping by several degrees.

"You've developed a smart mouth, Faith, it could get you into trouble," he warned her, his voice low, irritated.

"And you've developed a domineering attitude that could land you on your ass," Faith assured him furiously. "Stay out of my business, Jacob."

Enough of this! Hard-headed damned man, there would be no way to make him see sense, to make him understand that she didn't need him to pave her way with Wolfe. And she didn't need Wolfe ordering her to fuck her mate. Damn him. Damn Jacob. What gave either of them the right to suddenly decide they knew better than her, after six years?

"You are my business," he growled, his voice rife with irritation as he faced her, his own anger growing.

"Am I?" she demanded. "Then why did he order me to fuck you, instead of the other way around? You are the one who left. Remember?"

His face flushed and for a second, just for a second, his gaze flickered. Faith narrowed her eyes, her chest blooming with pain.

"Don't worry, Jacob. You're off the hook. You and Wolfe both can go to hell." She moved to rush from the room to get away from him, and the unbearable pain suddenly radiating inside her.

Jacob stopped her as she went to pass him. He pulled her to him, his hands sliding down her arms in a slow caress. His hands touched her. Faith drew in a hard, shuddering breath as his fingers moved further, dropping to cup her hips, pulling her into his thighs until the hard length of his erection was pressing against her lower back. Heat seared her body, burst through her veins like an explosion of wildfire. She gasped, flinching as her womb contracted hungrily and her clitoris began to throb in need. Dear God, only a touch and she was ready for him to mount her.

She could barely breathe for the physical demands of her body. Could barely stand the agony of suspense, the overriding needs, both emotionally and physically, that ripped through her.

"You feel it," he growled, his hands tightening on her hips. "It can only be denied for so long, Faith. I know. I have fought to run from it for six years; awaiting Wolfe's call, praying daily that you would reach the maturity of your body, and be ready for me. Do you think this was easy for me? Do you think my lusts have not nearly destroyed me?"

"You were with others," she cried out, her hands going to his where they rested on her hips, even as her head fell back on his chest.

His breath was doing wicked things against her neck, sending shivers of pleasure coursing over her body. It was heated, whispering over the mark he had left on her while still a captive within the cursed Labs. She burned in response. So long, she had dreamed of his touch, so long.

"I could not come to you before," he whispered as his lips stroked over the small mark. "I could not trust myself, Faith. I remembered too well the taste of your honey flowing into my mouth as I shoved my tongue inside your tight channel, sucked at your clit and heard your screams of climax, your pleas for more. You were so young. Not ready for the mating our natures demand. Too young to know the violence of my passion. I had to leave, or I would have taken you and harmed you far more than I already had."

Where had he got the idea he had hurt her? She wanted to protest his feelings, but she couldn't for the pleasure suddenly washing over her.

"No." She didn't know if she was protesting that decision, or the hand slipping slowly inside the waistband of her pants as the other eased beneath the loose folds of her shirt.

"Yes." His teeth raked her neck. "I would not have been able to wait. I would not have been able to allow you the time of growing, of learning that you needed. Do you know, do you have any idea the hell I endured trying to stay away, to wait until you were ready for me?"

His voice was strained, ferocious in its hunger. As he spoke, one hand cupped her swollen breast, though the other paused at her lower stomach rather than traveling further to her throbbing cunt. She was on fire. She needed his hand to touch her, stroke her. The lightning arcs of tortured arousal were not unlike the drugs she had been injected with so long ago.

"I didn't ask you to restrain yourself." Her eyes closed as she moaned with her need. She had forgotten how strong the needs could be, how they attacked, stroked and flamed through her system with just the threat of Jacob's touch.

"I would have hurt you, Faith. I had no other choice but to leave." His tongue stroked over the mark.

Faith cried out, her neck bending further to grant him greater access as the hand holding his wrist applied pressure, trying to push it from her abdomen to between her thighs.

"You did have a choice," she whispered, she could barely speak. She was breathing hard, heavy, her body was flaming, sensitized and aching almost painfully.

The anger and fury was dissolving beneath the onslaught of a fury of lust. She was shaking, needing so desperately she didn't know if she would survive the ache.

"God, Faith, you feel so good. You taste so good," he whispered, his own breathing rough, heavy. His chest rose and fell hard beneath her head, his tongue stroking over the small, sensitive scar he had left below her neck. "I want to mark you again. I need to, Faith."

His voice was desperate, so hot and dark she could only melt against him, a prisoner of her body's needs, held by chains of arousal so strong, so hot she could only tremble against him.

She felt the scrape of his teeth, the sharp canines as they rasped over her skin, sending sensual daggers of erotic sensation through her body. She knew what was coming, remembered with perfect clarity the all-consuming, raging lusts that would fill her body. Sharper, more intense than even the needs that tormented her now.

Emotions she had so long denied, swamped her now. Her chest tightened with them, her flesh prickling with enjoyment at his touch. She was weak, too weak to fight him, and her own body.

"No," she whispered her denial of such tormenting sensations even as her neck arched for another scrape of his teeth, and her hand bore down on his to push it closer to her tormented cunt.

His hand slid in further, beneath the edge of her silk panties, glancing over the honey-slick, bare lips of her pussy. She arched on her tiptoes to get closer, feeling the heated rasp of his fingers over her clit.

"More," she whispered.

He growled, breathing hard, fighting the same battle she was for oxygen amid the growing, painful arousal rising between them.

"I'm going to fuck you. I'm going to take you, Faith, and show you all the things I could not before," he promised her heatedly, his fingers sliding through the slick, honey coated slit. "You're so hot," he panted at her ear, nipping at the lobe as she bucked against the pad of his hand. "So hot and sweet you burn me alive."

"It's too much," she cried out, barely able to breathe, her body no longer her own, uncontrolled, riding a crest of pleasure that terrified her.

She could feel her vagina spasming, her juices leaking from her entrance, coating his fingers, soaking her panties. She wanted more. She needed relief for the overwhelming hunger now attacking her body.

His fingers moved further. Faith lost her breath as she felt one circling the entrance to her vagina, spreading the thick cream of her arousal, teasing, taunting her.

"Please—" her whispered entreaty became an agonized gasp of pure sensation as he penetrated the entrance to her burning core.

Jacob groaned at her ear. She felt his finger filling her, pushing inside her, hard and hot. She was trembling, her knees weakening, her breathing loud and rough in the silence of the room. Oh God, it was better than she had ever thought it could be. Hotter, more intense, searing her from the inside out. Oh hell, control. Where was her control?

"Mine," he growled at her ear, his tongue laving the lobe with a slow, sensual sweep. "My woman. My mate."

The words penetrated her dazed senses slowly as his hand moved from her soaking flesh to push at her loose pants.

"No." She shook her head in dazed rejection, denying his claim. If he claimed her now, took her, she knew she would never survive another desertion.

"Yes," he snarled at her ear, ignoring her weak attempts to keep him from lowering the material over her hips.

He was claiming her. Taking her over. Anger surged through her once again. She couldn't allow him to do this. If she let him claim her now, she would never escape the hold he thought he should have on her.

"Stop." Gathering her strength, Faith pushed away from him roughly, fighting not just Jacob and his lust, but herself as well.

Moving jerkily, her flesh protesting loudly at the separation from Jacob's body, Faith quickly put several feet between them, watching him closely. He looked intent, dangerous. Brooding sensuality stamped his features, giving him a dark, erotically dangerous look. That look speared through her womb, causing it to clench almost painfully.

"Faith, you are mine," he breathed in roughly. "You know this—"

"I belong to no one, Jacob." Amazement and anger surged through her. "You cannot just decree this, you and Wolfe, after six years, stinking of other women, and claim your rights as a mate. I will not allow it."

She shook her head, unwilling or perhaps unable to understand his assurance he could just take her.

"You want me as well, Faith. You cannot deny it," he began to advance on her, his body tense, ready to spring.

Breathing hard, Faith watched him warily. If he touched her again, if he drew her to him, she would not be able to resist him further.

"Jacob, I will not be forced into this," she told him furiously. "You cannot order me to your bed, and I will not allow you to try."

Jacob moved closer, his intent to seduce her into giving into him was reflected in the brilliance of his pale blue eyes.

"You want me, Faith, just as much as I want you," he growled. "I have suffered six years waiting for you to mature—"

"Oh, poor Jacob," she snapped out as she backed away from him, ignoring the fuming look on his face. "Why, he's just fucked his way through the world waiting on poor little Faith to grow up. Well, news flash, Big Boy, Faith grew up a long time ago. Without you, or your help."

For a second, astonishment flashed in his eyes.

"Faith, I left for your sake," he argued, irritation cording the muscles of his shoulders.

"For my sake?" she questioned him furiously. "Did I ask you to leave, Jacob?"

"You were too young."

"You don't know that," she bit out. "And how was Wolfe to know that? You and your damned know-it-all attitude. It wasn't up to you to decide if I was ready to have sex. Well, tell you what Jacob. I was ready six years ago. I'm not ready to fuck you now."

That lie was a whopper. She sent up a quick, fervent hope for forgiveness. Some lies were just too damned big not to.

"Your body says differently." He began to advance on her again.

Faith didn't back up from him. She wasn't going to run from him. She wasn't afraid of him, and she would be damned if she would lie beneath him, the stink of old lust still clinging to his body.

"My body does not control me now, Jacob," she fired back. "You do not control me. You had best figure that out now."

Jacob reached out to touch her. Faith smacked his hand away immediately. She couldn't afford the lust firing through her to blaze further. Jacob's lips tilted in a half grin as the lids lowered over his brilliant eyes.

"Will you fight me now?" Amusement laced his voice. "I can take you, Faith. You know I can."

"You can try," she told him softly as she relaxed her muscles, preparing herself for his next move.

"I'll mount you as I take you down, Mate," he promised her. "You won't get away."

"Go for it," she whispered with a smile.

Adrenaline surged through her. Fiery, blazing lust pulsed in her cunt. Her eyes narrowed on him, her body preparing for him.

He wouldn't be ready for her. She knew he wouldn't be. When he moved, it was a smooth flex of muscle, his arm circling around her waist. Faith ducked under the arm, hooking her ankle around his in a lightning move that pushed the foot off balance as she pushed her body into his back and delivered a quick, hard push to the opposite shoulder and moved quickly out of the way.

"Shit." He fell. She knew he would.

Flipping around, she watched as he came to his feet, his eyes narrowing on her, his big body graceful and dangerous as he prepared his retaliation.

"Good move," he complimented her. "I'll remember it."

She tilted her head mockingly in acceptance of the compliment.

"You should have run when you had the chance," he warned her, the soft growl in his voice making her heart rate pick up with excitement. "Because when I get hold of you, Faith, I'm going to make you pay for that little maneuver."

"Rape is a dirty word, Jacob," she jeered. "I told you 'no', and I meant it."

He paused, suddenly seeming uncertain. "You want me, Faith."

"My body is reacting to you," she corrected heatedly. "You are my biological mate, Jacob. Not my lover, not my love or my friend. And I refuse your claim to me. You left, lived your life and gained your experience as you saw fit. I believe it is now my turn to live my life as I see fit. I demand you release me."

Chapter Six

Shock held Jacob immobile. She sounded serious, furious. He shook his head in instant denial. Release her? It had been the one thing he had never considered in all the years they had spent apart. Jacob realized then that he had always hoped she would forgive him for hurting her, it had never occurred to him that she would be angry that he had given her time to get over the violence of the act.

He cringed, even now, as he thought of how rough he had been with her. He had not eased her, had not shown her the warmth he felt for her. He had been unable to. Had they not been rescued, then Bainesmith would have used it to torment her, to hurt her.

"I won't release you, Faith." He shook his head as he met her angry gaze. "I can't release you. I wouldn't know how."

"Why?" She dragged her fingers ruthlessly through her hair, sending the silken strands in every direction. "You don't want me, Jacob. Not really. If you did, you would have come for me."

"I didn't want to hurt you," he bit out. "Is this so hard to understand, Faith? I had no idea you weren't terrified of me. That you didn't want to be left alone. I practically raped you…"

"Oh, for God's sake." Disgust filled her voice, censure lighting her expression. "Do you take me for a fool, Jacob?"

He crossed his arms over his chest, watching the anger building in her as he sensed her arousal rising. He could smell it, just as he had the night before in the jeep. And despite Wolfe's letter, it still confused him that she could want him, desire him, despite his rough treatment of her. But she did, and he would be damned if he would hold back any longer.

It was different when he thought she feared him. Now that he knew she didn't, there wasn't a chance in hell that he would do without her much longer.

"I don't take you for a fool, Faith," he assured her smoothly. "But do not take me for one either. I may have been wrong in my reasons for giving you time to grow, but that doesn't mean I will compound my mistakes by giving you more time. Consider yourself mated, Faith. I won't let you go."

He watched her eyes widen. Saw the surprise that filled her expression. She had actually expected him to somehow release her. He ignored the sharp pain in his chest at that thought. Nature had given her to him. Had taken a creation of man and made it perfect, delicate, soft and gentle, and given it to him for his own. He may not have handled it well starting out, but he would be damned if he would attempt to help her find a way to escape it.

Jacob more than admitted that she could have done better than him. He was a killer, an Enforcer. It was his job to seek out the captive Breeds, rescue them, and destroy the monsters who created them. He had more blood on his soul than he could ever clean away. But the scent of her need, the heat of her body, wiped away the memories of that bloodshed.

"You can't force me, Jacob," she bit out, facing him furiously.

He had never seen her so angry. Had never seen that flush along her cheekbones, the glitter in her eyes, both of fury and of arousal. Her body was tense, primed for battle and for sex, and he was more than willing to give her both. Just not at the same time. He would be damned if he would let his own savage nature take control of him again.

"I will not rape you," he corrected her. "But neither will I let you go. I have a job to complete here before we can return to the Pack. But when we return, Faith, we will return as mates."

Her eyes narrowed. He could see her mind working, the arguments she was trying to come up with.

"And if I do not agree to share your bed?" she asked him, her teeth gritted.

Then he would slowly become a blithering idiot, he groaned silently.

"Can you honestly deny wanting me?" he asked her instead. "And before you speak, let me tell you now, Faith. I can smell your need, the lust that fills your body even now. Will you lie to me, merely to save yourself embarrassment?"

A bitter laugh escaped her. Bitter and angry.

"I never denied wanting to fuck you," she bit out explicitly, causing him to flinch at the description. "That doesn't mean I have to do it."

Jacob frowned. Dealing with this new, aggressive Faith was more difficult than he had first thought it would be. Wolfe's letter hadn't quite gone into enough explanation to prepare him for her.

"This is true. It's not something you have to do." He shrugged. Hell, what did she expect him to say? He wasn't going to order her to do it.

Her lips firmed then, her eyes narrowing further. She still didn't look pleased. He was just trying to find stable footing amid the tempestuousness she was displaying. He couldn't make her share his bed. Though it was an intriguing thought.

"Not something I have to do?" she asked him slowly, propping her hands on her hips as she watched him. "Tell me, Jacob, exactly what will be required of me during this enforced stay with you? Or am I here for you to merely torment?"

"Torment?" Jacob shook his head, confused and finding it more than difficult to follow her reasoning. "Faith, I have no desire to torment you. Did I not just let you dump me on my ass? Did I retaliate? Did I mount you and force you to take me?

Dammit, you're my mate, not my slave. Do whatever the hell you please, but you will stay." His voice slowly rose as his own frustration began to get the best of him.

He advanced on her until they were nearly nose to nose. He had to forcibly restrain himself to keep from touching her, tasting the heat that rolled off her in waves. In all his life, his control had never been tested in such a manner. He could not remember a time when he had been so filled with conflicting desires and needs that his body nearly shuddered from them.

"You are too bossy, Jacob," she yelled back fiercely. "You are arrogant, lordly, and an asshole to boot. I have no desire to be under your thumb for one day, let alone seven."

"Do you prefer my thumb or my body?" he growled back. "Don't push me, Faith. My control has never been at its best where you are concerned, and infuriating me in this manner does not help."

"So it's my fault now?" she argued back, her black eyes bottomless, hot and excited. Damn her, she didn't even bother to hide the fact that his anger was arousing her. "Poor Jacob can't control himself, so it's all Faith's fault. Come on, Jacob, surely you don't expect me to fall for that?"

"Faith, you are pushing me." His voice lowered, the rough rumble that echoed from his chest surprised him. Only during extreme stress or fury did the animalistic growl vibrate in his chest in such a way.

Faith's eyes widened, and damn her, he could literally taste the heat flowing from her core. The smell of her arousal was wrapping him in a bond of lust he was finding hard to deny.

"Jacob, you are pushing me." A slender finger poked into his chest. "This big bad Alpha Enforcer persona is growing tedious."

"Tedious?" he snarled. He was a big bad Alpha Enforcer. Did this now make him tedious? He didn't think so. "I am about to show you, Faith, that I can be very untedious, if you do not get that pretty little finger out of my chest."

She looked down at her finger, then back up at him. A slender auburn brow arched in challenge. Her finger pressed deeper as a daring expression crossed her face.

"What will you do Big Bad Alpha Enforcer? I've already dumped you on your ass once. Are you looking for a repeat performance?" she asked him softly, amusement and calculated female challenge filling her expression.

Before she could react, before he even knew what he had intended, his arms reached for her. She was lightning fast in her attempt to avoid him, to pull another of her little stunts designed to throw him off balance. Before she could get her legs in position he had her arms behind her back, her body sprawling beneath his as he forced her to the couch behind her.

He moved quickly between her thighs, pressing his thick erection against the heated, jeans covered cunt that tempted him past sanity. He stared into her shocked face, seeing the excitement that flared in her eyes, the flush of angry arousal on her cheeks.

"Be very careful, Faith," he whispered warningly as he arched her swollen breasts into his chest, relishing the feel of her hardened nipples. "I remember well how hot and wet your cunt gets, and how tight your ass wraps around my cock. It's your choice, which takes you when the time comes, the man or the beast. Push the beast much further, and you may well learn the conclusion of the act forced upon you in that damned Lab six years ago. Do not, Faith, push my needs for you in this manner."

She stared up at him, her lips parted, her breathing rough and hard. Then she licked her lips. A slow, wet swipe of her tongue, the act deliberate, challenging.

There was nothing left to say. Jacob's lips slammed down on hers as a groan was ripped from his throat. His tongue forged into her mouth, the heated depths soothing the sudden ache of it as her lips closed on him. He slanted his lips over hers, the hand holding hers behind her back arched her closer as the other curved ruthlessly around her breast, his fingers gripping the hard little nipple poking against the cloth of her shirt.

She moaned, a sound rich with longing and arousal as she met his kiss with a force of her own. Her thighs tightened on his, driving his cock tighter against the wedge of her thighs as her hips arched into him. She was a live flame in his arms, burning him, searing his body as he fought to take his fill of her lips.

And he would have. He would have taken his fill of her body, her lusts, if he had been but given a chance. As his hand went to burrow beneath her shirt, the low drone of the house alarm began to beep imperatively.

* * * * *

Jacob was on his feet, jerking Faith up behind him a second later as he rushed to the walnut wood cabinet in the corner of the room.

"Visitors," he bit out at her surprised look.

He jerked two revolvers, and matching comm. links from the chest and pushed them to her.

She didn't speak, but the brief glance he shot her assured him that she was following his lead efficiently. The revolver was in a readied position at her shoulder, the comm. link attached securely to her head.

"Expecting someone?" she asked him, barely a breath of a sound as they moved into the foyer, edging along the wall to the slender, tinted double windows that looked out to the front gate.

Jacob grunted sarcastically as he flipped his own unit to a private channel. He didn't want Faith aware of the fact that the whole compound was being watched. He wanted her comfortable, relaxed, and protected.

He didn't have to speak. When he switched over, he knew the others would be aware of it, and ready to report.

"Can't see shit, boss." Stygian's voice was disgusted, angry. "I got the alarm the minute it came through, but there's nothing out here."

Not possible. The alarms extended fully around the hacienda's boundaries, and were set to go off only in certain instances.

"No animals, no nothing. We found the tripped unit, and it's definitely been tripped, but I'll be damned if there's anything around here," the other Enforcer continued. "If it's Coyote Breeds, then they're getting smarter, or the alarm units are malfunctioning."

The Coyote Breeds were smart enough as it was, Jacob thought furiously, they didn't need to get smarter.

"Figure it out," Jacob told him softly, his voice hard as he continued through the house, secure that Faith was covering his back. "Now!"

"We're on it." The link was broken when Jacob switched back to the private channel with Faith.

"What's going on, Jacob?" Her voice was suspicious as they went through the lower level of the house.

"I don't know yet," he grunted. "Just stay behind me, and stay ready. I don't know what tripped the alarm but I want to be sure nothing got in the house. We'll check every room."

* * * * *

The house was clear. There were no breached windows, no sign of trespassers. Faith moved carefully behind Jacob, her back to his, her eyes covering every inch of the rooms they moved through. They finally ended back up in the living room, where Jacob hit the switch that closed dark shades over each window and left the interior gloomy, intimate.

"So." She turned to him, wanting answers now. "Exactly what mission are you on right now, Jacob, and who the hell were you talking to when you switched over on the comm. link?"

Chapter Seven

ॐ

Jacob sighed roughly.

"The mission isn't the problem, the possibility of Coyote Breeds are." He raked his fingers through his hair as he faced her. "There's a Lab around here somewhere, we just haven't found it yet. Evidently, the Breeds they're holding are pretty damned important too, because anyone who could have had information has been killed before I could get to them."

A quick, thoughtful frown creased her face. "How many Enforcers do you have with you?"

"The Elite force is working with me, as well as Danson," he told her, speaking of the team of eleven other Breeds known for their intelligence and savagery. "We've been working on this for a year now, with only the time to aid Wolfe taken off of it. But I think it gave them the time they needed to hide more effectively."

She pulled the comm. link off her head, but tucked the revolver into the back of her jeans. It should have looked out of place, awkward on her, but the gesture bespoke a quiet confidence, a strength he had never thought she had. He had always felt that Faith needed to be protected, that she was unable to protect herself. Seeing differently shook him a bit, he had to admit. She shouldn't have to defend herself. Shouldn't have to live a life that required it.

"They'll target you eventually. Have you set yourself up as a target?" she asked him. He had known she would figure out quickly, and as expected, she didn't like it.

"Security is in place, Faith," he assured her. "We're targets no matter where we are. At least this way there is a measure of control."

She knew this as well as he did. Her arms crossed over her chest, her hands rubbing at them as though to warm herself.

"This place is a security nightmare, Jacob," she told him coolly as she paced to the closed shades of the largest window. "Whose is it?" She rubbed her arms again.

Jacob narrowed his eyes, wondering if perhaps her skin was irritated. The price he paid for that damned lotion she used, it shouldn't itch, chafe, or develop a rash. The stuff was outrageous.

"A friend's." He shrugged, giving her the same answer as before. "He uses the place only rarely, and he's one of the Pack supporters."

Actually, Caleb's father had been a higher Genetics Council member. After his death, and Caleb's subsequent fury at learning of his parents' depravities, he had become one of the Breed's staunchest allies.

"How much trouble are you expecting?"

Jacob grunted. "Not much. Evidently they're pretty secure in their ability to hide. We haven't seen any signs of Coyote Breeds, and the perimeter breach could have been anything, including faulty equipment. But it's the best we have for now."

She nodded slowly, thoughtfully. Knowing that he was on a mission would not have surprised her. As an Enforcer, it was his life. It would become her life as well, and that scared the hell out of him.

Finally, she sighed deeply, rubbing at her arms again.

"What's wrong, Faith?" Jacob leaned forward in his chair, frowning at the way her arms seemed to be bothering her. "Did you hurt yourself earlier?"

"When?" She looked around at him, confused for a moment before her lips quirked into a small grin. "When I dumped you on your ass? Naw. That didn't hurt me." She tucked a strand of short hair behind her ear nervously before going back to the late evening view outside.

She rubbed at her arms again.

"Faith, what's wrong with your arms?" He stood up from his chair, stalking over to her, intent to find out what was wrong.

"Nothing is wrong with me." She turned on him, frowning as he came near her.

It hit him then. Hard. Sweet, hot and so damned tempting he could barely stand it. Her lust was a palatable thing; he could almost taste it on the air around her.

He lifted her arm, his fingers running over the soft skin. Damn, that lotion was worth every penny he had paid over the years. Her skin was soft as satin, with a healthy, glowing sheen. It was warm, the feel of it unlike anything he had ever known.

"You keep rubbing them." He cleared his throat, unable to release her.

She pulled away from him, rubbed her hand over it again before allowing her arm to fall to her side.

"Restless, I guess. I need to get home," she announced, almost desperate now. "There are things I need to do there. I really don't have a week to spend here, Jacob."

"Things that can be taken care of until your return," he assured her, watching her breathing escalate until she moved carefully away from him. "No one will invade your home, Faith. I promise you that."

She pushed her fingers through the short strands of her hair. Jacob admitted he liked her hair shorter. Liked the way it framed her face, the layered strands framing her elfin features perfectly. It did nothing to detract from her appearance of delicacy, though.

"Why are you forcing me to stay here?" she asked him, her earlier irritation threatening to return. "Why didn't Wolfe order you home? Why not come to me?"

"It's just a week, Faith," he reminded her. "We've been apart six years. Wasted years, I'm starting to suspect. Give us this time to get to know one another again."

He watched as she drew a deep breath. She turned her gaze from him, her lips moist and tempting as she ran her tongue over them nervously.

"I need clothes," she told him firmly as she moved to the large recessed bookshelf on the other side of the room. "Hawke was nice enough to have lost my pack nearly a week ago. What changes of clothes I had were in his pack. You sent him away."

Clothes were a must, but something easily taken care of, he thought.

"I'll take care of it," he promised her. "Anything else you need?"

She sighed again. "Lotion, but there's not a hope in hell of my brand being here. I could kill Hawke for losing my pack. Should have known better than to trust him."

Jacob frowned. She seemed melancholy. Was this one of the mood swings Wolfe had talked about? Damn, she was wearing him out.

"I believe I saw several different brands in the cupboard, in the bathrooms." He shrugged. He knew her brand was there. Caleb's sister also preferred it. "Check there when you shower tonight and see what's available. My friend uses the house for meetings and large get-togethers when he's here, so I'm certain there's something there for everyone."

She turned around. Her eyes broke his heart. They were somber, sad.

"Faith?" he moved slowly toward her. "Can't you tell me what's wrong?"

A bitter smile shaped her lips as her hand ran over her neck, down her arm. She seemed to want to shiver, but held back the action.

"I waited six years for you," she told him softly. "Six long years, Jacob. And I guess I'm just now realizing what a fool I've been. How many women have you been with while I waited, Mate? How many times have you fucked another woman while I waited for you like a fool?

* * * * *

Jacob wondered if the truth would surprise her. True, he had decided the night she had shown up at the bar that he was tired of waiting. Tired of wishing he was different, that she wasn't as soft, as delicate as she was, and had decided a night of raunchy sex was the cure. But honestly, in six years, there had been no other women.

When they escaped the Labs, the males had already gotten their fill of the emptiness involved in screwing just for the pleasure of those who watched, or even for the need to "get off" as the case may be.

From early manhood to adulthood, sex had been a daily diet in his life. Not having to worry about it had been a relief. Until he had seen Faith again. Until the sharp, bitter bite of lust had gotten its hold into him.

"Would you believe me if I said there had been no other women?" he asked her softly.

Her eyes widened. "Is that what you're saying?"

There was a spark of hope in her gaze, a flash of fear.

"Hell, Faith, you remember what the Labs were like," he growled, running his fingers impatiently through his hair. "It was years before I got the stink of that place out of my head. Sex was a damned training exercise, like fucking pushups. Hell no, there haven't been other women. There hasn't been time. I'm too damned busy fighting and finding the hellholes those scientists call Labs. Who has time to fuck?"

He knew it was his own guilt for the plans he had the night before that caused his ire. But dammit, it was her fault too. She had gone from a raging woman bent on breaking bones, to a woman so soft, so fragile, that her dreams whispered through the air around her. Like a damned fairytale princess. How did you fuck a fairy princess? He wanted her hot and sweaty, slick and wet and begging him to fill her. Princesses weren't supposed to do that. Were they?

"I remember many things about the Labs." Her lips thinned as she shrugged tightly. "I'm tired. I'm going to bed."

"Not yet, Faith." Impatience warred with desire as he moved to stop her. He wasn't about to let her leave like this.

He caught her as she made to walk from the room, his arm curling around her waist as he turned her, pressing her tense body against the wall beside the doorframe as she stared up at him in startled surprise. Her hands braced against his broad chest, her slender, graceful fingers trembling over the cover of his shirt.

"There are things I remember as well," he told her, surprised at the rough quality of his voice. "Things that awaken me in the deepest parts of the night, my cock throbbing. Demanding my mate. If I was wrong about your need to grow first, then I can accept this. But I will not allow you to hate me for my need to protect you."

"Where have you protected me, Jacob?" she bit out, though he could feel her body softening, smell her desire for him growing. "I've needed you. Needed to be with you, and you never came for me. Never called for me to come to you. I would not be here now had Wolfe not demanded it."

"But you are here." His fingers tangled in her short hair as he pulled her head back demandingly. "And I'll be damned if I'll let you leave."

Lust, thick and hot swirled in the air around him. The scent of her sweet, female need was like an aphrodisiac, driving him mad. Jacob's lips covered hers, his tongue pushing into her mouth to claim the velvety depths demandingly. She moaned against him. A whimpering, needy sound that made his body flame.

He felt her body conform to him, so delicate and small, as her hands gripped his shoulders, her nails biting through cloth, pricking at his skin. Fire arched from nerve ending to nerve ending in Jacob's body as he pulled her closer to him, his lips devouring her. He couldn't get enough of her. Her sweet taste, her heated passion.

Her lips were satin fire, her tongue a jolt of electricity, and when her lips closed on him, drawing on his tongue, easing the throb in the thickening glands along its side, he nearly came in his jeans. His cock pulsed, throbbed, until he gripped her hips, lifting her closer to wedge the hard length against the heated mound of her cunt.

He braced her between the door and his body, his hips pressing into her, flexing, stroking the sensitive, jeans covered folds of her pussy. He wanted to rip her pants from her body, lift her closer and push hard and deep into the fiery channel that awaited him. He wanted to devour her. Ravage her. He wanted his lips and hands on every part of her body at once.

"Damn you," he cursed as he jerked back, tearing his lips from hers only to move them along her cheek, her neck. "You're like fire, Faith. Fire and lightning and you're burning me alive."

They were both gasping for air now, straining together, loins grinding into each other.

"Jacob." The sound of her tremulous voice, fraught with equal parts fear and desire, whipped through his body with a surge of sensation that left him fighting for air.

He could feel his muscles trembling as he fought to control himself, felt his need for her reaching a peak he had never known existed. She was hot and sweet, and his. His mate. His woman.

Jacob allowed his lips to move with quick, ravenous kisses and strokes of his tongue along her neck, dipping under the neckline of her shirt as she strained against him. He loved the way her body arched to him, her neck tilting, giving him better access, her breasts flattening against his chest as she fought for breath. He could feel the hard points of her nipples burning into his flesh, making his mouth water to taste them.

One hand moved from her hips as he tore the shirt from the waistband of her pants. His hand moved beneath the cloth, stroking over skin so soft, so fine that he shuddered in awe.

"I want you," he growled into her neck as his hand smoothed around her side, his fingers glancing the curve of her swollen breast, his lips aching to stroke it in turn. "I want you now, Faith."

He heard her whimper, felt her as she tensed, striving for control. Her hands gripped his shoulders tightly, her breath shuddered through her body.

"Now," he whispered again. "You're mine. You know this as well as I do. Mine, Faith."

He didn't expect her to tear away from him. Didn't expect the surge of strength that would give her the impetus needed to jerk from his arms, stumbling weakly as she put several feet between them.

Jacob's eyes narrowed, his fists clenching as he watched the swollen, hard-tipped mounds of her breasts moving rapidly beneath her thin shirt.

"Why now?" she cried out, her dark eyes glittering with emotion. "Why do you want me now, when you haven't in six years?"

Jacob paused, frowning. "I've always wanted you, Faith." He shook his head, confused by her anger. "There was no question of that."

"Oh really?" she bit out sarcastically. "Funny, Jacob, I've been questioning it for years. Maybe because I never saw proof of this desire you suddenly have for me."

Jacob felt like snarling in frustration. His cock was swollen, demanding release, his blood pumping through his veins, his flesh demanding release, and it was more than obvious that she was just as aroused. Yet she stood here arguing with him, rather than choosing to satiate the need?

"Does it matter?" He raked his fingers through his hair in irritation. "We can make up for the time we have lost, Faith. If you would stop arguing with me long enough."

He wished he knew how to soothe her, how to ease the glimpse of pain that flashed in her eyes. He had a feeling his declaration only made the situation worse, though.

Chapter Eight

** හ**

Faith shook her head. "Sometimes, Jacob," she said bitterly, "men are so stupid." She literally stomped from the room, rushing up the stairs and out of sight.

"Shit!" he cursed, wondering if he was going to please her with any damned thing he had to say.

He paced the room long after she left, fighting the need to go to her, to force her to admit she wanted him. He started after her twice, then turned around, growling impatiently. How was he supposed to know how to handle this woman? When had she developed such stubbornness, such temper? It aroused the hell out of him, and confused him to no end. It made the urge to dominate her, to mount her, nearly uncontrollable.

His cock was throbbing impatiently beneath his jeans, reminding him forcibly that his mate was there. She was here now, man. Strike while the iron's hot. Show her who's boss. Give it to her now. Damn cock.

He shook his head, almost laughing at his own thoughts. She was driving him insane. Just what he needed, a crazy woman whose insanity was contagious. He was doomed.

Breathing in roughly, he growled out a curse before deciding that his best course of action was to just go to bed. Go to sleep. Forget she was in the house. Yeah. Like that one was going to happen.

He started up the stairs, intent on just that. And he assured himself he would have done just that, if the soft, muted sounds and the light scent of heat and arousal hadn't hit him the minute he stepped close to her bedroom door.

Jacob stepped silently into the bedroom, spellbound by the sight that met his eyes.

She lay on her back, her head arched back on the pillow, breasts swollen and hard, her thighs opened, her slender fingers moving gracefully, desperately over the slick folds of her pussy. Her fingers slid through the narrow slit, softly, so slowly he was panting by the time they pushed into her vagina. His breath exhaled roughly when they retreated and returned to her clit as she gasped out in needy lust.

The inner lips glistened with thick dew. It was so slick, it clung to her fingers, glistened on her inner thighs, and the sweet scent of it sent his cock into raging demand. He licked his lips, his eyes narrowing on her hand, his body tensing at her ragged, nearly silent cries. Clenching his teeth, cursing his cock, he walked to her.

* * * * *

Eyes closed, her lower lip clamped between her teeth to halt her cries, Faith moved her fingers over her swollen clit, her body shuddering from the delicious sensation, her legs tightening as she felt the tension gathering in her clit and in her vagina. Heat flared through her womb, her stomach, her veins. Her blood seared through her body, pounding harsh and loud in her head as she stroked the tender knot, fighting for release.

The fingers of her other hand tweaked at the nipple of one breast. The exciting flare of pinching pleasure almost broke her control. She could feel the moan welling in her throat, the need to call out Jacob's name was nearly overwhelming.

Behind her closed eyes, she imagined him as she wanted him to be. His face hard, savage, drawn into lines of pleasure. She imagined his lips on the slick folds of her cunt, rather than her fingers. His tongue licking her, lapping at her. Her hips jerked in response, a lightning stroke of sensation traveling through her body as her vagina contracted.

Her breathing was hard, heavy, her need rising by the second and still she could find no release. She wanted to howl in pain. How was she to bear the pleasure/agony of such arousal? Her breasts were swollen, her nipples fiery pinpoints of exquisite sensation. Her flesh was sensitive, her body sheened with sweat. Her cunt throbbed, pulsed, her slick juices coating it as her fingers moved faster on her aching clit.

She moaned. She couldn't help it. Desperation wracked her body as it never had before. Arousal was like a ravenous beast lurking just under the surface, crying out to be free. Release, no matter how minor, was now imperative.

She arched to her own stroking fingers, Jacob's name finally gasping from her lips as tears built behind her closed eyes. She needed, needed him so desperately.

"Faith." She heard his voice as it had been that night in the Labs, deep and dark, resonating with power and arousal. A figment of her imagination. How many times had she heard it before? How many times had the sound of it sent her over the edge into a climax, not completely satisfying, but enough to make the needs bearable?

"Now," she whispered, her head tossing on the bed, her hips arching, her need pounding through her bloodstream with the force of a tidal wave.

Then her fingers were halted. Not by choice, but by the force of a large male hand enclosing it tenderly.

Faith's eyes flew open in horror, widening as she saw Jacob standing over her, compassion reflected in his eyes, the temptation of his cock standing out hard and heavy from his body. It was so thick, engorged, the flared head wide and tempting. He would fill her. She moaned, biting her lip in agony, in embarrassment as she jerked her hand from his clasp and scrambled to jump from the bed. She had to get away from him. She couldn't bear the pity in his eyes.

She screamed out silently at fate, at the cruel circumstances that left her at the mercy of her own body and the wracking desires that twisted her loins into an inferno of lust.

"No, Faith." His voice was hard, thick, as his arm caught her around the waist, dragging her back along his body as he knelt on the bed.

Like a shaft of fiery steel, his cock was cushioned against her back.

"Let me go." She felt strangled, gasping for air as his touch sent such incredible, heated pleasure through her body that she had to fight to breathe through it.

Her hands gripped his thick wrist at her side, pulling at it, trying to force it from her. She had to get away from him. To humiliate herself in front of him, twice in one lifetime, was too much to bear. Her nails dug into his wrist, she felt her tears dampening her cheeks and hated herself for it. She hated the weakness that flowed through her body, the desperate need to fall forward, offering herself to him, begging him to mount her, to take her with the pounding force her body was screaming out for.

"Let you go?" he whispered at her ear, the thread of amused arousal in his voice tearing at her heart. "I don't think so, baby. When did you start taking me for a fool?"

"I'm sorry," she gasped, her head falling back on his chest as his other hand cupped her breast, his fingers enclosing the turgid point of a nipple and pinching it lightly.

Weakness flowed through her. She arched into the miniscule pain, needing more, but determined to hold the plea inside. Furious shame and agonized lust battled inside her for supremacy. She wanted to beg him to let her go, she wanted to demand that he fuck her into oblivion.

"Sorry for what?" he whispered at her ear as his mouth slid to the small mark he had left on her neck years before.

He licked at the proof of the wound he had made so long ago. Faith trembled. So good. Her flesh tingled, electrified as his tongue rasped over the rough area. Faith shook in his grip, hating the weakness of her own body, the strength of his steady control behind her.

"Jacob." Her voice was strangled as she felt perspiration slicken her skin further.

Heat raged through her body, stroking the volcano that seethed inside her pussy.

"You should see how pretty you look right now, Faith," he whispered at her neck. "Your head thrown back, your breasts so swollen and firm. Your cunt glistening with all that sweet juice."

How could he see? Her eyes blinked opened as she struggled to raise her head from his shoulder. She instantly met the dim reflection in the large standing mirror across from them. She saw the desperation in her own reflection and fought the cries that welled in her chest. She didn't want this. She didn't want Jacob once again, because he pitied her for the uncontrolled arousal she couldn't fight.

"Do you know what I'm going to do?" His eyes met hers in the mirror, glowing, the light steel-blue color blazing with heat. "I'm going to eat all that sweet syrup from your body, Faith. I remember how good you taste, how hot that pretty cunt gets."

She trembled violently. She could only gasp for breath, she was beyond coherent speech.

In the mirror, with only the light of the full moon to brighten the bedroom, she watched as his hand moved at her waist, sliding down, over her abdomen, the broad, dark fingers moving unerringly to the glistening lips of her sex.

When the touch came, Faith didn't think she could bear it. His fingers whispered over her clit, nearly throwing her into climax. If she could speak, she would be screaming for the ease. She could only whimper in desperation, arching to his fingers.

She watched in the mirror, unable to stop herself, unable to believe it as she watched his fingers part the bare folds and slip through the small slit that ran to the entrance of her vagina.

Faith's breath strangled in her throat. She didn't want to watch, to see her own shameful ecstasy reflected on her face, but she was held helpless by the image, erotic and more sensual than anything she had ever known.

"See how much you enjoy my touch, Faith," he told her, his voice husky, his own breathing rougher than before. "How hard your nipples are, how soft and wet your pussy is. Feel, Faith. That's all you have to do."

It was all she could do. She strained in his arms, whimpering as his fingers rolled her nipple between them, pinching lightly. Then crying out as the other hand moved back, his fingers circling the swollen nub of her clit with torturously slow strokes.

"Can your vibrator do this for you, Faith?" he asked her, his voice seductive as his fingers pressed against the side of her clit, rubbing gently.

Her strangled moan was loud in the sultry silence of the room as her nails bit into the outside of his thighs where her hands gripped now. She bucked against him, feeling the flame of sensation that built there before washing over her body.

"Please. Jacob, please." She hated the strangled plea that erupted from her throat. Despised her weakness and her body as she fought for release.

"Not yet, baby." His fingers moved again, sliding through the thick juices of her cunt until they were poised at the hungry entrance to her vagina.

Faith's vision blurred as she felt the insertion of two broad fingers into the snug channel. She felt her flesh part, stretching, felt the burning agony of an arousal so intense she could only cry out against it.

She pushed against his hand, thrusting against his fingers, desperate for a deeper, harder penetration. She needed more, and she needed it now. She could feel her juices building inside her, soaking his hand, dripping from the folds of ultra sensitive flesh as her body burned for more.

"Burn for me, Faith." His voice held a rough rumble, a command he was determined she would obey. "You don't have to control this, baby. Let it go."

She shook in his arms. She couldn't let go. She had humiliated herself enough. She would not willingly give up what little control she had over her own body. Then his fingers retreated, only to plunge shallowly, forcibly, into the tight channel once again. The upper part of his hand pressed into her clit, grinding against it with a gentle twist that destroyed her.

Faith knew it was her scream that shattered the night, her pleas as her body came apart in an ecstasy she had never known before. She bucked against the fingers, desperate for more, despite the climax rolling over her body in waves. She needed his cock filling her, stretching her.

She gasped out roughly as he pushed her forward, his voice rough as he ordered her into position.

"Watch the mirror," he ordered her savagely. "Watch it, Faith. See the man who possesses you."

Her eyes rose, widened. She was wild, wanton, on her hands and knees before him, her buttocks raised for him, leaving her open, inviting, beseeching him to possess her however he would.

Faith could feel her arousal like a beast, roaring inside her, transforming her, remaking her. She tempted him with her eyes, with slow undulations of her body, desperate for him to take her. She wanted to possess and be possessed. She wanted the heat and strength of his possession, his shaft pounding into her.

Jacob's hand was wrapped around his cock, the unusual thickness of it appeared menacing and promising all at once. He moved forward then, bending to her, covering her as he lodged the head at the entrance to her cunt.

"Jacob. Now." She pressed back against him, fighting the sudden grip he had on her hips as his much wider, taller body came over her.

His lips feathered her shoulder.

"Are you still a virgin, Faith?" he growled. "Have you taken your own innocence with those damned vibrators or is the shield still in place?"

"I didn't." Her breathing was strangled, her voice weak, desperate. "I didn't, Jacob. I swear."

She felt his teeth nip her neck, his head bending until his mouth covered the mark he had left so long ago. His sharp canines raked, scratched, then he bit her with enough force to wring a cry from her throat. At the same time, his cock pushed inside the tight channel of her body, causing her to scream out at the combined pleasure/pain.

One muscular arm wrapped around her hips to hold her in place as his shaft began to invade her, pushing through the tight muscles as they tensed, burned with the exquisite sensations that rioted through her body. He worked the broad length back and forth, his hips rocking against her as he tunneled further inside her.

She could feel the broad head parting her, easing her open for the thick shaft behind it. His cock was fiery hot as he slid through the slick frothing cream that soaked her vagina. Working the broad shaft with shallow, gentle motions, he eased into the heated core of her. He thrust forward then retreated before returning with another slow, heated thrust until the proof of her innocence was met.

Faith cried out pleadingly. She bucked against him, trying to force the heavy cock further inside her. She needed him, now. She wanted to feel him driving inside her, powerful and hot as her muscles clenched around him.

She felt him pause as he reached the shield of her virginity. Her eyes rose to his in the mirror, seeing a savage satisfaction wash over his face.

"Mine," he snarled, then pushed forward with a hard thrust.

There was no pain. There was a flare of heat so blinding, so intense that Faith felt as though her heart would stop. It pulsed from her vagina, flowed through her body and seared her flesh. Her cunt was stretched, filled, so tight around his erection that she could feel the hard beat of his pulse in the thick shaft. His canines were locked on her neck, his tongue laving the wound and Faith felt herself enter a maelstrom she could have never envisioned.

As his teeth released her, heat seared her. Her body trembled, the blood rushed through her veins and her last vestige of control shattered with the incredible arousal that tore through her body. And Jacob didn't seem unaffected. He growled low and rough, and began a hard driving rhythm of thrust and retreat that had her screaming for more. His cock pounded into her, huge, unbearably hot as her flesh tightened on it, spasming, trying to lock the heat and hardness into her body.

Sweat dripped from Jacob's brow, from her body as they fought for release now. His hips pistoned against her buttocks, his cock buried inside the slick, soaked flesh of her snug channel repeatedly, stroking the sensitive tissue, firing sensations that licked over her entire body. She tightened her vagina on him, heard his groan, felt a heated spurt, then another inside her, and he kept thrusting, driving her closer, harder. Until Faith felt her body dissolve. Her climax tore through her, ripped through her womb and cut a path of destruction through the rest of her body.

She lost her breath, could only gasp as she tightened in his arms. And then she felt more. Her eyes flew open in alarm as she heard Jacob curse. His cock tunneled inside her, then thickened further, then further, until each time his hips jerked, the unusual thickness that seemed to have grown at the point where her channel was narrowest, only lodged him inside her tighter. His cock was spurting repeatedly as he cried out her name, his body jerking against her, triggering flaring, multi-orgasms as the hard ball wedged inside her tighter, hotter than before.

Reality was only Jacob's flesh locked inside her. It was only the hard, deep pulses of release that ripped repeatedly through her body. The heat and hardness, the lash of pleasure/pain, until she could do no more than collapse beneath him, fighting for breath as he followed her, catching his weight on his arms as his hips jerked against her buttocks, driving the steel hard knot that had grown in his cock only deeper.

Time was a meaningless concept. She lay beneath him, shuddering each time he pulsed inside her, each time his hips jerked, his cock tugging at her flesh.

"Jacob," she whispered his name repeatedly, the word so soft, so breathless she doubted he even heard her.

Finally, with a last shuddering groan, she felt him tug once more, his cock popping free of her vagina as he leaned back from her. She expected him to fall beside her. Had thought he would hold her. She didn't expect him to jerk from her and stomp across the room. As she turned quickly in surprise, she saw only his sweat dampened back as the door slammed furiously on his retreat.

Chapter Nine

ഇ

Fury flared in Faith. It surged through her body. As hot as passion, as destructive as a climax, it tore through her body as the last vibrations of the door slamming died down. Shock had held her motionless, silent, but the pain that ripped through her tore her from the frozen moorings of silent disbelief.

"You bastard!" she screamed as she came to her knees, her fists clenched, tears falling down her cheeks as she felt the slick moisture of her body, and his seed dampening her thighs.

Her body still hummed with her release, and he just walked away? He couldn't spare a hug or even a damned thank you? Something broke in her chest. A hollow center of hope that she had always held, always nurtured. Dark, vivid dreams of Jacob holding her, touching her in heat and gentleness, taking away the ache, the lonely core of misery that seemed to fill her. She felt it all shatter, and in its place a hard, cold core of fury replaced it.

She didn't know what had happened, didn't know how to deal with the desertion. He had just walked away. As though she were nothing, as though she meant that little to him. Once again, her own desperation, her sickening needs and love for him, had driven him away from her.

A sob broke from her throat as she jumped from the bed and strode quickly to the bathroom to clean the proof of her lack of control from her body. It wasn't the first time he had left her like this, she reminded herself, but damn him to hell, it would be the last time.

Her teeth clenched on her pain-filled, enraged screams. The sounds locked in her chest, the small whimpers no more than the hard rasp of her breathing as she fought for and maintained her control.

This was what she had waited six years for, she raged silently. This was what she had dreamed? She didn't think so. She would be damned if she would accept it.

She pulled her clothes on, her body vibrating with anger and a hopeless pain born of yet another rejection by Jacob. It would be her last, she promised herself. When she managed to get out of this damned place and return home, she would make certain Jacob never had a chance to hurt her again.

As she slipped past his room, she heard glass shatter, and a curse, dark and violent echo from it. She sneered. Poor baby was upset? Over what? She would like to shatter glass over his head.

She collected her jacket from the kitchen and rushed for the front door as she pulled her cell phone from the pocket. Jacob's SUV was still sitting there in the driveway, waiting on her, keys in the ignition. To hell with him. She would be damned if she would walk back to town, or hike out of this dirty little hole. She would drive out in style and he could sit his ass there until he found other transportation.

As she jumped into the driver's seat, she keyed in the number to Hawke's cell phone. She tucked the phone between her ear and shoulder as she started the vehicle, counting off each ring as she put the vehicle in gear and headed for the gates.

Remote. She reached over and flipped open the door to the glove box. Thankfully, she had paid attention to Jacob earlier when he keyed in the code. The gates swung open smoothly as a victorious snarl curled at the edge of her lips.

"What?" Hawke finally answered, his voice drowsy and cranky.

"Meet me in the parking lot of that damned bar," she bit out. "I'm not searching for you. If you aren't there, then I head home on my own."

"Faith?" Shock colored his voice. "What the hell are you doing? Stay with Jacob."

"You heard me, Hawke," she bit out. "I'll be there soon, you have one hour to meet me and then I'm headed out of there. Do you understand me?"

She didn't give him time to answer before she disconnected the phone. She wiped at the wetness on her face, amazed at the tears that still fell from her eyes. Why was she crying? She should have known what to expect. She had known, she had just refused to face it. Jacob was the classic lone wolf, he didn't need her. He never had. Her breath hitched, infuriating her. Damn him, he had made her cry. He had made her cry when all the long, desperately painful nights aching for him had never pushed her to that point.

She drove the SUV down the rough track that led back into town, there she found herself helplessly lost amid the back roads and narrow alleys she managed to enter. She cursed Jacob, Wolfe and the damned cell phone beeping its battery operated little brain out beside her.

"What?" she snarled into the device as she turned along another side road.

There was a small silence; enough to make her frown as she sniffed back her tears.

"If I don't pass you heading back to the house, then you may not like me much once I get hold of you, Faith." She had never heard Jacob's voice so cold, so furious.

"I don't like you much now," she bit out. "I did my job, you have your papers, now I'm going home."

"Faith, you won't get out of town before I catch up with you, baby," he growled. "And I promise you, you'll regret leaving like that."

"Catch up with me then, you son of a bitch," she told him furiously. "Come on, Jacob, find me. I promise, you'll be the one who won't be pleased."

She disconnected, pressed her foot to the gas pedal and eased onto the main road leading directly into town. She accelerated the vehicle as fast as she dared, racing to the bar. If Hawke wasn't there, then she swore she would leave his ass sitting.

He was there, with Danson, standing beside a vehicle identical to the one she drove. She squealed to a stop beside them and waited impatiently as Hawke strode quickly to the door. He had it opened before she could stop him, jerking the keys from the ignition and facing her furiously.

Surprised flared through her.

"What are you doing?" She snatched at the keys, jumping from the vehicle as he moved back quickly. "Damn you, give me the keys. What the hell are you doing this for?"

"Faith, you can't leave, dammit," he told her angrily. "Do you think I spent two months busting my ass to get you in shape to meet up with Jacob just to have you turn tail and run? I never took you for a coward."

Faith stilled. She felt a chill race over her spine as she faced the Enforcer, seeing the steely determination in his dark blue eyes as he stared down at her. This wasn't the friendly, charming soldier she had fought with for two months. This wasn't her friend or her partner. He was an Enforcer, and answerable to Wolfe and Jacob before anyone else.

"You called him," she whispered hopelessly.

"Hell yes, I called him." He raked his fingers through his short black hair and stared down at her. "Faith, honey, you can't leave him yet. You know that. Dammit, you're so fucking hot any Breed in a two-mile radius could track you. You're becoming a danger to yourself and to the Pack."

She shook her head desperately. "I don't live with the Pack." She should know, she suffered that isolation every day of her life. "I'm alone, Hawke. All alone for a reason, damn you." Because the man who had marked her had deserted her.

"And soon you'll be alone and dead, woman," he growled. "You know as well as I do there are still Breed soldiers out there following the commands of their puppeteers. Goddamn it, the smell of your lust will see you raped before they ever get around to killing you. Is that what you want, Faith? Do you really think those vibrators are easing your lust enough to still the scent of it? I promise you, it's not."

Faith fought to breathe. She wanted to scream, to rush him, hurt him. She still held enough control, just enough to realize it would serve no purpose.

"Please give me the keys, Hawke," she whispered desperately as she heard a vehicle speeding towards the parking lot. "Just let me go home. Please, Hawke, before he destroys me."

She could feel fear clawing at her insides. She wasn't afraid of Jacob, she was terrified of herself. The demands of her body, the surge of her desires, her emotions, were tearing her apart.

"Faith, your death will lay on my head if I let you go," he told her gently. "Fight this out with Jacob. It will work out."

"He doesn't want me," she screamed out as a motorcycle's headlight speared through the area. "Why are you fucking doing this to me? If I have to be pity fucked, then you do it. Goddamn it, it wouldn't hurt nearly as bad."

There was silence as her words struck each man. Jacob, who had just halted and switched the motor off to the lethal black cycle he rode, and Hawke who stared at her in shock.

"If he touches you, Faith, I'll kill him." Serious as death, and just as dark, Jacob's voice sliced through the tension already building in the parking lot.

She turned on him. She saw the savage fury on his face as he lifted himself from the motorcycle and advanced on her slowly. She snarled at him, fury filling every cell in her body as she tensed for the fight she saw in his face.

"Not yet, baby," he promised. "Unless you want me to mount you here, in the parking lot, with Hawke and Danson as witnesses."

"I'll kill you first," she bit out.

He shook his head, mocking amusement crossing his face.

"Get in the jeep, Faith. Now."

"Make me." She backed away from him, searching desperately for a weakness in his stance. She saw none.

He stopped in front of Hawke and held out his hand. Betraying bastard laid the SUV's keys in that broad palm. Jacob slid them in his pocket, never looking away from her.

"You see that cycle, Hawke?" Jacob asked him carefully.

"Nice little thing." Faith sneered at the other man's awed voice.

"I expect to see it outside the gates of the hacienda come afternoon. Then I want that job I gave you completed."

"Hawke, you leave me here with this sadistic son of a bitch and I'll kill you next time I see you," Faith bit the words out furiously, her breathing rough, and damn her body all to hell and back, but her pussy was throbbing with a beat more desperate than that of her heart.

She could feel her clit swelling, arousal stark and blinding flaring through her body.

She watched as Jacob inhaled softly, his lips quirking.

"I hate you," she snarled viciously, her fingers curling into fists as Danson and Hawke drove away. "You just signed his death warrant, Jacob. I'll murder that betraying bastard when I catch up with him."

He tilted his head, his expression curious.

"Faith," he chided her a little too sweetly. "Why darlin', I never saw you so bloodthirsty. It's arousing."

She trembled violently from the hard edge of pure rage that shot through her.

"Arousing?" she asked him with a sneer. "Sorry baby, I don't like your brand of fucking. Find someone else."

"Well darlin', I guess I'll just have to see if I can't do better next time." He advanced on her, his eyes narrowing.

Faith backed up again, seeing no advantage, no sign of weakness in him. He was dressed in form fitting black pants, boots, and a sleeveless white T-shirt that he had tucked into the snug waistband of his pants. There was no body hair to mar the perfection of his muscular body. Nothing to dim the sun bronzed sheen of flexing muscles and a body ready for any move she would make.

"I don't want you," she assured him heatedly.

"Your body is desperate for me," he argued. "I can smell it, Faith, sweet and hot, so damned addictive it makes my mouth water with the need to taste you."

"And you think I'm desperate enough to let you touch me again," she bit out. "I don't think so, Jacob. I'd rather suffer."

She stared up at him as he stopped before her, standing still, forcing herself to relax. He watched her for a long moment, and she didn't hide the fury, or the resounding pain in her expression.

"Faith," his voice gentled, his hand reaching out to touch her face.

Instinctively, the flat of her palm slammed into his stomach as she twisted, ducking under his arm, her foot slamming into the back of his knee as she gave a hard shove to his shoulder.

She heard his curse, but didn't wait around to see if he recovered. With a burst of speed and desperation, she headed for the edge of the jungle. If she couldn't outfight him, then maybe, just maybe she could outsmart him.

He caught her just inside the perimeter of the jungle. His arms went around her waist, dragging her back against his hard body, his legs braced apart enough that there was no power to the desperate kicks she aimed at them. His hands caught hers, twisting them to her sides as he held her securely against his chest, maintaining her struggles.

"I ought to fuck you here and now," he bit out at her ear. "I should take you to your knees and rip those pants off you and take you now, and I would, Faith. I swear to you I would if I weren't terrified that while I was locked inside you we could get our asses killed."

They were both breathing hard now. She could feel his heartbeat thudding at her back, just as she felt hers thumping desperately in her chest. Her breasts rose and fell with her short panting breaths, but it wasn't from the exertion. She could feel the lust zinging through her body, turning her cunt to liquid fire.

She could feel his erection against her ass, pressing against her, hot and throbbing even through the layers of their clothing.

"Another quick little fuck where you can walk away in disgust," she cried out, struggling against his grip, against the heat his touch evoked. "No thanks, Jacob, two in one lifetime is enough."

Then she screamed out in fury as he quickly turned her around, hauling her into his arms, tossing her over his shoulder as he held her legs firmly to his chest. She opened her mouth to bite the bunching muscles of his back when a hard, resounding whack to her rear had her screaming out in fury.

"Bite me and I'll whip your bare ass good when I get you back to the house," he warned her. "Now settle the hell down."

He covered the distance across the parking lot quickly, his long legs moving purposely, his tight ass bunching attractively beneath her dangling head. Damn him to hell, nothing on his body should be attractive to her right now.

"Get in." He set her down in front of the passenger door as he jerked it open. "And if you get out, I promise you, Faith, you'll regret it."

A firm push at her shoulder had her jumping furiously into the seat, as anger raged through her. Her body shook with it, with the need to pounce, to hurt. He slammed the door on her and moved quickly to the other side as he dug the keys out of his pants pocket.

He jerked his door open and jumped in. A second later the motor roared to life and the jeep peeled out of the parking light as dawn began its gentle appearance.

Chapter Ten

∽

The black jacket, pants and shirt were lying in a dirty heap on the floor when Jacob walked into her bedroom later that morning. He could hear bath water running in the next room and the sound of Faith muttering furiously.

Damn, he had never seen her that mad before. With her cheeks flushed, her eyes almost glowing with rage, and her lips pulled back in a snarl, displaying her pert little canines, his body had hardened with such immediacy it had shocked him. He had wanted to throw her down on the dirt parking lot and fuck her into submission without delay. And the angrier she got, the hotter she got. The scent of her arousal had wrapped around him as sultry and hot as the jungle itself.

"Son of a bitch, dragging me around, ordering me around, fucking me and walking out on me—" Water splashed furiously in accompaniment to her angry voice.

He picked up the clothes from the floor silently, and laid the short summer dress he had borrowed from Caleb's sister on the bed. Faith appeared to be about the same size, so he was certain it would fit.

Caleb Sanchez owned the house, but rarely used it. His sister, Catherine, used it mostly during the milder months and kept clothes on hand at all times. He had picked several outfits, as well as matching underclothes that still had the tags hanging from them. He doubted Catherine would even miss them.

"Stubborn bastard!" He grinned at her strangled rage.

She wasn't settling down at all. Damn if Wolfe wasn't right. She was more hormones and need right now than she was common sense. And he hadn't helped matters.

He pushed his fingers through his hair in irritation. He had been in shock. There was no other way to describe it, no excuse for it. The mindless, searing pleasure that washed over him when his cock swelled further, his orgasm exploding through his body as he locked inside her, had been more than he could handle. It had frankly terrified him. He had never experienced anything like it.

On top of that, he had lost his control with Faith. He wasn't certain how it had happened. Watching her in that damned mirror, her face a mask of desperation and need, feeling her cunt so hot and slick, smelling her arousal like a potent drug wrapping around him, he had lost it.

He tossed the clothes down the recessed laundry chute inside the walk-in closet with a reminder to himself to throw the damned things away. They were torn and dirty, and carried traces of Hawke's scent. He wanted no other scent of any man attached to Faith. When he was finished, her body would be so infused with his scent, his need, his possession of her that no other man would dare try to touch her.

He left the bedroom as he heard her leave the bathtub. He wasn't prepared for another confrontation with her. His instincts were already pushing him to force her submission to him, to see her kneeling before him, no longer fighting him. His cock clenched at the thought. He remembered the night in the Lab, the way her anal entrance opened for him, allowing him to sink inside her, possess her in the most primitive manner.

Until the night before, Jacob had not realized how close they actually were to the animal side of their DNA. The sexual training in the Labs, the women, the drugs, none of them had produced such a reaction in him. He would have to be certain to thank Wolfe for mentioning this little phenomenon.

* * * * *

"What in the hell did you do with my clothes?" Jacob turned from the stove at that question and lost any thought he could have had to answer her.

The soft white silk dress clung to her full breasts, emphasized her narrow waist and flared hips, as it lovingly fell just below her thighs. It was a stretchy, clinging silk that held her breasts seductively in fragile cups, leaving the upper curves temptingly bare and making the delicate tone of her satin skin glow. But what surprised him the most were the high heels she had managed to find to go with it.

A matching pair of white, three inch heels that she moved naturally, gracefully in. This wasn't his little Faith. This was a temptress, a seductress.

"I didn't give you shoes," he felt the need to point out. And he sure as hell wouldn't have picked shoes that would turn her legs into a work of art that he only wanted to spread and slip between. And since when had that dress been the one he laid out for her? He was certain it wasn't. "Where did you find them?"

"Same place I got the dress," she snapped. "I'm not a child, Jacob, and I refuse to wear something that makes me look like a damned teeny bopper. Now answer me, where are my jeans? I don't know who lives here, but the silly twit doesn't own a single pair."

Jacob wanted to shake his head and try to clear the fog of lust rising within it. Those breasts were killing him. And he prayed to God she didn't decide to turn around. He had a feeling that dress was hugging her sweet ass just as lovingly.

"The dress I laid out was fine," he grunted, turning back to the soup to still the haze of aroused confusion growing in his mind.

"It was at least twenty years old and so out of date it reeks," she snarled. "If you're going to borrow clothes for me, borrow something decent, at least."

"You don't wear clothes like that," he bit out. "You wear jeans." Damn, the thought of other men seeing her dressed like that had a red haze of fury clawing at his vision.

"Yeah. Sure, Jacob, whatever you want to believe," she snorted behind him. "So where are my jeans?"

"In the trash," he growled, stirring the soup. "They were nasty, torn and the stench of them offended me."

When she didn't say anything, he turned back to her. Sweet heaven, he was going to end up fucking her on the kitchen table. A frown had her dark brows lowered over angry eyes, her arms were folded beneath her breasts, pressing them up in a temptation he was hard pressed to ignore. And those legs. He wanted them wrapped around his waist, holding him tight while he fucked her into a screaming orgasm.

"You are starting to irritate me." Her voice was calm, even, despite the fire in her eyes, and the obvious arousal in her body. And he was aroused, he knew.

"Sit down and eat. You're worn out, and hungry, that's why you're so irritated. You can rest after lunch."

He spooned the soup into bowls, and set it with two thick ham sandwiches on the table in the middle of the room.

"I'm irritated because you are being a typical, bossy, irrational male Breed," she snarled, though she took her seat anyway.

"You're irritated because you're hungry, horny and sleepy, and I will address each issue in that order." He took his own seat, exasperation filling him.

She stared at him, her eyes narrowed, her expression so filled with stubbornness it immediately made him want to force her to admit to each point.

"You have a point." She surprised him. "Looks to me as though you may as well get used to it as long as you're forcing me to stay here. I have no problem with eating your food, or sleeping in this house, but I'll twist your dick off if you try to touch me."

Jacob had to forcibly restrain his chuckle and his immediate impulse to show her otherwise. She didn't wait for his answer, but lifted the sandwich and bit into it hungrily. Jacob applied himself to his own food, but watched her carefully to be certain she finished. One of Wolfe's main concerns was the weight she had been losing over the past months. And she had lost a considerable amount. She wasn't skin and bones, but she appeared too delicate, too fragile for the savage needs pulsing through him.

Thankfully, she finished the meal. After taking the last bite, she took her saucer, bowl and empty milk glass to the sink and started searching the cabinets.

He watched her for several moments, curious as to her intentions.

"What are you looking for?" He leaned back in his chair, unable to take his eyes from the rounded curves of her tempting ass. The bunch and flex of the rounded flesh had him clenching his hands into fists to keep from touching them.

"Coffee," she muttered. "Where the hell do you keep it, anyway?"

"There isn't any." He shrugged. Of course, Caleb kept a supply on hand, but it was in the supply closet rather than the cabinets.

She turned around, her eyes wide with shock. "You don't drink coffee? What are you, an alien? Order me some. Now."

How cute. Her eyes were rounded in distress, and he could have sworn she actually paled a bit. Love her heart, she was definitely addicted.

"The caffeine isn't good for your system right now, Faith," he told her patiently. "Neither is alcohol, come to think of it. You're going to have to watch what you drink and eat for the next few weeks."

She drew to her full height, her brows snapping over her eyes in a frown as she stalked to the refrigerator door and jerked it open. He knew there was no longer any beer there. He had gotten rid of it hours ago. She closed the door slowly.

"You have five minutes to call someone, anyone, I don't care who, and order me the finest blend of coffee that rat hole town has, and a dozen beers. If it's not sitting on this table…" a slender finger pointed furiously at the table in question, "…in one hour, you die."

She appeared perfectly serious. Jacob leaned back in his chair, watching her warily.

"Faith, I am not bringing coffee or alcohol into this house for a while, and neither are you. I'm telling you, right now, your system can't handle it." He crossed his arms over his chest and waited to see what she would do.

Her lips thinned, her face flushing as anger flooded her system. Anger and lust. As though the heat of her fury made her lust burn higher. Damn, he loved the scent of it.

Her breasts rose above the low cut of her neckline as she took a deep breath. Her head raised, her shoulders straightened, then she was walking purposefully from the room. That was not a good sign.

"Dammit, Faith," he growled, jumping up from the table and following her as she entered the foyer and headed for the front door. "Come back here."

He caught her halfway through the wide entrance hall, his hand catching her arm as he pulled her to a stop. She stopped easily enough. Long enough to reach down and bite him.

"Son of a bitch," he yelled, jumping back to stare at his arm, then at the woman who had refused to bite anyone at anytime during training. He was fucking bleeding! Two perfect punctures marred the skin of his arm and oozed a small amount of blood. Dammit, he was partial to his blood and he preferred to keep it in his body.

She didn't appear surprised or shocked at her own actions. She stared at him, her dark eyes glittering with fury, her cheeks flushed with it.

"I want my coffee, and my beer. You can be as much an ass as you want to be, and you can hold me here till hell freezes over, but there are some things I refuse to live without. And while you're ordering, get on whatever Internet connection this stinking jungle has and order me a vibrator. I want seven inches long, three inches around, D battery. Use that ineffective male brain and hunt up a vibrating egg as well. Preferably, white. I refuse to stay here without my necessities."

Jacob stared at her incredulously. His gaze went to his arm, then back to her again.

"You bit me, Faith," he growled, ignoring her demands.

"And I'll bite you again," she assured him fiercely. "Don't manhandle me, Jacob. This isn't the Pack, and contrary to what you think, I refuse to acknowledge you as my mate. Mates do not desert each other. They do not walk away after fucking them, and they do not refuse them the few pleasantries their life has to offer. Namely, my caffeine and my beer. But since you are a typical Breed ass, you can supply my vibrators as well, because I refuse to fuck you." Her voice rose with each sentence.

Her breasts were heaving, her eyes glittering, and he knew her cunt was so wet he could knot her there and then with no trouble.

"You're in heat, Faith. Caffeine affects it adversely, as does alcohol. And you need me, not fucking vibrators," he yelled back, furious that she would think she could deny him now.

She staggered just enough to assure him that he had effectively shocked her. She stared at him, fear and horror flashing across her eyes before her features settled into a mask of cold hard fury.

"Then I've been in heat for six fucking years," she growled. "Guess what, Jacob, I survived it without you then, and I will now. So, do you order what I need or do I walk out of this comfortable little prison you have set up and find it myself?"

"Did you hear what I just told you, Mate?" he snarled the title. "You are in fucking heat. You need to be fucked. My seed splashing inside your tight pussy. My touch, my taste. A vibrator will do you no good, and the caffeine and alcohol will only make the symptoms harder on your body. I will not tolerate this childishness from you. The least you can do is take care of yourself."

"My childishness?" she asked him furiously. "Shall I show you childishness, Jacob? Shall I show you just how childish I can get? You better never sleep. You better never turn your back on me, because the minute you do, I'm out of here. If I can't steal a vehicle, then I'll walk, hitchhike, whatever it takes to go somewhere to get what I need. And since I know for damned sure there's no adult stores anywhere in the flea infested towns that you situate yourself in, it might be a while before I get back. Because I will have my fucking vibrators!" she screamed the last sentence at him.

Jacob blinked, staring at the miniature apparition that seemed possessed by some vile, horrendous demon. How did you exorcise a caffeine addiction from such a damned little shrew? Damn Wolfe to hell and back, he could have at least warned him properly of what to expect.

"There will be no vibrators brought into this house," he snarled back at her. "You need relief then you can come to me for it, Mate. No vibrators. No coffee, no beer."

Jacob had a feeling that should he show the slightest weakness now, then there would be no end to her demands. She snarled, displaying those cute, though vicious little canines as she made for the door once again.

114

"No. Faith." His arms went around hers, trapping them at her sides, wrapping around her waist. No way in hell was he getting near her mouth right now. Bloodthirsty little shrew.

He pressed his cock into the cheeks of her ass as he lifted her against him, turned and walked into the living room. He dumped her on the couch, then pushed her back when she would have jumped up. He stood over her, frowning down at her, becoming drunk on the sweet scent coming from her luscious cunt. He had fed her, now he was going to fuck her. Fuck her until she couldn't fight, couldn't argue and sure as hell wouldn't have the energy to go after coffee, beer or a fucking vibrator.

Chapter Eleven

ഏ

Jacob came down on top of her, his body stretching along the length of hers, long and hot, all male and sending her senses into riot. She could feel the heated length of his erection as he settled over her, his legs on each side of her, holding her captive beneath him as he caught his weight on his arms. His hard chest cushioned her breasts, his hair falling forward, framing the savage features of his face.

"Hurry and do it, and get off me," she bit out furiously, hating her body's response, her need to feel the driving length of his cock separating her, penetrating her, only to have him desert her seconds after climaxing.

She needed more than just the sex. Faith had always known that, had always realized that what she needed from him, he likely couldn't provide. She needed him to hold her, touch her. She needed more than the rough ride and the desertion later. She needed the warmth of his body as the tremors of release shook her. She needed his voice, soft and gentle as he held her.

As he lay over her, six years of fantasies and loving daydreams drifted through her head, her heart. They pulsed in her soul as bright and hot as the lust throbbed in her pussy.

"I'm sorry about last night," he whispered down at her, his eyes brooding, heavy lidded as he watched her. "Do you even realize what happened, Faith? What I did to you as I climaxed inside that sweet, hot body of yours?"

She frowned, breathing roughly. She didn't want him to talk. She wanted him to fuck her, to love her and hold her. Explanations could come later.

She stared up at him in confusion. "Does it matter? Just do it again."

She didn't need explanations, she needed relief. She needed him to ease the fury of arousal, the ache of loneliness, and the dreams that had shattered over the years.

A strained laugh escaped his throat. His hands framed her face, one thumb smoothing over her lips in a slow stroke.

"Faith, I locked inside you," he told her, his body tightening against her as she stared up at him, wondering if it was supposed to be a bad thing.

"You're large—"

"I knotted inside you, Faith," he bit out. "My cock swelled further, until the middle was the size of your fist or larger, baby. I couldn't pull free. Like an animal, Faith."

She fought to breathe. He sounded furious, enraged over it. She swallowed tightly. She had known that was coming, if Jacob took her. Hope had already warned her.

"Hope handles it," she whispered. "Wolfe didn't get angry with her—"

His body tensed further

"You knew this would happen?" he asked her carefully.

Faith stared up at him, anticipation pounding through her body. He was pressed to her from thigh to breast, and the heat of his body was driving her crazy.

"I thought you knew," she told him breathlessly. "Hope told me about that when she found out Wolfe was sending me after you. She said I needed to know. I thought you knew. There have been other women—"

"It's never happened before, Faith," he growled. Damn, that harsh rumble from his throat made her entire body tremble.

Her heart was racing out of control, she could feel the slow slide of her juices coating her cunt, preparing her, pleading with her to open herself, to force him to take her again, to fill her, burn her with his heat and his hardness.

She licked her lips, trying to ease the dryness that assailed them. She looked up at him hesitantly, meeting his hungry gaze, aching for his kiss.

"I liked it, Jacob," she whispered, her hands moving beneath his shirt, touching the tight, muscular flesh at the side of his abdomen. "You didn't hurt me."

She felt and heard his indrawn breath as she touched him. She paused, wondering if she should. How she had always dreamed of touching him. Was it like the cuddling afterward, forbidden?

"Don't stop," he whispered as she paused.

He levered up, allowing her hand to work under the T-shirt. Instead, she drew back, hooked her hands in the material and ripped it. Excitement flared over her as she heard the rending material, saw the hard muscles of his chest and abdomen finally revealed. The rush of blood through her system seemed satisfied by that small act of savagery. The need to assert herself, her desire, screamed through her body.

He smiled. A small half smile that looked sexy and inviting as he tossed the remains to the floor, rising to his knees, his legs encasing her hips as he watched her.

"Are you finished?" The dark suggestion in his voice had her breath coming quicker now, her curiosity overwhelming her.

"No." Her hands flattened on his abdomen, watching the muscles clench as he drew in a hard breath. "I want to touch you, Jacob." She heard the throb of longing in her voice, the need inside her that was more powerful than the demand in her vagina.

"Then do it right," he told her heatedly as he moved back. He pulled up until she was kneeling in front of him.

Jacob gripped her dress and pulled it roughly over her head. The thong was ripped from her hips, leaving her naked in a matter of minutes. Then he was watching her, his pale eyes filled with hunger as his hands fell to his sides.

Faith watched him, wary, uncertain what to do. He was breathing as roughly as she was now, his chest rising and falling laboriously. Tension lay thick and hot around them, drawing her into a maelstrom of sensations that assailed her both inside and out.

His hands moved again, gripping hers, laying them back on his hard stomach. Faith heard her own whimper of longing, distantly shocked at the desperate quality of it.

Faith's hands slid to his chest, her palms tingling with the feel of smooth, hard muscle. But as much as she wanted to touch him, she needed to taste him. She leaned forward, her lips pressing against a rough male nipple, her tongue stroking over it, wondering if it would bring him the pleasure that his fingers on hers had.

He groaned, his body tensing further, his hands going to her head, clenching in her hair. She braced herself against him, then raked her teeth over the hard point before nipping it seductively. His indrawn breath was hard, loud.

She moved to the other side, giving it the same attention, amazed that Jacob was allowing her the freedom to touch him as she pleased. She wasn't about to argue the opportunity though. Her mouth slid to his neck in a slow heated stroke, her tongue rasping over the skin, then her canines raking it as he shuddered against her. Her mouth trailed over his jaw then, her hand moving timidly to his head, needing his kiss.

"Faith, you're killing me," he whispered as her lips stroked across his.

She opened her lips, her tongue pressing against his, begging for his kiss. She needed him so desperately, needed the hunger and heat that she knew was a part of him.

As her tongue stroked over him, a growl, rough and deep, vibrated from his chest. His hands tightened in her hair, holding her still as his lips closed softly over her tongue, drawing it further into his mouth, stroking it, suckling at it until she was moaning into his mouth, fighting for more, unable to get enough of the erotic, sensual caress.

His muscles were tight with the leashed power of his body. His lips slanted over hers, his tongue driving into her mouth as she pressed the soft mounds of her breasts against his chest. The fiery pinpoints of her nipples were rioting with the added sensation of his hard flesh cushioning them. Her body was vibrating with arousal. Pleasure streaked over her skin like arcs of lightning as, with a desperate sound of her own hunger, her lips closed on his tongue. Her tongue stroked the swelling glands at the side, knowing the hormone they contained would send her streaking further into ecstasy.

His taste was dark and rich, like the earth, like a summer lightning storm, like all the heat and madness that burned her body for the past six years. She couldn't get enough of it. She stroked at the invading, thrusting tongue, suckled at it, fought for more and still craved him.

Her hands wouldn't lie still at his chest; her hunger wouldn't stay timid, restrained. She stroked his chest, his hard stomach, then moved to the snaps of his jeans as her lust finally overpowered her.

"Faith," he cried out her name softly as the last metal snap came undone, and her hands were pushing frantically at his hips, drawing the material down, until they cleared the massive erection awaiting her.

He was huge. Too thick for one hand to encircle, heavy and pulsing with heat. The head was thick and flared, tapered, perfect for a slow, easy penetration. She remembered how it felt, sinking into her vagina, spreading her, stretching her with a sensual pain that had her begging for more.

Her hands stroked the shaft, her fingers exploring the heavy veins, the steel hard heat as she felt her cunt weep with anticipation, her mouth water with the need to taste, to stroke that heavy cock.

She pulled back from him, her eyes rising to his. He stared down at her, his gaze heavy lidded, his lips sensually swollen, his breathing hard and rough.

"I want to—" she whispered, almost tearful with her inability to express what she did need. She didn't want to disgust him, didn't want to shame herself, but she needed—

"Faith." His hips moved, pushing his cock further into her grip, as his hands clenched in her hair. "You'll kill me, baby."

Then his hands were pressing her head down, pushing her to the jutting, demanding erection below her. Faith licked her lips, then licked the pulsing head rising to meet her.

He jerked against her. His grip tightened in her hair as his harsh, dark voice whispered his explicit encouragements. Her mouth opened, sliding over the tapered tip, stretching as her cunt had stretched the night before, taking the full width into her mouth and sucking at it hungrily.

He tasted male, rich and heady, strong and hot. Her tongue laved the area just under the hooded edge of the head and she felt him jerk.

"Yes, baby," he groaned when she would have moved back in fear that she had done something wrong. "It's okay, Faith. That's it, baby. Lick me there. Oh hell—"

His body arched as she sucked him back into her mouth, flattening her tongue to allow it to stroke the area as her hands caressed the length of the shaft, his smooth, hairless balls. She slurped at him, licking and sucking as her hunger intensified. She wanted to feel the hard throb of him as he tightened for his orgasm. She wanted to taste him, wanted to know the taste of him in her mouth as he came.

He whispered her name repeatedly, the muscles of his thighs clenching as she felt him jerk.

"Faith." His voice was shocked as he tried to draw her head back.

She refused to move. Her fingers stroked the hard shaft, her mouth sucking desperately at his cock now as she moaned in a desperate denial as he tried to pull her from him.

"Baby, please," he growled, his body shuddering.

Then the head pulsed, shooting a small stream of moisture into her mouth. It was a bit salty, a bit sweet. She growled then when his hands tightened in her hair, her teeth scraping the flesh warningly. She wanted more. She needed more.

"Damn you," he cried out with sensual fury. "You want it, baby? You want it all that bad? Then take it."

He held her firm then, his cock thrusting into her mouth, burying the wide head repeatedly into her mouth, fucking her mouth with hard strokes. Another pulse of fluid shot into her mouth. Her lips tightened on him as she swallowed greedily, her tongue stroking him, her hands now slippery with her own saliva as his hips continued to drive his flesh into her mouth.

Four pulses, small, sweetly addictive, then he growled hard, heavy, his body shuddering. He hadn't climaxed. She knew the jetting fluid was merely a precursor. She drew the head deeper into her mouth then, sucking at him, hearing his moans, his growling whispered directions as she led him closer to his orgasm.

When it came, she gloried in his rough cry, stroked him with her tongue as she sucked at the now throbbing head. When the hard jets of his salty, earthy taste shot into her mouth she couldn't halt her own cry, or her hunger. She drew on him, needing more, needing all he could give her. He was crying out above her, his body drawn tight, his hips arching to her as he shot several more explosive streams against her tongue as she swallowed desperately.

"Enough," he cried out.

He jerked her away, his hands on her shoulders as he pushed her back, following her down as she fell to the couch.

His hands were hard as he parted her thighs. She expected him to fill her, to drive the still-hard cock deep inside her.

Instead, his hands framed her face and his head lowered until his lips touched hers with a soft possession that seemed to sink into her soul. They slanted over her lips, his tongue penetrating, as she cried out into the kiss. One hand moved into the hair at the side of her head, holding her close, the other smoothed over her shoulder, then cupped the swollen curve of her breast in its calloused heat.

Faith could feel the sensations building in her body as never before. She was on fire, burning from her head to her toes. His lips swept over hers, then he rained kisses over her cheek, her neck, moving unerringly to the smooth mound of flesh his hand held imprisoned.

She writhed beneath his touch, inflamed, so desperate to feel him driving inside her that she could do nothing but whimper each plea. When his mouth covered her nipple with heated suction, his tongue flickering fire and arcs of lightning through her body, she screamed out for more.

She could feel the pull and tug of his mouth in her cunt, her womb, spasming her body with the driving demand to be fucked. She needed it, wanted it now. Her sex wept with its demand, the muscles inside tightening, needing. Her clit was a tortured, aching pinpoint of sensation as she ground it against his thigh. She was close. Oh God. So close to the orgasm, she needed to still the screaming beast intent on satisfaction.

"Jacob, please, stop torturing me," she cried out desperately as his lips moved from her breast, his tongue licking its way down her taut abdomen.

"You're so sweet, Faith. So sweet, and so soft—" he muttered as he lowered his shoulders between her thighs, his lips going immediately to the soaked, aching folds of her pussy.

His tongue drove deep inside her vagina as his hands lifted her thighs to his shoulders, opening her further for the fierce thrusts. He was growling into her flesh as she arched to him. She could feel the vibrations in her vagina, against her clit. Her cunt was a fiery, torturous ache demanding satisfaction.

Her hands gripped his hair as he licked her, then moved to her clit, circling the hard, swollen bud, then suckling it into his mouth. Her hands clenched, her thighs tightened on his head. She could feel her body shaking, perspiration slickening her body further as she screamed out at him.

"Jacob," her voice echoed around her as she felt that her clitoris was about to explode.

His hands were hard on her thighs, his tongue a marauder as he stroked her higher, destroying her with her desperate need for release before he finally rose to his knees, holding her legs in hard hands, spreading her as he came to her.

"Mine." He stared down at her possessively, savagely.

Her hands reached for the steel hard strength of his cock, needing it inside her, wanting only to encourage him in his possession of her. He grabbed her hands, forcing them to the cushions of the couch as he came over her, snarling down at her.

"Mine. Say it, Faith," he bit out, his canines gleaming wickedly above her.

"Prove it first." She snarled back at him. "Make me yours, Jacob, and then we'll see."

"You'll pay for defying me," he bit out. "Tell me now, Faith. Give me what I need, or I promise, I'll make you scream it before I give you your release."

He had no idea how close she was. If his tongue plunged inside her vagina one more time, then she would come, Faith knew. There would be no way to hold it back when his cock surged inside her.

She licked her lips slowly, staring into his eyes as she lifted her hips, the ultra slick folds of her pussy sliding over his hot cock in a long kiss. She felt him tremble, his body tightening further.

"Make me scream then," she whispered.

Chapter Twelve

 හ

Jacob's eyes narrowed on her. Faith felt a thrill of excitement, of exhilaration as her challenge was accepted. Jacob was taller, stronger than she was. His instincts were more ingrained, more savage than she could ever attain. But here, she was just as powerful as he was. She could feel the head of his cock, nudging at her cunt, throbbing at the tight entrance in its own demand as her juices heated it, the clenching muscles at the mouth of her vagina kissed it.

"Dangerous, baby." His smile was sensual, daring as he nudged the thick head closer, parting the narrow mouth of her cunt.

Her breath whooshed from her chest. He was so hot, so hard. She twisted against him, trying to drive him deeper, to trigger the climax boiling at the edge of ecstasy.

"Greedy, baby," he whispered, holding her hands to the couch cushions, resisting her twisting hips. "No, baby. Slow and easy. I want you to feel every inch of my cock stretching that tight pussy of yours. I want you screaming for it, begging me to heed your declaration that you belong to me."

He would kill her. She had forgotten that he had learned the sensual, torturous arts of forcing erotic submission under tutors who made no allowances for innocence. She doubted her defiance did more than heighten his own anticipation.

She licked her lips, staring up at him as he nudged deeper. A small measure only, causing her cunt to grip desperately, pleading, weeping its slick juices as it demanded her acquiescence to him.

His eyes narrowed as he watched her tongue, his hips jerking before he could control the response. Faith allowed her eyelids to drop slumberously, her head raising as she lapped at a hard male nipple above her. He groaned, and she could feel his muscles trembling as he fought for control. Her teeth raked the hard male flesh.

Faith whimpered at the need she had to sink her teeth into the muscle above it, to lick him, taste his skin again.

Jacob's growl was deep, animalistic, his cock driving a tenuous inch inside her gripping heat. Almost. Oh God. She wanted to throw her head back and scream for more, to scream out her acceptance of his dominance and her plea for the hard, driving length of his cock.

He reared back on his knees then, his eyes going to the slick lips of her cunt. Faith looked down, seeing his length, so thick it looked threatening, the mushroom shaped head buried between the lips, lodged in her vagina.

"Cheating," she groaned, falling back to the cushions as her legs encased his hips.

Her hands strained at the grip he had on her.

"I won," she announced. "No matter what you force—" She bit her lip, panting as she tried to bring him further inside her. "No matter what you make me say. I won." She forced the words past her lips, her head tossing as the desperate cry welling in her throat was forced free. "Oh God, Jacob—"

It was agony. She could feel the deep throb, the heat spearing into her, the rush of blood pounding in her cunt, tightening her, pleading with her to give him what he wanted, so he would give her what she needed.

"Does it matter how I win?" he asked her, his voice graveled, deep from his own arousal.

Faith's eyes opened, barely able to stare into the erotic savagery of his expression.

"Where is your victory?" she asked him, breathless, trembling from her need. "There is none with no resistance, Jacob."

His eyes narrowed further. His hips flinched, driving him no further, but forcing his cock to caress the stretched muscles it now possessed.

"There is victory in the attainment," he assured her.

"Is there?" She ground her hips against him, succeeding in tormenting herself further, but also causing the flush that mantled his cheekbones to deepen as the pupils of his eyes flared. "Could I defeat you, Jacob?" she cried out, no longer able to still the urgency that pounded demandingly through her body.

She needed to touch him, to taste him. God help her, she would give him whatever he demanded for that alone.

His breathing was hard, heavy now. His own control becoming shaken. Tears rose in her eyes, her body surged with the knowledge of his dominance at this moment. His experience was more than she could fight. More than she could deny.

"Let me touch you," she screamed out finally. "Six years I waited on you. Damn you, let me touch you. I am yours. For now, Jacob, I am yours."

His cock pulsed, buried inside her an inch deeper as he groaned out roughly, fleeting confusion crossing his face.

"Always mine," he whispered roughly.

"No." She shook her head, fighting the need to lie, to give him whatever he demanded, if only for the moment. "For now. Yours for now, Jacob. You cannot defeat what cannot fight back. Where is your victory? Where is the belonging when it is taken?"

She jerked against his hold, her legs tightening at the small of his back, fighting to force his cock inside her, to feel the pinch, the separation of her aching pussy.

"Damn you," he bit out roughly, his voice darkened with exasperation and an arousal as hot as her own.

But he released her hands, his palms sliding up her arms then beneath her shoulders, holding her in a gentle vice. He lowered himself against her, his expression filled with a wariness, a hesitancy, as though releasing his hold on her was an alien concept. Alien and not entirely comfortable.

Faith wasn't about to give him time to rethink the decision. As he moved to hold her close, her hands flattened at his hard stomach.

"I want to touch," she cried out. "Touch as you touch, Jacob."

Her hand moved over the perspiration-dampened flesh, her hips undulating against him as a hard, tortured growl ripped from his chest. Her vagina clenched on the scant inches buried inside it, and though he refused to bury more of his length inside her, he allowed her hands to smooth down, over the tight muscles of his abdomen, lower to the damp width of his cock.

Her fingers smoothed over the pulsing flesh as his hand moved to her breast, the fingers tweaking a painfully hard nipple. She arched, moaned for more.

"Give to me," he demanded. "I have not forgotten what you must pay to receive your pleasure, Faith."

The words were distant, a warning, a growling threat she chose to ignore. His release of her did more than free her hands. It freed the agonized, howling lust that had been chained inside her for six years. Her mouth went to the smooth muscles of his chest, just above the dark, male nipple that had drawn her attention earlier.

Her mouth opened, her lips moving over the area, her tongue licking, flickering over the salty male skin as his head dipped closer and he licked the mark along her neck. Sensation piled atop sensation. Her pussy gushed, her clit felt explosive as she arched to him. Then, unable to deny herself further, her teeth raked his skin, her canines scraping the flesh as his did similarly to her neck.

Before Faith could think, halt herself, or explain the compulsion, she allowed the sharp points of her teeth to draw blood, her mouth clamping to the wound as he jerked, cried out, his own teeth and mouth re-possessing the area he had marked at her neck. She could feel her body screaming, agonized cellular wails of an arousal so destructive she felt as though her head would burst. Her tongue swiped, her mouth sucked at the wound, the glands at the side of her tongue pulsing, releasing their moisture as her saliva was laved over the primitive scratches.

Heat built around her as Jacob's mouth caressed her neck, his tongue cool, then hot, his mouth sucking at her as her hands went to his back, her nails digging into the smooth taut flesh as he suddenly cried out hoarsely.

His hips bunched, his hands caught her hips, then he was surging hard and hot inside her. Her body bowed as a soundless scream came from her throat, her head falling back from his chest as she fought for breath.

He didn't pause. All control was gone, an inferno raged between them now. The sound of his cock plunging into the frothy slick tunnel of her pussy echoed around them as she fought for breath. Then his heated groans mixed with her desperate scream as his flesh raked the swollen bud of her clit and sent her body into a rioting orgasm so intense her teeth locked onto his shoulder. As the first pulse of her release began, she felt his teeth as well lock onto her shoulder as his cock began to swell, harden further.

The unbearable tightness grew, stretching her cunt tight, driving her climax so high, so hot her body felt blistered, singed by the surging wave of fiery pleasure/pain tearing through her. Her eyes were wide open, but she could see nothing but the bright flares of her body burning, exploding as the hard pulse of his cock echoed through her body. His hips continued to jerk against her, lodging the swollen shaft deeper as he released the hot, jetting streams of his sperm deep inside her clenching channel moments later.

His hands held her hips still as she shuddered and writhed beneath him. She was unable to catch her breath, unable to find a hold on reality as she spiraled out of control. Deep, hard explosions shaking her body, destroying her last grip on reality as he cried out her name, shuddering as hard in her arms as she did in his.

Then with one last pulse of his cock, one last hard tremor of her own release echoing through her body, Faith gave herself up to the exhaustion, and finally, the satiation of her primal lust.

* * * * *

The couch was wide, but still a tight fit with Jacob's body. He turned on his side, holding Faith tight in his arms and finally rested against the back of the couch with a weary sigh. He was drained. So damned exhausted he didn't really want to breathe.

She drained him to the point of no return. His lips lifted in a grin, surprising him with the lightness of the feeling inside him. He felt free, which was confusing to him. Even after the escape from the Labs, Jacob had never felt completely free. Until now.

He looked down at her sleeping face, his hand lifting so he could smooth his finger over the gentle flush along her cheekbone. Damn, her skin was soft. The finest silk, sheened with a satiny glow that never failed to mesmerize him. He loved touching her, feeling her against his body.

His hand smoothed back her hair, drawing several stray strands from her face. It was soft, thick and silky. Every part of her amazed him. To him, she was the most perfect creature God had ever assembled. And she was his. A small, compact little bundle of fire and heat that warmed every part of his body, inside and out.

He tucked her closer as he dragged the light blanket throw from the back of the couch and flipped it over them. He allowed himself to relax, his eyes closing as exhaustion claimed him. She was his now. He smiled as he slipped into sleep. He should have no further trouble from her, he thought in satisfaction. Surely by now she knew his dominance over her. She would submit as easily in all matters as she had in this one.

He frowned then. She had submitted, hadn't she?

Chapter Thirteen

ဆာ

The incessant beeping of the phone finally roused Jacob from the deep sleep he had slid into. He rolled over on the couch, instantly missing Faith's warmth, the heat of her body curled against him. Frowning, he looked around the darkened room, then growled as the phone refused to stop ringing.

His shoulder still tingled, a pleasurable warming, reminding him of Faith's new bloodthirsty tendencies. Those cute little canines were sharper than they looked. But along with the tingle, he could also feel his cock thickening, hardening with the thought of having her beneath him again, locked tight and hard inside the snug volcano of her slick cunt. He would have to find her first. He frowned as he looked around the room.

The dress still lay in silken disarray on the floor, the torn thong several feet from it. Jacob's jeans were thrown over the coffee table, his ripped shirt was half under the couch. Everything was there but Faith. And that damned phone was driving him crazy.

He stumbled to the tall walnut cabinet, jerked open the door and pulled it off the hook with a violent motion.

"Hello?" he barked, his eyes moving around the room, wondering if Faith had gone to bed without waking him. Surely, she would have wakened him to join her.

The muted sounds of raucous laughter filtered through the receiver.

"Jake, its Hawke," the weary, wary voice identified itself.

Jacob shook his head. Hawke was supposed to be miles into the jungle, not at a damned bar.

"Why the hell are you calling? And why are you bar hopping? You aren't supposed to be anywhere near a town." Irritation flared inside him.

"And I was heading out, I really was," Hawke assured him easily. "We had to wait on some supplies and extra ammo, and we were heading out of town when I just saw the most amazing sight."

Jacob's stomach dropped. His trouble barometer peaked.

"Such as?" Jacob asked carefully.

"Well, this pretty little auburn-haired spitfire rode up to the bar on a beauty of a black cycle, just like yours. Dressed to kill and happy as she could be, she walked right in as though she owned the place.

"What?" Fury pulsed, raged. She had sneaked out on him, damn her to hell. He was paddling her ass for sure.

"Right now, she's parked in front of a pot of Columbia's best, and a pitcher of the finest brew she could sweet talk the bartender out of. And ole son, let me tell you, a fine piece of ass dressed as soft and silky as she is tonight, can talk a man out of some prized brew. She has the best in the house, on the house, and a table surrounded by many male admirers."

Jacob didn't wait around to hear more. The phone was jammed back on its base. He jerked his jeans on, then ran upstairs and pulled a fresh shirt from the closet, pulling it on hastily. He pushed his feet into leather sneakers without socks and he rushed from the house. The garage was open and the motorcycle was gone. He groaned. Hell, it would be gone for sure by the time he got there. No way would that baby escape the thieves that regularly hung around that particular place. Saldora was a hot bed for the worse dregs that any society could offer.

He dug the SUV keys out of his pocket and within seconds was roaring out of the driveway as the gates slowly swung closed behind him. He pushed the vehicle as fast as he dared down the dangerous track, cursing Faith every bone jarring, back breaking bumpy inch of it. He cursed her loudly, violently. Damn her stubborn ass. Did she think this was a game?

More hormones than common sense, the words jumped through his mind. He would give her some common sense right fast, in the form of his hand applied to her well-rounded ass. Better yet, his cock, tunneling into it hard and fast until she screamed the knowledge of his dominance. He would be damned if he would let her get away with this.

What the hell had happened? He had spent hours fucking her into exhaustion. Hell, she had nearly passed out on him again when he finally locked inside her that second time, his body shuddering violently with his release. Where had she found the energy to sneak out like that?

Pack leader or not, Wolfe had a hell of a lot to explain next time Jacob saw him. Like why he neglected to inform him that the once placid, almost timid Faith had turned into a damned hellcat. The transformation was destroying him and his self-control.

He roared into the no parking area in front of the bar, jerked the keys from the ignition and jumped out. Rage bubbled through his veins like an effervescent explosion of mini nuclear bombs. His heart raced with it, his muscles were tight, violence surging through him.

Jacob stopped just within the door and snarled. The sound was so primal, so lethal that the patrons close enough to hear beat a hasty retreat out the swinging doors he had entered. And there was his Faith. Dressed to kill in a pair of snug silk knee pants and a sleeveless yellow blouse. And she was wearing sandals. Sandals that showed her delicate feet, her pretty, perfect little toes with their rounded nails that were painted a hot, fire engine red. When the hell did she start painting her toenails? Dammit, this was not the Faith he remembered.

But then again, the Faith he remembered had never seen high heels, nail polish or silk. Still, some things should stay constant. Faith's adoration, and her soft shyness were two of the things he had thought would never change.

Hawke and Danson were standing against the wall behind her, watching stoically as men crowded close, their eager eyes watching in amazement as she drank alternately from a cup of steaming coffee, and what appeared to be a chilled pitcher of beer. Dammit, Ramirez, the bartender never served chilled beer. He shot the bartender a dark, furious look, satisfaction flaring inside him as the other man paled slightly.

He would take this up with him at a time when there was no danger of ripping his throat out. Right now, Jacob knew if he confronted the man, he would kill him.

The only thing saving the lives of the bastards milling around Faith's table was that she ignored them. She was sitting back lazily in her chair, her legs crossed at the ankles as she tipped back a mug and finished off the last of the dark, potent brew that filled it. She breathed in deep, fighting the grimace that wanted to cross her face.

"About time you got here," Hawke bit out as he walked over to Jacob. "She's put away a pot of that damned coffee and almost a full pitcher of beer. What the hell did you do, cut her off?"

Jacob shot him a brooding look.

Hawke sighed, pinched the bridge of his nose then groaned roughly. "Man, do you even imagine the hell I went through when Wolfe ordered me to lose her damned vibrator? You don't cut Faith off of her necessities, man. She has her needs. I survived the vibrator, barely. I still have the scars in payment for losing the damned backpack. You just can't do this shit."

"She's in heat," he bit off. "The effects are too hard on her."

"Well, tell me something that even those ignorant full-humans over there can't figure out?" he said mockingly. "They've been sniffing around her like hounds after a bone.

Get her the hell out of here. I'll bring out the stuff she needs in the morning before I leave with Danson. That is if we can get her out of here without a damned fight. Give her the coffee, just make sure and sneak in a decaf blend. The alcohol doesn't seem to hit her as hard as the caffeine does."

Jacob growled. He was looking forward to the fight. He was praying one of those prancing, eager morons got brave enough to give him what he needed. He moved away from Hawke, and strode quickly, furiously to her table as she finished the last glass of beer.

Perspiration glistened on her face and dampened the shirt she was wearing. Her breathing was fast, her eyes glittering in her pale features. She was so aroused he could practically see the white hot heat rising from her body, steaming around her.

"Are you insane?" he asked her, his voice low enough, pulsing with enough anger that the males around her beat a hasty retreat. "Didn't you hear a damned word I told you earlier?"

"I heard every word you said. Evidently though, you didn't hear me." She shrugged as though her condition were nothing unusual.

Jacob could see the blood rushing through the vein at her neck, pouring the caffeine through a system already overloaded with adrenaline and lust.

"You're making yourself sick," he bit out. "Why would you want to do that, Faith? Are you so damned stubborn now you don't care if you're killing yourself?"

Surprised laughter came from her throat as she shook her head at him. "I'm not sick, Jacob, nor am I about to be. You're overreacting to the fact that I refuse to obey you. I told you earlier, you do not own me, despite your opinion to the contrary."

She rose to her feet, and he was the one surprised to see that she did so gracefully, without stumbling. "I've arranged for my deliveries in the morning. As I figured, adult toy stores are scarce as hen's teeth here, but I figured, as long as you're willing, what the hell, you can take the place of my BOBs. Are we ready to go now?"

The calm innocence in her expression had his fists clenching to keep from strangling her or kissing her into silence. If he touched her, he was afraid he would end up giving the bar a show they would never forget.

"My motorcycle?" he gritted out, furious.

She waved her hand towards the bartender.

"Oh. Ramirez locked it up in his garage. Hawke or Danson can bring it back to you in the morning. They have the keys." She shrugged as though she hadn't just handed his prized machine over to the biggest thief in the territory.

"Hawke," he gritted out.

"Yeah, Jake," Hawke's voice was wary.

"Get my fucking cycle. Now!"

"Uh, sure, Jake." Hawke's voice was carefully controlled, but Jacob heard the underlying laughter in it.

"Let's go." He gripped Faith's arm, careful to keep an eye on her. He wouldn't put it past her to bite him again.

Docile, her small smile more worrisome than comforting, she followed him out to the SUV. He opened the door for her, watching with a slow burning anger as she jumped pertly into the seat. His hands were clenched into fists as he stared down at her.

"Are you ready to pay for your pleasure now, Faith?" he asked her, fighting for control.

She looked up at him, her gaze slumberous, sexy.

"Jacob, I always pay, one way or the other, for my pleasures. I learned that lesson the last night in the Labs."

The husky, sensual tone of her voice, the cynical cut of her words was a double-edged sword spearing into his loins. His cock throbbed, reminding him of the near to bursting erection contained in his pants. How the hell could he get hard again, this fast? His cock would soon be raw if he didn't do something to contain Faith and her damned impulses.

He leaned forward, noticing that she did nothing to shrink away from him. Her eyes narrowed, and damn her to hell, she licked her lips with a slow, wet swipe of her tongue that had him nearly coming in his pants.

His lips covered hers, hard, savage, his teeth nipping at them when she didn't open immediately to the hard thrust of his tongue. When they parted, he surged forward, his hands going to her shoulders, pulling her closer as he growled into the kiss.

Hesitantly, her tongue stroked his, washing over the fevered glands that pulsed at the side of his tongue. She knew what he wanted. Knew what it would do to her. His hand tangled in the short strands of her hair, pulling her head back as a whimpering moan issued from her throat.

"You know what I want," he bit out, nipping at her lips again. "Do it, Faith."

"Not yet, Jacob." There was a plea in her voice, and a hunger that fed his own.

"Now," he ordered against her lips, his voice hard, unrelenting. "Now, Faith, or I won't be responsible for what happens right here, in front of this damned bar. Now do it."

His tongue plunged into her mouth again as a moan ripped from his throat. His tongue throbbed almost as hard as his cock, the glands at the side aching with the need to release their potent intoxicant into her system.

Her tongue stroked over his, igniting a lust that would have blinded him had his eyes been opened. Then her lips tightened, her tongue stroked again, and then she began a gentle sucking sensation that had his entire body tightening, raging with such unbearable need and pleasure that sustaining control became a gamble as each second went by.

He felt the pulse of the glands, the emission of the hormone that would send her body into such heat, such lust, that he knew she could never deny him. She moaned into his mouth, her hands moving from his arms to his head, spearing into the thick strands of hair as she fought to bring him closer, to draw more of his taste, his essence into her.

"Damn, Jacob, you're going to incite a gang rape if you don't get her the hell out of here." Hawke's voice was furious. Jacob pulled reluctantly away from Faith, and glanced over his shoulder at the crowd that had gathered.

He slammed Faith's door and stalked to the other side. When he pulled away from the bar, he looked over at her. His teeth clenched hard, his fingers tightening on the steering wheel as he saw her breasts, swollen and hard, moving beneath her shirt. Her nipples were hard and the scent of her arousal was drowning him in lust.

"Bastard," she whispered.

"Had you left the alcohol and the coffee alone, you could have handled it," he bit out, furious with her and with himself, for his own lack of control and his reluctance in forcing his dominance on her earlier. "I told you, Faith, your system will not tolerate it right now."

"You just might be surprised at what my system can do," she muttered heatedly, crossing her arms under her breasts and sitting back in her seat with an unladylike snort.

Jacob could smell her anger, almost as crisp and hot as her arousal. He wanted to shake his head; confused by the creature that had taken the place of the soft-spoken woman he had once known. This woman was proud, tempestuous, and so damned reckless it terrified him.

"Trying to ignore me will not help the situation, Faith," he bit out as he headed for the hacienda. "You know what you did tonight cannot be tolerated. Do you think you are not in any danger? Have you forgotten the Coyote Breed mercenaries who hunt us like rabid dogs? Or the Council Soldiers who would love nothing better than to rape a Breed female in heat?"

"Now would be a good time for either of them to try me," she growled.

She literally growled. Jacob flicked a quick look in her direction, surprise and his own arousal surging through his body. She sounded as though she would relish taking on either danger right now. She should be terrified, not prepared to fight.

Jacob felt like banging his head on the steering wheel and howling in exasperation. The woman had no care for her own safety now. What was he to do about her? How was he to protect her? Better yet, how was he to ensure her good sense long enough to keep her alive until the effects of the 'mating frenzy' wore off? Damn her. Being mate to this woman would end up killing him.

"Faith," he muttered. "You are riding very close to the edge of my control."

"Oh really?" she asked him sweetly. "I just love pushing boundaries, Jacob. Let's see if I can't skate a little closer." And then she moved.

Chapter Fourteen

✂

Jacob allowed her to take her place between him and the steering wheel. Her cunt settled nicely against the swollen hardness of his erection beneath his jeans, searing it with her arousal. He ruthlessly tamped down the desire to release it. If he did, he would rip the pants from her body and force her to ride him to completion before they made it to the house. That wouldn't do. No, he had other plans in store for Faith, and satisfying the arousal coursing through her body right now was not included in it.

She terrified him with her willfulness, her impulsive recklessness in defying him. She controlled the man, the part of him that wanted only her satisfaction, the heat of her passion and her desire. But nothing controlled the beast that lurked just under the skin. The male predator that demanded submission demanded her protection above all things. She was his woman, his mate, and while in heat, she was at her weakest.

Faith couldn't know how arousing, how seductive the fragrance of her arousal was. It was a scent capable of possessing the mind and the loins of any man not strong enough to heed the stamp of his mark on her neck. A scent that roused a near violent lust.

It also made her easily tracked. There were still Breeds out there who followed their creators. Those who had broke, who had fallen beneath the cruelties and training of their merciless masters. Jacob couldn't stand the thought of losing her to such rabid creatures.

Her head lay on his shoulder now as her fingers pushed aside the edge of his shirt. He steeled himself against the soft tongue that stroked over the mark she left on his broad shoulder.

"Mine," she whispered, her hands sifting the strands of hair at the back of his neck as she lapped at the wound.

Jacob maneuvered the SUV through the narrow roads and back alleys, tortured, tormented by the softness of the woman who had draped herself over him. But he refused to lose himself in her touch. In her caress. He smiled tightly. He knew what she was doing, all soft and seductive on his lap, and he knew it wouldn't work. Not this time.

"Am I, Faith?" he asked her seductively as he turned onto the rough track that led to the house. His tongue stroked over her neck in turn, rasping the mark he had left on her.

"You are now." There was a thread of amusement, of confidence in her voice.

"And you are assured of this, how?" he asked her dryly. He refrained from allowing her the knowledge that she was, of course, right.

"My mark, Jacob." His hand clenched at her hip as he heard the note of hope, of wistful longing in her voice. "You took my mark."

Jacob felt his heart clench. There was an echo of loneliness, of pain in her voice that disturbed him.

"I am your mate." He kept his voice soft, even. "Of course I took your mark, Faith. Just as you took mine."

He felt her sigh, the whisper of her breath across the wound. It was a sigh of regret, of longing. Suddenly it hit him, that he had truly left her alone for the last six years, unaware of the repercussions to her, the hell her body would have put her through as she waited for him. And she still came to him. She had allowed him to touch her again, only to have him leave her, when he should have comforted her, eased her through the aftermath instead of fighting his own demons.

And still, she had come to him. Perhaps not in sweetness and need, but with a lust and demand he could not have refused even had he wanted to.

"I missed you, Jacob, while you were gone." She was soft, aroused, and so hot the heat of her pussy burned through his jeans to his straining cock. He pressed closer to her, wedging his erection tighter against her saturated heat as he held her against him with his hand at her hip.

"I'm still paddling your ass, Faith," he promised her, his lips quirking into a smile as her laughter whispered over his neck.

She was not taking him seriously. And though Jacob had no intentions of hurting her, he knew that the sexual punishment to come would assure that she would give second thoughts of defying him in such a manner again.

His body tightened at the thought of it. The memory of taking her, dominating her in that damned Lab cell had haunted him for six years. He remembered clearly the impulse that had pushed him past his reason, and forced him to take her in the most primitive way. Submission. She was his mate, his sexual weakness, his sexual strength. He was determined that she know him for his strength and his dominance over her sexually. It was that need that had pushed him into the act. They were the same impulses pushing him now. She would know that he would not tolerate such defiance.

"Promise?" she asked him seductively.

"Oh, I promise you this and more." His hand smoothed over the rounded cheeks of her ass, clenching his teeth against the thought of driving his cock between those rounded globes.

Damn. He could feel the damp heat that wept from her vagina as she rubbed against him. Silk covering satin and hot wet woman. Was there any combination more seductive to man or beast? But it didn't still the dominant surge of possessiveness pouring through his veins. Ahh, sweet Faith. She thought she could tempt him, seduce him once again from forcing her submission to him? She had much to learn about her mate.

"Oh, I definitely promise," he assured her again as he brushed a kiss over her forehead.

She nipped at his shoulder then. A second later her tongue laved over it. He could feel the smile that curved her lips.

"You are pushing your luck, Mate," he told her softly as he fought to maneuver the bumps and gullies in the path he was driving over.

"Not yet I'm not." One small hand went to the buttons of the shirt he wore, slipping several free as he fought for breath. Her mouth moved along his collarbone, her tongue licking over him like a wash of sensual lightning.

Resisting the soft, needy allure of her body wasn't easy. The dominant core of him was outraged that she would try such maneuvers to get past her punishment, but the man who knew her, who finally realized the years of loss and lonely heat she had lived through, clenched in self-anger. How was he to punish her, when he could not get past the years she had needed him? Years he had spent fighting, and trying to still the hunger for her in his very denial of its existence.

He had left his mate. It didn't matter that he had not realized the ramifications of the mark he had left on her. It didn't matter that he would have gone to her if he had known the need, both physical and emotional that she had for him. It mattered that he had not. And now, his natural possessiveness would force her to face another part of the animal that fucked her, that locked inside her, forcing her body to accept his seed, to hold it with the hope of nurturing it.

He sighed as he reached the closed gates of the hacienda. Reaching over to the glove box, he retrieved the remote to the gates, watching as they opened slowly. He pulled through them, set them to re-close and the security system to reset. He watched the rearview mirror carefully, assuring himself that no one had slipped in behind them.

His trouble indicator was flagging a warning, but nothing too serious. Damned good thing it wasn't too insistent, with his arms full of Faith, her hot cunt grinding against his erection, her body heating in his arms, it was damned hard to concentrate on anything but Faith.

"Tell me, Jacob," she whispered sensuously, her soft voice filled with husky arousal. "Have you ever fucked anyone in this SUV before?"

* * * * *

Faith felt Jacob's cock flex between her thighs as he drew in a hard breath. She suppressed a small smile of triumph as his hands flexed on her hips and a rumbling growl sounded from his throat. Her fingers caressed the back of his head, sifting through the fine strands of hair as her lips caressed the sensitive skin beneath his ear.

She felt bold, adventurous. Serious, quiet little Faith was gone, and in her place was the woman she had always longed to be. A temptress. How far could she tempt Jacob? Could she make him lose that precious control of his? Make him take her again as he had taken her that night in the Labs?

She was a seductress. She would seduce him, make him burn as she had burned for so damned long. Could she make the blood sizzle in his veins, make him forget any ideas he had of anger or punishment and fill his thoughts, his mind with nothing but her?

Well, maybe not. But she could definitely tease the hell out of him, which was what she meant to do. And it seemed she was off to a running start. She felt the buttons at the side of her pants slipping free, and Jacob's hands as they caressed her bare hips. He was breathing deep and hard, his head lying back against the seat as her lips whispered over his neck.

146

"The bed would be more comfortable," he told her roughly, his hands running up her back, pushing beneath her shirt as his fingertips skimmed her spine.

"But not nearly as much fun," she whispered, smiling against his jaw as her tongue peeked out long enough to taste the rough, beard stubbled skin there.

He tasted wild and spicy, with the hint of a thunderstorm, lightning and fire. She wanted more. Her teeth scraped along his chin, her head raising, her tongue peeking out to lick at his lips. Faith opened her eyes, her breath catching at the expression on his face. Lust, raw and bare, and awe. He was watching her as though she had given him some gift, some rare and precious treasure.

"Jacob?" She questioned the look tremulously. What could she have given him that could be so special?

He stared at her, his eyes nearly glowing, heavy lidded, awash with pleasure.

"Kiss me, mate." There was a hint of desperation in his voice now. "Kiss me, Faith, before I die for your taste."

He didn't give her time to comply. Faith whimpered in eagerness as his lips covered hers, his tongue pushing past her lips as he groaned in his own need. His hips surged forward as his hands moved to her hips once again, holding her in place as his erection ground against her sex.

Faith wrapped her arms around his neck, her fingers never still, learning each contour of his neck, his shoulders. She loved the strength she could feel, the heat and hardness of the man who held her mesmerized her. His flesh was completely free of hair, but the skin wasn't smooth, soft like her own. It was weathered, tough, and made her feel more feminine, conquered and protected. He made her hornier than hell.

As his tongue tangled with hers, an imp of seductive mischief took hold of her. She allowed her lips to close on his tongue, to draw on him, at the same time, her fingers smoothed down his chest until she encountered the hard nubs of his male nipples beneath this shirt. She gripped the little point, massaging them tightly as she drew on his tongue.

He arched with a short, convulsive move. His body shook, shuddered with pleasure as he cried out at the caress. Yet, his hands moved in a lightning swift move, gripping her wrists and pulling her fingers back.

Faith moved back, watching him, breathing roughly, confused by his actions.

"Why?" She tried to pull her hands out of his grasp, watching as he fought to catch his breath.

His face was flushed, his eyes glittering with some emotion that tugged at her heart. Vulnerability? Hunger? She watched him, fighting to hide her amazement. Was she not supposed to please him, touch him?

"Let me touch you," he growled, his hands going to the hem of her shirt.

"No." Her hands caught his now. "Why don't you want me to touch you, Jacob? Don't you enjoy my touch?"

He had fought her before, on the couch. Forcing her to blackmail him, to challenge his strength to allow her freedom to touch him. Perhaps she was so untutored, so unknowing…

"You could teach me how to do it right." She hated how her voice trembled, revealing her weakness, her needs to touch him. "Did I do it wrong, Jacob?"

He swallowed tightly, his eyes closing for a brief moment.

"Faith, any better and I would cum in my jeans," he gritted out, his forehead resting against hers as he stared into her eyes. "I have never known such a lack of control."

She could hear the confusion in his voice. A need to understand what was not understandable.

"I want to touch you too, Jacob," she told him fiercely. "It is my right to touch you. My need."

"I won't rape you in the front seat of this damned vehicle, Faith." His hands clenched at her thighs, almost bruising in their strength.

"So you can only rape me in a bed?" she taunted him.

"I can only control you in one it seems." She could hear the frustration building in his voice.

Faith bit at her lower lip, watching him with a mixture of surprise and confusion. Was he angry at her? If he was, who the hell cared? She had needs as well. As her mate, he was required to satisfy those needs, and she was tired of waiting on him.

"Are you certain you can control me there, Jacob?" she asked him softly, watching him, filled with a sense of power, of knowledge. Her fingers raked over his tight abdomen, her female soul reveled in his harsh, indrawn breath.

"I could tie you to it." His voice was raspy, desperate.

"Hmm," she breathed out, licking her lips slowly. "Now that sounds interesting. But where would your sense of challenge come in?"

He grunted, trapping her hands as the nails scraped over a sensitive spot.

"Should there be a challenge?" he asked her as her fingers wiggled beneath his, releasing several of the buttons to his shirt.

His muscles jerked as her fingers stroked lightly over his flesh.

"God, Faith. Have mercy," he groaned, his hand tightening on hers.

"Mercy?" she asked him rocking against his hips, caressing his cock through their clothing. "What is mercy, Jacob?"

Where had her mercy been in the last six years? Her eyes narrowed as she remembered the nights she had spent longing for him, her cunt soaked and weeping as she fought for some small measure of satisfaction.

He groaned, his head falling back against the seat once again as the heat of her body rocked against him. For indescribable minutes he arched against her, giving her maximum sensation, wedging his cock tighter, harder against the notch of her thighs.

"Faith, you are teasing the wrong man," he told her, his voice deepening, darkening. "Your power only extends to the limits of my control."

"And you think I cannot handle your loss of control, Jacob?" she asked him, her fingers releasing several more buttons so she could spread the shirt apart, revealing the heavy muscles of his chest.

Unable to control herself, Faith's head lowered, her need to taste him, to caress him now paramount. She blew gentle breaths over the smooth flesh, then ran her tongue in a moist trail around the flat, darker area of his nipple.

She felt his body stiffen, heard the low growl in his throat as he fought for control. His hands clenched at her thighs, then moved higher, dragging her shirt up her stomach, his hands running a path to her breasts.

"I will retaliate, Faith," he promised her, groaning. "I refuse to lay back, my control a sacrifice to your explorations."

Faith smiled, her lips brushing closer to the hard nub of his male nipple. He had nearly come out of his seat when her fingers had touched him. What would he do if her mouth surrounded him, as he did to her?

"Faith, do not do it," his voice was heavy with warning as she brushed closer, her tongue swiping around the darkened area.

"Why?" she murmured against his chest, her hands laying flat on the bunched muscles of his abdomen. "Tell me, Jacob, why should I show you mercy, when I have been given none?"

His eyes speared into hers. She saw a maelstrom of emotions, conflicting needs and regrets in his expression. His hands rose, cupping her face with a tenderness she had never though Jacob capable of.

"Had I ever known how you suffered, had I suspected it, Faith, I would have ignored the dictates of my conscience and our Pack Leader to have you with me. But God's truth, Faith, I thank God I did not know. For the horrors you would have seen would have shredded your soul."

As they had shredded his. Faith stilled, seeing the pain, the horror of his memories as they clouded his eyes, darkened his expression.

"Perhaps, Jacob," she said sadly, painfully. "Perhaps your mistake was your lack of faith in me. To shred my soul, you would have to take my anchor. Had I been with you, that anchor would have been secure."

She moved from his lap now, breathing roughly, aware that the pain of both their pasts twisted between them, dulling the edge of lust with bitterness. "As it was, there was no anchor, no mate, nothing but a memory, or a dream. I was never certain which." With trembling fingers she re-buttoned her pants, shaking from her lusts and the emotional storm swirling between them.

He started to speak. She looked at his face, saw his indecision, the words coming to his lips, and she knew she had to escape. God help her if he apologized for that hour in the Lab, or if he expressed his regret. There had been so little for her to hold onto over the years. If that was taken as well, she didn't know if she could bear the blow.

She jerked the door open and ran for the house. She ignored his curse. Ignored the anger in his voice. She ignored the need, the desire, and the rush of tears that fell from her eyes.

Chapter Fifteen

ʂɔ

"Faith." He caught her just inside the house, his arm wrapping around her waist, dragging her against his body, holding her tight against his chest. "Baby please, I didn't mean to hurt you. Please, Faith…"

Her nails bit into his arm, pain and anger lashing at her heart as she tried to twist away from him. The feel of his body, so warm and hard against her sent her blood thundering through her veins, throbbing in her cunt. She was a seething mass of lust, and damned near ready to beg him to fuck her. But even stronger than her lust, was her need for Jacob himself. His heart, his love. He was holding back the intense emotions she knew he kept hidden. Protecting himself and his heart.

"It was my place," she bit out. "My place to be there for you. To soothe the horrors you faced, Jacob. To comfort you. You took that from me."

And it had tormented her over the years. Wondering if he needed her, if he was lonely, hurting, if the things he was forced to do, the blood he was forced to shed was further scarring his soul.

"No, Faith, I protected you," he protested roughly. In his voice she heard her worse fears confirmed. "Do you think I wanted to remind you of what we escaped? Remind you of the horrors you had already known?"

He turned her in his arms, staring down at her, furious now. His eyes darkening with the intensity of his emotions.

"It is my place to protect you."

"It was my place to protect you as well," she blazed back at him. "To protect your heart, Jacob, and your soul. To comfort you, to heal you. This was my place. And you took it from me. Instead, you're scarred, so hard inside that you cannot even open up to me."

"Open up to you?" he questioned her roughly as he released her, his fingers tunneling through his hair in agitation. "What do I hide from you, Faith? You have only to ask me and I will provide for you."

Faith stared up at him, seeing his confusion, his attempt to understand what she felt he should have already seen.

"Then give me your heart," she demanded. "Can you do that, Jacob?"

He stilled. He went so still, that Faith felt a shaft of raw fear surge through her body. His eyes lost their heated anger, chilled until she felt frozen to the bone.

"Bainesmith cut it out, Faith," he finally told her softly. "Long ago, far away. Didn't you know that, baby? There's no heart left."

Faith strangled on the cry that welled up from her throat as he passed her, stalking through the foyer and then bounding up the stairs. There was no regret in him. No anger. He had cut himself off from her as though she no longer existed.

Her fists clenched in pain. She had known better. Known not to push him, not to mention his heart or his love. Like Wolfe and Aiden, Jacob's life had been much harder than hers as the younger member of the Pack. As the oldest, the strongest, they had taken the responsibility of protecting the others. She shuddered as she remembered the cruelties of the scientists and soldiers. Then her eyes narrowed. She stared up at the second floor, her lips firming. He was wrong. He still had a heart, she could feel it beating, feel it hurting. She could see the pain in his eyes when he remembered the Labs, the helpless fury that even six years later, had not dimmed.

He was hiding his heart from her. He was hiding his emotions, and his soul. It had become such a habit with him that he no longer even realized what he was doing.

She sighed wearily, wiped the tears from her cheeks and debated the best way to deal with it now. She loved Jacob. She had always loved him. But she needed his love as well, and Faith knew that he would fight letting go of the protective shield that sheltered his emotions. She understood the need to do so. She had been doing it herself ever since he left her after their escape. But that didn't mean she would allow him to hide any longer.

Faith knew if she didn't act and break through his reserve, then he would eventually walk away from her again. He was an Enforcer, a fighter, a warrior. That part of him would never settle down to Pack life, and Faith knew she wouldn't want him to. There were too many Breeds out there crying out for their freedom. But she wanted, needed to be a part of it as well.

Gritting her teeth, she snarled silently and stomped through the wide hallway into the kitchen. She was horny and hungry, and evidently Jacob had little intention of satisfying the first need right now, so she would take care of the second. She would need her strength to deal with his stubbornness anyway.

Male breeds were simply impossible. Alpha male breeds were the worst, of course. Domineering. Intractable. Much too sexy for words. She sighed, she hoped he had the hard-on from hell and found it impossible to find relief. It would serve him right for leaving her so needy.

Chapter Sixteen

ॐ

He was a coward. Jacob stared up at the ceiling over his bed and admitted that soul shriveling knowledge as he listened to Faith toss and turn in her bed in the other room. The woman terrified him. She was equal parts aggression and female softness, and the combination was destroying him. His desire for her was destroying him. Hell, he couldn't believe he had walked away from her. She was hot, wet, and every sexual fantasy he had ever had in his life, and he had walked away from her because her needs terrified him.

Love wasn't a concept he could accept, even with Faith. He cared for her, deeply. He respected her abilities, her courage, and her tenacity. He wanted her until his cock was so engorged he didn't think it would be possible to come hard enough or often enough to ease it.

Love terrified him, he admitted. The very thought of loving Faith threw him into a panic. If he loved her, could he survive it if he lost her? Could he even attempt to continue living? And the chances of losing her would become higher when word spread that the invulnerable Alpha Enforcer had a weakness. How would he protect her?

He frowned, a sudden sharp pain tearing at his chest at the thought of losing her now. His fists clenched at his sides as he pushed the feeling away, pushed the fears back. There was no love left inside him, it had been ripped out years ago, he assured himself. For surely if there was any love left, then Faith would be the one to suffer for it. She had nearly suffered for it already. That night in the Lab could have scarred her, could have made her hate him forever, instead of longing and aching for him.

He had lost control. Losing control in such a way wasn't acceptable. But he couldn't stop the rising heat of need that came from the memories. He had dominated her, and yet her willingness, her need to submit to his desire had done nothing to ease the hunger for more.

Was it instinct, he wondered? Had the added DNA of the savage wolf somehow given him needs, hungers he had previously been unaware of? Jacob thought back to the years of sexual training the scientists had insisted on. The different partners, the variety of setups. Women hired because of their ability to dominate men, other women for their ability to submit, and some who had fought. He pushed the memories away. He had done what he had to in his fight to save their lives and his own. Just as Wolfe and Aiden had done. Each day there had been hell. Each decision had been a matter of life or death.

Those decisions had made him, though. Those experiences had carved his heart from his chest and bled him in ways he still fought to face. And they would now scar Faith. Scar her because the very things she needed from him had been destroyed years before.

He silenced the curse that would have slipped past his lips. Forced back the howl of agony that wanted to escape from his chest. He couldn't protect her. No matter how hard he tried, or how he fought, he would never be able to fully protect her. And neither could he let her go. It wasn't love, he assured himself. It was the mating frenzy, the sexual heat that was driving him crazy. Somehow, she had managed to infect him as well. His cock had never been so hard, so agonizingly desperate to sink inside her. He had never been so terrified of anything in his life than he was of the needs she had and the needs growing inside him for her. Jacob had a feeling he was fighting now, not just for his life, but for his soul as well.

Enduring Faith's hurt, her pain was harder than he had thought it would be. The next day, he watched as she stood in the side courtyard, going through the exercise maneuvers

Wolfe had always insisted on after they left the Labs. Sunlight gleamed on her auburn hair as she stretched, sheened her golden skin with moisture, and made him hunger to taste her. He stood silently in the shadow of several low trees instead, merely watching. She moved like a dream, a sigh of pleasure. Graceful and enduring, she performed the intricate turns and karate exercises as though she had been born to them.

The borrowed sports top and lycra shorts conformed to her body, the dark blue color complimenting her creamy skin. He blew out roughly, hanging onto his fragile control by his fingernails.

Finally, with a slow exhalation of breath, she stilled as she completed the exercises. Bending over she grabbed the towel she had left on the ground and wiped at the perspiration on her face. She opened her eyes, her gaze spearing into his. Jacob stiffened, anger lashing through his body at the quiet emotion he read in her eyes. Love and demand. She wasn't hiding a single damned emotion that she felt for him, and was demanding the same in return.

His fists clenched at his sides as he fought the ache in his chest. She smiled then. A slow, almost victorious smile that terrified him. Shaking his head, he forced himself to turn from her. Forced himself to retreat. Damn her to hell. She was destroying him.

* * * * *

Faith was hot, and she was horny. She was tired of laying in her bed, waiting for sunrise, and enduring another sleepless night. She hated sleepless nights, hated it when her body burned, and her needs throbbed through her bloodstream like a drumbeat of agony.

She turned over on the bed, wide awake. That was nothing unusual, the past years she had spent more time fighting for sleep than she had spent actually sleeping.

She could have slept the other night, she reminded herself, if she hadn't let her anger and her determination get the best of her and force her into that drive into town. She grinned, the taste of the beer and the coffee had damned near been worth it. Withdrawal was a bad thing. Not that she was seriously addicted. It was just one of her few pleasures. Her morning coffee, her evening beer. The first to keep her going through the day, the last to settle her nerves after dealing with stubborn Breeds and suspicious informants.

She rolled over on her back, sighing roughly. Dawn was peeking through the window, and she had done little more than nap since coming to her room the night before. Her nerves were wired, her flesh sensitive. She would try to ease the ache herself, but she knew she would never find satisfaction. And she sure as hell wasn't going to find sleep either.

Breathing out an angry sigh she rolled from the bed and stomped to the shower. Fifteen minutes later, after shivering under the cold spray, she toweled off, and smoothed lotion quickly over her body before dressing in a borrowed dress of butterfly light, pale green cotton, and matching sandals.

Sunlight filtered strong and bright through the shades of the bedroom, and she wondered a bit angrily if Jacob had managed to drag himself out of his lair yet. She had heard him tossing and turning in his bed for most of the night as well. For a while, she had entertained the notion of going to him, riding him to her own satiation and walking off as though his desires, his needs were unimportant. Unfortunately, Jacob had the strength to hold her to him, and her reaction to him would ensure that she would be more than willing to satisfy him.

She grimaced at the thought as she slipped from her bedroom, keeping a wary eye out for him. This being mated business was the pits. She made a mental note to be certain to warn the other females of Wolfe's pack against it. No man deserved to have such control over a woman who loved him. Especially not a man who has spent six years separated from his mate. Six long, horny years, she reminded herself. Though her body forcibly reminded her of it whether she needed it or not.

Her first priority was coffee. Danson had made some comment to Hawke at the bar, wondering why she had been forced to search out coffee, because the owner of the Hacienda kept plenty on hand. That meant she just had to find it. Jacob was more than obviously hiding it from her. And that fake decaffeinated stuff Danson kept trying to pawn off on her was getting tiresome.

Twenty minutes later, practically humming with pleasure, Faith measured fresh ground coffee into the coffee maker, poured the water into the reservoir and waited with greedy anticipation as the dark strength of the fresh beans began to curl around her senses.

Her eyes closed in ecstasy as she bent near to the pot, inhaling the heady aroma.

"It's not sex." Jacob's voice startled her, causing her to jerk and turn to him in surprise.

He wore a disgruntled expression, his chest was bare, risking an attack by her overly amorous hormones, his feet were bare, and he was dressed only in jeans, the top button of which had been left undone. Her mouth watered, and this time, not for coffee.

"Well, since the sex isn't available, it's the next best thing," she assured him, flicking a glance at the impressive bulge in his jeans once again.

Her vagina contracted at the thought of the thickness and length confined there. Her mouth watered. Dammit. He didn't have to be so sexy, did he?

"Who said sex wasn't available?" he growled as he padded into the room, hooking a cup from the shelf above the coffee maker as she poured her cup and moved away.

Faith shrugged, turning to watch him curiously as he poured a cup of her coffee and brought it to his lips for a tentative sip. He grimaced, but went back for more.

"Sugar and cream is said to taste rather good in it," she suggested, restraining her urge to grin.

"Cats drink cream. I'm not a damned cat." He carried his cup to the table.

Faith rolled her eyes. "You don't have to be a cat to enjoy cream. Even full humans like it."

"That should tell you something," he grumped, sipping at the liquid again.

Faith could only shake her head. Going to the refrigerator, she pulled out two steaks she had set in it the night before to unthaw, eggs, canned biscuits and milk.

"I'm fixing breakfast. Want some?" She asked, glancing back at him questioningly, ignoring the clenching muscles in her vagina, the itch in her hands that pleaded with her to touch the smooth skin of his shoulders.

He grunted. Faith took it as an affirmative and set about getting him fed.

"You're a grouch in the mornings," she informed him as she turned the stove on and dug around for a decent skillet. "Are you always like this, or just put out with me?"

"You are unreasonable," he growled.

"So you've said before." She rolled her eyes as she turned from him. "Maybe you're the one who's unreasonable and you just don't realize it."

That made better sense to her. She didn't consider it unreasonable to want the heart of the man who had taken her as his mate. Nature and chemical reactions be damned. She had loved Jacob since she was a child, and she was tired of sitting back and waiting on him to decide it was time for him to love her back. He could get as grumpy as he wanted to.

She needed to be fucked, but she needed love too. If she couldn't have his love, then his cock was next to useless to her. Well, almost next to useless. She was in heat, after all.

"I am never unreasonable," he assured her arrogantly. "I'm an Enforcer, Faith. I was trained to be logical at all times. To be prepared. An unreasonable Enforcer is a dead one."

She turned back to him, her eyes narrowing. She walked over cautiously, staring at him, ignoring his frown as she bent close.

"You really look alive, Jacob," she assured him. "Perhaps you're one of those anomalies we keep hearing about. You know, the Breeds that could be more human than Breed. Or in your case, more alive than dead, despite your flashes of unreasonable behavior."

She jumped back with a laugh before he grabbed hold of her. His eyes had darkened dangerously, the muscle at his jaw tensing in anger or in arousal, she wasn't certain.

Her body was burning for him, but for once, there was no fury springing from it, no anger at his overbearing attitude or at the years he had spent away from her. She was determined there would be no more separations though. She would achieve her needs during this time she had with him, or she would break from him forever.

She frowned, wondering if it were possible to become un-mated. It wasn't like marriage or a contract. The chemical and psychological bonds were a mystery to scientists and Breeds alike. There had been no record so far of any pair becoming separated after the complete physical mating had occurred.

"What's wrong with you this morning?" He was almost snarling as she hummed while placing steaks and eggs in separate plates long minutes later and placing light, fluffy biscuits in a large bowl.

She set his plate in front of him, refilled both their coffee cups and took her own seat.

"Should something be wrong with me?" she asked him, frowning. "Sounds more like something's wrong with you."

"You've been a shrew for two days straight, done everything but invite the Council to target you in that damned bar, and now you act like Miss Mary Sunshine cooking breakfast and playing mate. You need to be consistent, Faith. All this jumping around is driving me crazy."

He cut into his steak with a quick, vicious swipe of his knife. Faith hid her smile and did her best to appear innocent. She wasn't about to let him know that he was in for the ride of his life if he considered her erratic to this point. The best way to beat a damned alpha male was by confusing him. Hope had assured her of that. According to her, Wolfe was still more than uncertain about how to handle her. And he had easily admitted he loved Hope.

As she ate her breakfast, she fought the despondency that wanted to weigh her down. This was her last chance, and she knew it. If he walked away from her again, she didn't know if she would survive the pain.

Breakfast was finished in relative silence. After clearing off the table and stacking the dishes in the dishwasher, Faith put on another pot of coffee, then went into the living room where she had placed her briefcase after finding it stacked by the fake coffee Hawke thought he was fooling her with.

He had returned the motorcycle as promised the day before, and dropped off the supplies Faith had ordered. A case of beer, and what he was trying to pass off as a can of coffee. Like she didn't know decaf from the real stuff, she snorted.

As she re-entered the kitchen, briefcase and cell phone in hand, she caught Jacob sneaking the bag of coffee beans from the pantry. He froze as she stopped, watching him with narrow-eyed intent.

"Jacob." She sat her briefcase on the floor and crossed her arms over her breasts as she sighed in resignation. "What would it take to get you to leave my coffee and my beer alone?"

His lips thinned, his eyes narrowing on her. She had the impression he was clinging desperately to some misplaced idea that he could actually control her.

"It's too hard on you. The tests prove it." He narrowed his eyes on her. "Until you come out of heat, you need to abstain from the coffee."

"It's not going to happen," she assured him coolly. "So let's negotiate here. You promise not to bother my coffee in exchange for what?"

Chapter Seventeen

ഇ

She watched him pause. He stilled, just like that, his eyes trained on her in a way that made her pulse leap in heated warning.

"Negotiations." He set the bag of coffee beans on the table between them. "I can handle that."

"Hm, I bet you can," she murmured. "So state your demands and let's get on with it."

There hadn't been an Enforcer yet that could outnegotiate her. Even Wolfe had to struggle to do so.

Jacob watched her carefully, suspiciously.

"No more than a cup a day," he stated.

Faith rolled her eyes. "If you aren't going to take this seriously, Jacob, I'll just carry the damned bag around my neck."

He frowned. "A cup is more than you need."

"And much less than I'll actually be drinking. The least I intend to settle for is four pots before late afternoon, if we are in the house all day. So let's go from there."

His lips thinned. "Four pots? Faith, no wonder you never sleep. The caffeine alone will kill you."

He looked so domineering that she wanted to chuckle. She kept her expression calm despite that need. If he saw a single weakness in her stance now it would all be over with.

"I never sleep because I'm too horny to sleep," she assured him, going for the jugular now. "You take care of your duties as my mate, and perhaps the coffee problem will take care of itself along with it."

Surprise froze his expression. "Not that I mind fucking you, baby, but I'm not your damned stud," he bit out, his tone edging on furious.

How had she known he would react just like that, Faith wondered in amusement.

She shrugged. "It would appear to me that perhaps there is a problem there. But that's beside the point. We're talking coffee here, not sex."

She watched his lips thin, his eyes darken. Not in fury, but in complete surprise. She would have laughed at the expression if she weren't more concerned with watching the swirl of emotions that suddenly filled his gaze.

"You believe the problem is with me?" he asked her incredulously. "You think I don't desire you?"

"Jacob, I don't think it's a matter of not desiring me, but a matter of keeping up with me. Coffee or no coffee, I just don't think it can happen. I've tried doing without. It only gets worse," she admitted with a shrug. "But we're debating my coffee..."

"Faith, I could keep up with you any day of the week," he growled in irritation. "Are you trying to insult me?"

"If I were trying, Jacob, then you would know it," she promised him with a frown. "Can we get back to the coffee?"

Faith tried to ignore the sharp, bursting heat in her vagina as he faced her. Her entire body was warming, preparing itself for him. She could see the determination to master her filling his expression.

"Forget the damned coffee." One hand swiped through the air as he watched her with an expression of male challenge. "I want to discuss the sex."

She propped her hands on her hips. "Forget the sex, Jacob. I wanted sex the other night and you stomped away like a spoiled child. I don't want the sex, I want the coffee."

He paused, his eyes narrowing as he considered her intently.

"If you want the coffee, then you have to give out," he informed her smugly. "It makes you hornier, remember?"

"And I've done without for six years, remember?" she reminded him sarcastically. "I'll make it another six if I want to."

Jacob frowned. He laid his hand on the coffee bag, but it was the bulge behind his zipper that made her mouth water.

"No sex, no coffee. That's non-negotiable." His expression settled into lines of male stubbornness.

Faith restrained her urge to laugh at him. Like she was about to turn down the sex.

"The sex is negotiable then?" she asked him, her head tilting as she considered him.

Jacob frowned, his eyes narrowed. "Do you have to negotiate everything, Faith?"

She snorted. "I haven't negotiated near enough where you are concerned, Jacob. If I had, I wouldn't have suffered with terminal horniness for the past six years. I get my coffee, you get the sex. No limits allowed. No crying foul if you can't keep up."

"How much coffee can you drink?" he asked her suspiciously.

Faith made certain her smile was innocent and non-threatening. "The question is, Jacob, how often can you fuck?"

* * * * *

How often could he fuck? As though he didn't have the stamina to keep up with a woman who until the other night had been a virgin? Jacob watched Faith as she poured a cup of coffee in unconcern. She had her back turned to him, and that dress draped her ass perfectly. She turned back to him, cup in hand, watching him with that damned expression of curious interest. As though she expected him to doubt he could keep up with her. He almost snorted in disgust. He wanted to growl in frustration. He reminded himself to question Wolfe about the alternate personalities she seemed to be displaying. Temperamental minx one moment, a nympho on a mission the next. She would drive him insane.

He owed his Pack Leader a forceful "thank you" for not apprising him properly of what to expect. And Jacob had no doubt Wolfe knew. As though the sexual revelations hadn't been enough to contend with, he was now forced to deal with an added aggressiveness from his once quiet, shy Faith that threw him completely off balance.

"You know, Faith, it occurs to me that in your role of negotiator and Liaison to the Pack, that perhaps you have come under the impression that you are somehow not limited by the same rules as the rest of us mortal beings." He crossed his arms over his chest, glancing pointedly at the coffee cup.

Her delicate brows lowered in a frown. "How so?" She sipped the coffee, and Jacob restrained his urge to smile with smug satisfaction.

The caffeine was proven to heighten the arousal, the adrenaline during the female's cycle of heat. The aggression and sexual longings could be tempered and controlled if she would listen to reason.

"You forget, mate. The males of our breed are naturally stronger, and highly sexed. I will have you pleading for mercy before you sleep tonight." And he had no doubts, caffeine or not, that he could wear her down.

She was baiting him, he knew. Holding against him his ignorance of her condition for the past six years and her disappointment in his emotional responses, and she was determined to make him pay, one way or the other. Her amused belief that her arousal was greater than his ability to temper it made him more than determined to prove otherwise.

That was a smile she was hiding behind the cup that she raised to sip at. A deliberate, knowing smile that made the beast in him roar in outrage. He knew it was. Added with her smug assurance was the scent of her heat driving him crazy. That had to be the reason for his own unstable emotions right now. That was the only explanation for this asinine game he was allowing her to draw him into.

"According to you, you haven't had any for six years, until the other night," she challenged him. "It's a proven fact that when men, even Breeds, do without for long periods, they have no control. And I think I read a man is good for only twice a night, and then only a few times a week. Those aren't good averages." She shrugged. "Perhaps ordering the vibrators in case you get tired would be a good idea."

Oh, how innocent she looked as she baited him. As though she had no idea what such a challenge would do. As a Liaison, as a female breed, Jacob knew she well understood what she was doing. Or at least, she should. Could her innocence, her needs, be allowing her to overlook this fact?

He narrowed his eyes on her, trying to see past the sweet delicacy her expression revealed for any hidden motives she might have. When he saw nothing but her utter belief in her own words, he felt irritation flare inside him once again. He would definitely show her that he was more than capable of keeping up with any desires she might have.

"Finish the cup of coffee now." He glared at her.

Faith froze. He liked that little glimmer of apprehension he suddenly saw in her eyes, the way every muscle in her body tensed, and the sweet fragrance of her arousal deepened.

"Excuse me?" She quirked a brow. It was a charming move, but his cock wasn't in the mood to be charmed, and neither was he.

The prickling along his flesh was only growing worse. The sensitivity of his skin, the need to touch her, taste her, was driving him crazy. He had spent the night tossing and turning in his bed, denying himself, staying away from her, intent on protecting her. She needed love and happily-ever-afters, and in his world, they just didn't exist. He wanted to be honorable; he wanted to protect her from the world he inhabited and in part, from himself. But he would be damned if he would deny himself any longer. She had come to him, that sweet ass flexing in front of him, her voice soft and husky, her need scenting the air around him.

And now, she had the utter temerity to challenge his manhood. Sweetness and innocence be damned. He would show her what it meant to be his mate, and if she didn't like it, then the blame could rest on her, and no longer mire his soul in guilt.

"Finish the coffee, Faith," he growled again. "I believe it's time to show you who can keep up and who can't."

He watched the pulse accelerate in her neck, the way her breasts quickened with her sharp breaths. She was intrigued, and just a little bit frightened. She was reconsidering her challenge, he guessed. He hid a short smile of triumph. It was too late for her to reconsider anything.

She sipped at her coffee again, and he could practically feel her searching desperately for control of the situation. She had much to learn about male breeds, and her own mate in particular. He would allow her very little control now.

"I have work to do. Sex is a nighttime sport, I believe." She finally recovered, shrugging elegantly, a smooth lift of her shoulders, an expression of unconcern. It was spoiled by the flush on her cheeks, the glitter of arousal in her black eyes.

"Sex has just become your vocation, mate," he promised as he stalked to her, lifting the coffee easily from her hand and smacking the cup to the counter.

She was opening her mouth to insult him again. He knew she was, and he had no desire to hear more of her opinions on male stamina. He covered her lips with his, his tongue spearing into her mouth as she gasped in surprise. He gave her no time to protest. He was learning that in giving her so much as a second to speak was his downfall every time. He would do best to keep her mouth filled, if not with his tongue, then his cock.

He was rewarded for his initiative when her lips closed on his tongue, drawing at the sensitive flesh, easing the ache of the swollen glands and filling both their mouths with the heady taste of spice and a rainstorm as they released their potent hormone.

His hand moved to her waist, then to the taut curves of her backside as he pulled her closer, lifting her hips until he could grind the heat of her mound against his erection. She was like fire in his arms now, her breathy moans caressing his lips as her tongue tangled with his, then followed it back to his mouth. It flickered over his lips, his teeth, tangled with his until he put a stop to her antics by allowing his lips to clamp onto it, drawing on it as she had done his.

Her body tightened, arching closer to him as she whimpered into the caress. Her hands weren't still either. They caressed his shoulders, tangled in his hair, her nails biting into his scalp as she fought to get closer. Jacob's hands tightened on her ass, lifting her closer.

He groaned in surprise as her legs lifted, her smooth thighs clamping at his hips as she moved against him, notching him higher, tighter against her hot pussy. And it was hot. It seared him through his jeans, the moist fire so tempting he had to grit his teeth to keep from releasing his cock and pounding it into her furiously.

The little minx. She had to know what she had done to him. She had to know how he craved her taste, her touch, like a man possessed.

"Oh yeah," he whispered against her lips, nipping at them as she began to ride the ridge of his erection.

His hands held her steady, holding her tighter, closer as she ground herself on him.

"That's good, Faith. So damned good," he groaned, unable to hold back his own sounds of pleasure as he felt the dampness of her panties through the material of his jeans.

"I can get better." Her lips went to his neck, caressed their way to his shoulder, then her canines raked the mark she left on him, making him jerk with the pleasure of it.

"Save me some sanity," he groaned, his lips returning the favor as he sipped at the fragrant skin of her neck.

Jacob could feel the need spearing through his body like tiny pinpoints of lightning. His muscles tightened with it, making control a tenuous concept as she moved against him, moaning out her pleasure, her moisture dampening the jeans over his erection. One hand moved from the curves of her butt, smoothing down her thigh.

Faith stilled, her breathing harsh, heavy in the steamy atmosphere of lust that rose between them. Jacob allowed his hand to caress her outer thigh, then around to the satin softness of her bare buttock, and down, down to where soft liquid silk awaited the touch of his fingers.

She cried out as his fingers pushed under the material of her thong, inserting itself at the humid entrance of her vagina. She bore down against it, trembling, heated cries breaking from her throat as he teased her with the possibility of his finger thrusting inside her.

"Jacob," she cried out his name beseechingly.

"Not yet, baby," he growled, his finger circling the tender entrance.

"Jacob," she whimpered tremulously. "Please, Jacob. It hurts. It hurts so bad."

He could feel the pulse of her inner muscles, the soft slide of moisture as it raced over his fingertips. She was so hot she seared him. And in pain. He clenched his teeth, fighting for control. He was so close to ravaging her, to taking when he should be easing. He knew she was in pain, literally. Her needs would rise so high, when unfulfilled, that the pain could be agonizing. The report Wolfe had sent had been very in-depth in that area.

And Jacob admitted that it wasn't much better for him. He could feel every muscle in his body tightening, nearly cramping with the demand for release.

He held her close to him as he turned her, stepping over to the table and easing her onto it. She gasped as the cool wood met her hot skin. Jacob's fingers went to the buttons of her dress and he swallowed a moan as hers went to the buttons of his jeans.

He tore the material in his haste to get her out of it, but finally he was tossing it to the floor, his mouth watering at the sight of her firm, up-thrust breasts and their dark pink nipples.

Faith's hands were pushing his jeans over his hips, releasing the swollen length of his cock as Jacob tore her panties from her. He wanted the foreplay. He wanted to taste her, to lick every drop of cream from between her thighs. He wanted to suckle at her breasts, nibble at her nipples.

"Easy, baby," he groaned as her fingers tried to encircle the width of his cock. "Slow down, Faith. Let me make it good for you, baby."

He wanted her to know how he cherished her body, her desire for him. He wanted to stroke her skin, just because it was so warm and so damned soft it made him think of fairy tales. He wanted to kiss her, stroke her. He wanted her pussy so damned wet he could drown in it.

"Hmm, maybe I'm the one who needs to make it good for you," she panted, her hand stroking his torturously hard shaft. "I'm not the one having problems in this relationship."

His hands were at her breasts. He could barely make sense of her words, he was so greedy to touch the full, swollen curves that beckoned him. He felt her gasp of pleasure as his hands filled with the warm flesh. He had to still the trembling of his body and his eagerness for her. He felt starved, deprived, at the edge of a banquet, terrified it would be snatched from him before he could sate his hunger.

"No fears," he growled, his head lowering to the tempting peaks of her darkened nipples. "Your pleasure is all I need, Faith..." He groaned, his hands tightening on her breasts as he licked at the hard pebble of her nipple.

He heard her whimper of need, felt her body heating and couldn't control the flex of his hips that drove his cock against her fingers. Her back arched, pushing the hard tips of her breasts to his lips and Jacob was in no frame of mind to deny her. He covered one hard tip with a hungry sigh of pleasure and proceeded to take his fill of her.

Chapter Eighteen

ᔓ

Faith fought to hold onto her control long enough to tempt Jacob, to tease him with her passion and his own needs. Holding onto any control with his lips at her breasts, his teeth nibbling at her nipples, was next to impossible though. She arched against him, his erection a heavy weight in her hand as she stroked him, drawing him closer to the slick portal of her pussy. She needed him there now. Not later. She didn't want the foreplay, not now, not yet. Maybe later when the sharp bursts of painful need weren't ripping her womb apart.

Right now, looking down at Jacob, watching his face slacken in lines of sensual pleasure, his mouth suckling at her breast as his teeth and tongue rasped it, she felt as though an inferno were building in her.

Lightning flared in her breast, traveled through her stomach and struck her vagina like a pending explosion. The muscles there spasmed, clenching in heated need. One hand speared into his hair to hold him to her as she arched closer, her thighs gripping his hips as the plum shaped head of his cock nudged at her slick entrance. She was so wet, so hot for him, she was desperate. She couldn't contain her cries, her need for the hard, stretching thrusts that would burn her, stroke her into a fiery orgasm.

"Jacob, please," she groaned as he nudged the entrance, then retreated.

He was so hot. So thick. Her thighs tightened on him as she pressed closer, desperate for his possession.

"Not yet," he growled against her breast, his lips stroking over her sensitive nipple as his hands caressed the swollen globes. "Not yet, Faith, I need to taste you, touch you."

His hands stroked to her hips, gripping them, holding them still as he moved back from her.

He would destroy her. Faith whimpered as he began to lower his body, his lips stroking over the flesh of her abdomen in a moist trail of lava hot sensation.

"You taste like fire and silk," he whispered as he pressed against her, indicating that she should lay back.

"Jacob, on the table?" she gasped, shocked. But the warm pulse of liquid from her vagina assured her that her body was more than willing.

"What better to place to make a meal of you," he muttered, his lips moving closer to the bare, slick petals of her sex. "Damn, Faith, I'm starved for you."

She felt his hands spreading her thighs further, his body lowering, his fingers smoothing down the plump lips of her pussy. Her hips jerked, arching closer to the warm puffs of breath that caressed the sensitive flesh.

"So sweet." His tongue stroked across her straining clit.

"Oh God!" she cried out, jerking against him, driving her hips closer to his torturously slow caresses.

"You taste exquisite. Like nectar and dreams, Faith," he groaned low, his tongue stroking along the sides of the swollen lips. "So hot and wet, and mine. Just mine, Faith. Every sweet, delicious inch is mine."

She would have protested. She really meant to. She would have if his tongue hadn't swiped slowly through her aching slit, circling the entrance to her vagina then moving back so his lips covered and suckled at her swollen clit.

Faith could barely breathe. It was all she could do to release the breathy, agonized whimpers of nearing orgasm as she strained closer to his touch. His tongue was a stroke of feathery lust, sensual, heated, licking at the thick cream of her passion, murmuring his appreciation as he ate her like a delicate treat.

She twisted in his grip, straining closer to him. She wanted his tongue deep inside her. Wanted to feel it plunging into her vagina, easing the aching emptiness there. She needed to be filled, fucked, held, driven into the insanity of release.

"Easy, baby." He lapped at her. Licked her. Sipped at the moisture that pooled along her cunt.

Like a greedy man. A man starving for her. A man desperate for her taste and her passion, he never let up. He placed her legs over his broad shoulders, her thighs parted now by his head as he lapped and sucked at her soaked flesh.

His hands weren't idle though. They cupped the cheeks of her rear, bringing her closer to his mouth, holding her still as she twisted against him, screaming out in need as he sucked delicately at her straining clit.

She could feel her body tightening to a bone breaking level. Her head tossed, her body thrashed and she could hear herself pleading. Broken, whimpering cries as he moaned into her pussy a second before he drove his tongue deep inside her flooding vagina.

Faith shuddered convulsively, her hips straining closer, her cunt erupting in fire as he fucked her hard and fast with his agile tongue. She heard herself screaming, begging. Oh God, it was too good. Too hot. She was dying. And when his thumb stroked over her clit, she exploded. Rapture rained over her body, sizzled in her blood until she couldn't breathe, couldn't fight, could only dissolve into liquid fragments of ecstasy as he tongued every flooding drop of her release into his mouth.

The eruptions sang through her body, vibrated through her cells. The repeated, pulsing eruptions in her womb were never ending, causing her body to jerk repeatedly as he continued to lap at the liquid heat that spilled from her.

Faith's hands were locked in his hair now, though she wasn't certain how they got there. Her body was taut, a seething mass of desires that demanded more of his touch as the greedy needs of her body only flared higher.

"More," she begged shamelessly. She knew no shame. She knew only the burning, the ache of emptiness inside her.

He rose between her legs then, his fingers unthreading hers from his hair, as he lifted her legs from his shoulders and wrapped them instead around his waist. His cock pressed against her opening as he stared down at her.

His eyes glowed. A brilliant pale blue in his flushed face, his eyelids were lowered, his dark lashes casting erotic shadows along his cheekbones.

"I need you," she cried out, her legs tightening around his waist as she squirmed closer, desperate to feel his engorged cock thrusting inside her. Deep. Hard. She wanted him, all of him, now.

"God, you're beautiful like this," he whispered thickly as his hands tightened on her hips, his cock sliding the slightest degree inside her hungry tunnel. "So flushed and moist, your eyes so dark. You make me hunger for you, Faith, as I have never hungered before."

His voice was thick, deep, until it rumbled in his chest and stroked over her senses like a caress. He eased deeper inside her, the thick, flared head of his cock parting the tight muscles of her entrance as his fingers clenched at her hips.

"Oh yes." She shuddered, needing more.

The pleasure/pain of his slight entrance wasn't enough. Never enough. She needed more. She needed all of him.

"You're so hot. So tight," he groaned, his hips burrowing the thick length of his tumescence an inch deeper.

He burned her, stretched her. She twisted in his grip, her cries ragged and hungry as she begged for more. She could feel her cunt gripping the head, milking it, fighting to tug him deeper. She wanted him deep, hard and hot inside her.

"Damn you," she cried out as he eased in just a bit more.

She felt as though she were burning alive from the inside out. Her muscles clenched in furious need, her cunt wept in lustful desperation. Pleasure lashed her flesh from head to toe, sensitizing her skin, tormenting her with her need for climax.

Jacob's face was creased in lines of strain. Perspiration soaked them both, dampening their bodies, making her wetter, making her lusts burn hotter.

"Ah, Faith." He grimaced, his teeth baring as he fought for control. "You're so tight. So damned tight and hot."

He eased in further and she screamed out her frustration. Her hands gripped his at her hips, her feet locking behind his back as she used him for leverage to push herself closer, to bury the hot length deeper. The head of his cock eased in further as her muscles clamped down tight, desperate to hold him inside her. She gripped him, relishing the stinging pleasure of his possession.

The tight grip undid Jacob though. With a heavy groan, a rough curse he surged forward, parting her with a thrust that stole her breath. She felt the heavy length forging inside her, eased by the slick essence of her need, burning with the lust that rose like an inferno between them.

And he didn't pause. He didn't give the tight grip time to ease, to accustom to the width of his erection. As though that thrust had been his breaking point, he held her tight and began to move, hard and heavy, repeatedly inside her as they both fought for breath.

The thick froth of her cream glided between them, heating them further as he forged back and forth. His cock tunneled inside her with long repeated strokes that kept the sensations building, the fire burning out of control. Tremors raced over Faith's body as the tension built to painful proportions inside her cunt. Her hips rose and fell, taking him deeper, feeling him part her, stretch her with each downward stroke.

The sensations were destroying her. She was hot, cold, her womb clenched; her cunt trembled around his erection as he began to increase the speed and depth of his thrusts. He bent over her, holding her close, pushing her legs closer around his waist as his lips covered hers with a hungry groan.

Lips and tongues battled together. They moaned against each other as Jacob's hand moved to her breast, his lips stroking over her jaw, down her neck to the sensitive mark he had left on her. He licked her there, groaned and began to thrust harder.

Faith could feel her body shattering. A storm of pleasure erupted through her blood stream, her nerve endings as everything inside her began to unravel. Prickling fire traveled over her flesh, bolts of electricity exploded in her cunt as she tightened on his thrusting cock and came apart within his arms.

She was only vaguely aware of his cry as it vibrated against her neck, but she was more than aware of the swelling of his cock, the way it stretched her further, drove her climax higher and locked him inside her. Exactly where she wanted him. Deep, hard, held at the very mouth of her womb as she felt the hard, heated jets of his sperm erupting inside her.

His hips jerked. The swollen knot tugged at the muscles it was locked inside of, causing Faith to gasp at the renewed vibrations of her own climax. Jacob's hands were beneath her, holding her close, his groans nearly sobs as his cock jerked, pulsed, with each eruption of his seed inside her.

Faith clamped her muscles tighter on the fully lodged knot. She shuddered at the sensation. The burning pleasure that bordered on pain, the deep shudder of yet another post climactic eruption. But Jacob's reaction was more intense. His hands tightened against her back as he hugged her closer, growling as his lips locked on the mark he had previously licked. His breathing shuddered from his chest, his hips jerked, his seed pulsed inside her again.

It seemed never ending, a pleasure that rocked her to her core, and bound her to him, body, heart and soul. She would never survive without him. Without his touch, without the deep, soul filling satisfaction of holding him to her, feeling him locked inside her in a way that he would never know with another woman. Only Faith. Only his true mate.

Chapter Nineteen

හ

Jacob pulled slowly from the hot, moist grip of Faith's body, his breath shuddering through his chest, his cock so sensitive that the smooth friction of his retreat had him shivering with pleasure. He had never known such pleasure. Had never known such satisfaction.

She was sprawled on the table, fighting to catch her breath, her hair damp, her lips swollen as they parted in the need to draw in air. And he still needed her. He was still erect, engorged with blood and lust. The repeated blasts of his seed inside her had done little but take the edge off his hunger for her.

He pulled her up until he could hold her against his chest, her head settling against him, her lips placing a soft kiss on his chest. He felt the muscles there tighten, felt his heart slam against his ribcage at the incredible tenderness her soft caress conveyed. She made him feel things he had never known before. Things he didn't want to delve into too deeply.

"I want you again," she whispered as her hands stroked along his tight stomach, his hard thighs. "I want you inside me forever, Jacob."

His throat tightened. Her voice was so soft, hesitant and yet unafraid of expressing her emotions. She was destroying him with her gentleness, with her silken kisses and her heated passion.

He held her close, his cheek resting against her hair as he stroked her back, her shoulders, and reveled in the tenderness of her lips at his chest, the heat in her hands along his thighs. He breathed in hard and deep when her hands circled his shaft, her slender fingers measuring him, tracing the heavy veins, the large plum shaped head.

"We have a bed we could do this in," he told her, his voice husky, rough.

"Mm, so?" She slid from the table, her lips and tongue painting a path of fire around a hard male nipple.

"Hell, Faith," he moaned her name as she nipped at his nipple, then stroked it with her tongue.

"I want to touch you like you touch me," she whispered. "I want to show you how good you make me feel, Jacob."

He heard the need in her voice, the arousal, and more. He heard her conviction, her belief in happily-ever-afters and romantic dreams that had to come true. And he wanted to believe. Even though he knew it didn't exist, he wanted to believe.

Jacob closed his eyes, fighting the sheen of moisture he felt there, the knot of pain in his chest, and focused instead on her explorations of his body. She weighed his heavy scrotum in her hand, murmuring her appreciation as she tongued the small bead of his nipple. Her other hand stroked his erection as her lips moved across his chest, attending then to his other nipple. Jacob was lost in sensation. Pleasure washed over his body in never ending waves, leaving him gasping as she caressed him.

He looked down as she began to travel lower, instantly transfixed by the pleasure that transformed her face. As though touching him brought her as much pleasure as his touch brought her.

Soft auburn lashes feathered her cheeks as her tongue stroked over the clenching muscles of his stomach. Her teeth scraped him, her delicate canines raking sensually over his tight flesh as he groaned heatedly at the touch.

His hands speared through her hair as his body hardened further, his cock beating a tattoo of agonized anticipation as her mouth neared it. Her breath blew over the sensitive head gently as her hand stroked the hard column with firm strokes.

Jacob's thighs tightened as anticipation curled in his belly and wove its way around his loins. His erection jerked in her grasp, eagerly awaiting the second her hot mouth would enclose the engorged head.

"Faith," he growled out her name when she skirted the pleading knob to kiss his thigh.

He felt her smile against his flesh, then a second later, the hot swipe of her tongue across his scrotum. He couldn't stop the startled moan of heated pleasure that broke from his chest. As he fought to recover, she chose that moment to move higher and to enclose the swollen head of his cock inside her hot, moist mouth.

Jacob clenched his teeth as he fought for control. His hands bunched in her hair, his back arched, driving him deeper into the humid depths as he felt her moan vibrate against the ultra sensitive flesh. She hummed her approval to his reaction, her tongue swirling over the thick head, then her mouth suckling him firmly.

He felt his muscles bunch as he fought for control. Her mouth was an instrument of torture. Her tongue a lash of searing fire. The suckling motion of her lips, her caressing moans were driving him to the brink of insanity. The slick, moist sounds of her suckling, the heat of her hands, the rasp of her tongue, was too much. Too hot.

Her short nails ran along his inner thighs, a prickling tingle that had his breath strangling in his throat. He felt his cock throb, felt the first pulse of fluid that would have eased her cunt had he been there. She took it eagerly into her mouth, humming against his taut flesh once again.

Jacob felt like whimpering, the pleasure was so deep, so strong. His muscles trembled with the force it required to hold back his climax, to relish the heat of her mouth moving on him, pleasuring him. Unselfishly, giving, taking nothing for herself as she touched him. Had anyone ever done such a thing for him before? It was all he could do to hold back his climax, to allow himself to cherish every moment of this unusual experience.

"Faith, so good…" He couldn't hold back his moan of praise as her tongue stroked the underside of his cock with slow, swirling licks. "Oh, baby. Oh hell. Faith, it's too good." She sucked on the bulbous head, her mouth moving back and forth, forcing his cock in and out of the snug grip of her lips with tender force.

He had never known such sensations in his life. A pleasure that tore through his body, his soul, wrapping him in warmth and in peace despite the agonizing need for release.

Another spurt of liquid shot into her mouth, and she took it greedily. His cock flexed, blood pounding through the thick veins as he felt the hard beginning contractions that signaled his climax and the swelling knot that locked him deep inside her cunt.

"Faith." His hands clasped her head as he forced himself back.

He groaned, agonized, grief-stricken as he was forced to ignore her disappointed cry and relinquish the liquid heat that was driving him to the edge of madness.

"Come here." He dragged her to her feet, lust roaring through his veins, pounding through his body.

He had to be gentle. He restrained the beast that roared out a demand that he take her now, pound into her hard and fast. He kissed her lips as he groaned her name once again, then he turned her, bending her over the table as he positioned his cock for the needed thrust.

"Faith. Baby. You destroy me," he whispered as he leaned over her, his erection nudging into the tunnel of fire between her thighs.

"Jacob, you tease me with that cock again and I'll hurt you," she cried out fiercely, backing into him, shocking him with the explicit need in her voice. "Fuck me, damn you. Before I die from the need…"

The kitchen echoed from their combined cries as he thrust inside her to the hilt. One long, smooth stroke into the very heart of her as her muscles parted, then clenched on his cock like a velvet fist. Control became a fragmented idea as her heat and wet silk poured over him. He held to her hips, steadying her, holding her in place as he began to pound inside her.

The sounds of wet sex, of soaked flesh, and gasping cries wrapped around him until he could hear her sobbing for relief. He felt his own cries ripping through his chest as his cock throbbed, pulsed, swelled so tight and hard inside her that he was locked deep, locked clear to her soul as he poured his seed inside her body.

Chapter Twenty

๛

The next morning, dressed in jeans and a dark T-shirt, Faith watched from the shelter of a low growing tree as Jacob checked the perimeter of the yard once again. He and several of the other Enforcers were going over the alarms and security measures they had placed throughout the compound, making certain they were still in working order.

What they expected, Faith wasn't certain. From what she could figure out about the present mission, they were at a stalemate. Unless they could get the Council or Lab soldiers to make a move, capture one, and pry out details, then they were screwed.

It was a risky enough business going after the small, independent Labs in this part of the world. South America was largely unpopulated, the jungles dense and capable of providing more places to hide than even the most experienced scout could name. Entire human expeditions had been lost within the mountainous terrain at one time or another.

Here, the jungle grew right up to the tall, stone walls that surrounded the hacienda. In many areas, it had grown over the perimeters and were once again attempting to reclaim its stolen land. Trees grew close to the walls, the smaller ones leaned over it, or their branches sheltered it. It was a security nightmare. But she had a feeling Jacob was aware of that, depending on it, actually.

Grabbing hold of the low branch above her, Faith lifted herself to the sturdy limb before staring around curiously. The Enforcers were busy with the minute details of checking out the equipment and preparing for a siege. She snorted. It would only take a few inventive Coyote Breeds to figure out a way into the house from here.

Moving slowly, her eyes narrowed as she tried to place herself in the enemies' mind frame, she looked around the back end of the gardens. Next to her, another handy tree afforded her another view. She crossed to it, stopped, then considered her next move. None of the others even realized where she was, or the danger inherent in the ease in which it could be accomplished.

Balancing herself carefully, she moved from branch to branch, tree to tree, feeling more like Tarzan's sister than Jacob's mate. Keeping a careful eye on the alarm that had triggered before, she worked herself over, then dropped down on the trigger area. Which was also closest to the house.

A shrill beep sounded instantly, causing the Enforcers to swing around as one, weapons cocked and ready. Faith didn't bat an eye, though she was more than thankful for the stringent training the Enforcers went through.

"Goddammit, Faith." Jacob's voice was furious, enraged and carrying a thread of fear. "Be careful where you step."

He strode up to her and as he neared, she lifted her weight, allowing the heavy branch she had pulled down with her to pull her back up as she flipped herself back into the sheltering leaves of the tree.

There was complete silence below her as she ignored the Enforcers and began a more thorough check of the tree. She found what she was looking for within minutes.

"There are scuff marks all along the branches, as well as broken bark. Your intruder is using steel points to make his away along the trees," she informed the men below.

"Not possible," Jacob bit out. "We would have heard something."

"Not if he knew what he was doing." She shrugged then frowned again as she pulled a large eagle feather from where it caught between branches.

She stared up at the tree carefully, looking for a nest, or any sign of a bird that could have been disturbed. There was something different about the feather that she couldn't entirely place. Shrugging, she tucked it into her back pocket as Jacob swung up into the tree in front of her.

He quickly found the areas where the bark had been skinned back, the evidence of metal prongs having been used.

"I'll be damned," he bit out as he raised his eyes slowly to her. "How did you figure it out?"

She arched a single brow coolly. "Liaisons have to think sneaky. Often. Alphas just power in. If you're dealing with Coyotes here, then they are the smartest ones I've ever heard of."

"Liaisons can be smartasses, too," he growled.

Faith licked her lips and lowered her eyes as she mimicked a pouty kiss.

"You can kiss my smart ass, Jacob. Your equipment isn't malfunctioning, your security setup is."

"And how do you suggest I fix it, Ms. Liaison?" he sniped. "We're in the middle of a freaking jungle. Besides, I just want advance warning, not a major alarm system."

"What you're likely to get is one of your Enforcers killed," she hissed. "They are using the trees, Jacob. And they've breached your defenses once. What if they figure out where the alarms are, now that they know there are alarms?"

"You think I am not considering this?" he asked her impatiently as he stood to his full height, towering over her as he stepped closer. "You think I have fought these bastards for six years without learning anything, Faith?"

"Well, evidently you didn't learn anything about using the trees for cover, or you would have thought about it," she retorted. "I've been out here half an hour and I figured it out."

"What does this make you, a damned cat?" he growled, his voice rumbling now.

"What is this thing you have against cats, Jacob?" She rolled her eyes mockingly. "Learn from them. Felines can be your friends, baby."

She heard a round of snickers below. Evidently Jacob did too, if the volcanic look on his face was anything to go by.

"Styx, he who laughs hardest can spend his night in the damned trees waiting on the bastards," he bit out coldly. "Get some rest and see if you can't make like a cat tonight."

Faith glanced down at the huge redhead. If a wolf could pout, then he was doing a fair imitation of it if his expression was anything to go by.

"Hell, boss. She's cute. You can't blame us." Stygian was openly laughing now. "Has you by your balls and you know it."

"Want to join Styx tonight, Stygian?" Jacob snapped, his eyes still on Faith.

Faith restrained her own grin as Stygian immediately cleared his expression.

"No way, boss," he answered quickly. "Never did care much for the feline way. Keep my feet on the ground if it's all the same to you."

"What is it with you people and the Felines?" she asked with exaggerated patience. "They are really very nice people, you know."

"And you would know this how?" Jacob snarled.

Faith's eyes widened. "I keep telling you, mate." She spoke clearly, hoping he would understand this time. "I am Liaison to the Pack between all informers. This includes members of the Feline Breeds. I deal directly with their Liaison, Tanner."

A real growl erupted from his throat now.

"Don't you start, Jacob," she warned him firmly. "There is nothing at all wrong with Tanner."

"He's a pervert," he snarled. "His mating affirms this. You have no reason to be around this person."

"He has a perfectly nice mate. She gave birth to twins last year. Perfectly adorable babies." She crossed her arms over her chest and narrowed her eyes. "Has a Wolfe Breed sired a child yet? Not that I've heard of."

"This is beside the point. When a Wolf Breed does sire a child, he will need no help from others, I can you assure you of this."

Faith drew in a hard, patience-restoring breath. "You have lost your mind. Is this an Alpha thing that comes with a male's mating cycle? Thank God all I have to deal with is perpetual horniness. And let me assure you, you are not keeping up today. Perhaps you need help after all."

Below, Enforcers scattered amid helpless laughter as she faced a more than enraged mate.

"I promise you, mate," he snarled as he came slowly forward, backing her into the thick trunk of the tree, his body aggressive, his voice dangerously sensual. "I need no help keeping you fucked. Not today, not tomorrow, not ever. All I need to do is get rid of the damned coffee that turns you into a nymphomaniac with more attitude than a rabid Coyote."

Her eyes narrowed on him as his hips pressed into hers, driving his cock against the softness of her lower belly.

"We have a deal," she reminded him heatedly. "You have to leave my coffee alone and keep me fucked. Not snipe at me, or take it out on me because I figured out something you hadn't thought of."

Her hands gripped the limbs above her to steady herself. She watched his eyes heat, his cheeks darkening with sensual awareness as her breasts brushed his chest.

Jacob's hands went to her waist as he lifted her just enough to grind his cock between her thighs suggestively.

"Mmm." She licked her lips again as she lifted her legs, allowing them to bend and grip his thighs. *"Wild monkey sex. Sounds like fun to me."*

Chapter Twenty-One

ಬ

"It would serve you right if I fucked you in front of the entire Pack," he growled as his lips went to her neck, his tongue stroking her skin.

"Exhibitionism? Sounds kinky, Jacob. I'm game if you are." Her head tilted back, her eyes closing as pleasure washed over her, heating the core of her body further, and leaving her longing for his touch, his taste.

There, in the shade of the huge trees, sheltered by the jungle, the mists of night still clinging to the air around them as the sun blazed in the morning sky, she wanted his touch, his heat.

Her hands tightened on the limbs of the tree as Jacob moved closer to her, his feet braced on two closely spaced limbs, his hips pressing tight against hers as his lips caressed her neck, and one hand delved beneath her shirt to the bare, swollen breasts awaiting him.

At the first touch, Faith felt ripples of sensation streaking through her body, caressing her womb and her vagina. She whispered a needy moan of arousal, desperate for more.

"Oh, you are hot," he nipped her ear as his fingers tweaked her breast. "Does it turn you on, Faith, sparring with me? Pushing me?"

It did. She knew it did. Pitting herself against him, watching his eyes flame, seeing emotion transform his face, the confused anger, the heated desire. The need to make her submit. It fired her blood as nothing else could, seeing that dominance rising to the surface. She had no desire to best him. Faith fully admitted she wanted to be bested.

"Does it turn you on?" she asked him, rather than revealing her feelings, her weakness for his emotions.

His growl was surprisingly strong as he jerked her shirt above her breasts and stared down at the bounty now offered up to him.

"Turn me on?" he said roughly. "Damn you, Faith, you make me so hot I expect to disintegrate every time I touch you."

She expected his mouth to ravish her breasts. To take what he was staring at so greedily. Instead, he took her lips in a kiss that destroyed her. His tongue swept into her mouth, conquering her, weakening her and yet filling her with a power she could have never imagined.

"Then take me, Jacob," she whispered beseechingly as his lips lifted. "We can burn together."

She needed him, needed him as she had never needed anything in her life.

"I won't take you where my men can see your lush body, or hear your cries," he bit out. "You are mine, Faith. Know this now. Mine."

"Yours," she cried out breathlessly as his hands cupped her breasts, fingers plucking at her nipples as he stared down at her in heated desperation. "If I am yours, Jacob, then prove it. Take me."

He stepped away from her, breathing in quick, hard breaths, his hands rough, shaking as he jerked her T-shirt back over her bare breasts.

"Go. Now." His voice was raspy, as dark and graveled as any she had ever heard. "I'll be in our bedroom in five minutes, and by God, you better be ready for me."

* * * * *

Ready for him didn't come close to describing how eagerly she awaited him, Jacob thought as he entered the bedroom to find her sleek, perfect body laying back on the bed.

She stared up at him, her eyes so black and hot they seared him further. His whole body throbbed. Not just his cock, not just his tongue. He watched as she licked her lips with a lazy, moist movement of her tongue. They glistened now, making him hunger with his need to taste them.

There was knowledge in her eyes. A burning satisfaction that confused him. As though some need in her were suddenly fulfilled. A need that did not involve his touch, merely whatever she was seeing in his expression, in his desire for her.

"What do you think I've done to you?" she asked with him a purely female smile of mystery. Damn her, it only made him want her more.

"Drove me insane," he suggested with a measure of amusement at his desires. He was nearly at the edge of his control, and he had yet to even kiss her.

Jacob lowered himself to the bed, coming over her, needing her. His mate. Her hands rose, flattening on his abdomen as the muscles there clenched at the agonizing pleasure of her touch. Jacob drew in a hard, deep breath as his cock twitched in reaction. Her touch smoothed from his abdomen to his chest, then back again, igniting a fire of need that tore a ragged groan from his chest. He wanted to eat her alive. He wanted to fuck her until she screamed. He wanted to love her, touch her with all the tenderness, all the heat that rose inside him for her.

The scent of her need enfolded him, infused his system now, just as she did. Just, he realized, as she always had. Had he ever been free of Faith? Free of the need, in some form, for her?

"You are so soft." He brushed his jaw, rough from the stubble that had grown there overnight, across her bare shoulder. "Your skin amazes me."

And it did. It glowed with the depth of a rare, perfect pearl. The sheen of satin, the warmth of life, that passion of a rising lust that amazed him. He brushed his lips over the curved area, loving the taste of heat and woman, the dewy drops of perspiration that began to cover her body.

She shifted beneath him, her back arching, her nipples hard and fiery brushing his chest. He grimaced, burying his lips in her neck, his tongue stroking the mark he had left on her as he settled cautiously beside her. He pulled her into his arms, fighting the overpowering need to take her quickly, urgently. His body, his mind was conflicted. He wanted her soft and easy, hard and fast, screaming in orgasm, crying out his name in release.

"Yours is warm, and strong," she whispered with a breathless arousal that strained his control as her hands whispered over his abdomen. "You make me feel warm and hungry, Jacob."

Jacob couldn't stop the need to press her closer, to feel her breasts with their fiery tips burning into his chest, the way her thigh lifted over his, the humid heat of her pussy burning into his skin. Damn her, he felt like a ravenous animal in his need. It was all he could do to keep from throwing her to her back. Instead, his lips took hers possessively. She was his woman. His mate. He would prove this to her this day. Before she left his bed, she would know she was his, heart and soul, body and life.

He caught her cry in his mouth as his tongue thrust past her petal soft lips, sweeping over hers, encouraging her to take him, to draw the pulse of his passion from the swollen glands there.

She didn't hesitate. Her lips and tongue twisted against his, then she closed over it, drawing it into her, relieving the minute pain of his need. Her tongue slid past his lips, a cry escaping her as her own need became paramount. Jacob's lips twisted against hers, taking possession of her, drawing the sweetness of her passion into him.

Her kiss was silken heat, satin lust, and a core of such vibrant emotion he wanted to shy away from it in self-defense. He, the lone wolf, the Enforcer that all Packs and humans who knew of him feared. With only her kiss, this woman stole his strength, his breath, his will to live without her. As though recognizing the dark needs he had refused to confront, and admitting they all stemmed from his need for her, suddenly made the difference in his very survival.

God help him, she had possessed his very soul. The more he tasted of her, the more he needed.

They fought each other for domination of the kiss; lips, tongues, muted moans of desperation as their arousal began to flame out of control. Jacob could feel his control fraying, just as it had the night in the Lab, when his desperation, his animal instinct pushed him past the edge.

He fought those same needs now. As though the first pulse of her heated, arousal laced kiss was just entering his system. His hand tightened at her hip, his lips drawing a desperate line of kisses over her jaw, her neck. He licked at the mark there, drew it into his mouth, laved it roughly. He wanted her as hot, as out of control as he was. He wanted her screaming. Or did he want her soft and pulsing? Hard and exploding? He wanted it all, and he needed it now. It made no difference that one contradicted the other. All that mattered was the need.

* * * * *

Faith couldn't help but plaster her body as close to Jacob as possible. She could feel her needs building inside her. They vibrated through her, setting up a steady palpitation in her cunt, her womb, beneath her skin as his kiss fired her body more heatedly than ever before. She strained to him, wanting every inch of their bodies to touch, to mate. One hand gripped his hair, fighting to hold him to her as he turned her to her back, rising over her. The other curved over his shoulder to his back, feeling the muscles there bunch, clench.

"The taste of you makes me crazy." There was that heated rumble, rough and sexy that growled from his chest as he spoke.

Faith shivered, her head tilting to give him better access to her neck as she licked over the wound at his shoulder. He tasted just a bit salty, very dark, and very male as his mouth left her neck, then traveled a heated path to her breasts.

She groaned, feeling his breath waft over a nipple, tightening it further, heating it until she felt her flesh burning from her needs. She arched to him, whispering her plea as her nipple raked his lips.

Eyes half open, drowning in sensation, Faith watched as his mouth opened then covered the stiff peak. Faith felt her breath catch for long moments as pleasure tore from her nipple to her womb, contracting the muscles of her abdomen. Her hips jerked, her cunt rippling beneath the onslaught of ecstasy that fired through her body. Her eyes closed as a tremulous moan whispered past her lips.

Her hands roamed over his sweat-dampened shoulders, into his hair, holding him closer, pleading as the deep suckling motion of his mouth had her burning alive. Her thighs tightened as she fought the demand in her vagina. Her body tried to turn, to find the ease of the hard male thighs that pushed between her softer ones as he came further over her.

"Stay still," he rasped roughly. "My control is shaky at best, Faith. Do not tempt me right now."

"I need, Jacob." She could feel the blood rioting through her veins, throbbing in her cunt as her body cried out in hunger.

He groaned at her breast, licking her nipple with a rough swipe of his tongue before he moved more fully between her thighs. Faith wanted to scream in denial when she realized he was not positioning his cock to sink into her heat, rather his shoulders to hold her legs wide as his head lowered to her cunt.

"And I need, Faith," he groaned, his breath blowing against the wet folds of her sex. "I need your taste, I need your heat—"

Faith wanted to scream as his tongue circled her clit, then pushed through the narrow slit below. It twisted, probed, licked at her with such erotic stimulation that she could only tremble in his grasp, her hips bucking against his greedy mouth. Heat seared her body, whipped through her vagina, and contracted her womb as she felt his tongue plunge deep inside her saturated cunt.

Her thighs tightened on his shoulders, her head tossing on the bed as she fought to get closer, to make him plunge inside her harder. She screamed out when he moved, his tongue running fiercely up her slit until it stroked her clitoris. Short, quick circles, the suckling action of his lips and mouth and Faith was driven past sanity. The feel of his finger, long and broad, slipping past her anal entrance then, sliding with burning pleasure into her ass pushed her over the edge. She bucked into him, then against the finger fucking her with gentle short strokes, and dissolved.

"Damn you." Jacob's voice was dark, as desperate as her body as he jerked her up, turning her quickly to her stomach. "Knees," he demanded roughly, his hands lifting her hips, positioning her body.

"Jacob?" She stilled, remembering clearly the night in the Labs, the sensual fire, the agony of unquenched lust.

"Mine," he growled, his hands clenching on her buttocks as his finger moved purposely along the line that led to her anal entrance. "Tell me, Faith. Tell me you are mine."

"Yours," she whimpered, unable to deny him, unable to deny the complete dominance of his position, the wild, animalistic lust surging through her.

She felt his fingers at the tight opening, probing gently, spreading a slick substance before two pushed in with excruciating heat and pleasure. She cried out, distantly hearing his groan, her name a rough entreaty on his lips.

His fingers moved easily inside her, stretching her, working the muscles, easing them into parting as he slid deeper, deeper, until he could go no further. He pulled back then as she cried out in protest and followed the movement. She backed into something much thicker, much harder than the two fingers that had prepared her.

The head of his cock nudged at her anus. A second later a small, hot jet of thick fluid shot into the anal entrance. Faith trembled, remembering Hope's confusion as she related this action to her. The ability the male had of providing the lubrication needed for his mate. A natural lubrication. One that aided in arousal, and the lessening of pain upon penetration.

Almost instantly she felt the tight muscles relaxing further. Hot passion surged through her veins, igniting an inferno of desperate lust as the mushroom shaped head eased into the passage. Fiery pleasure/pain began to build there as she felt her muscles separate for the broad length pushing into it.

"Jacob." She wanted to scream, but barely had breath for a whisper.

"Faith. God. You're so hot. So tight." His voice was tortured as he held her hips still, worked his cock further into her ass.

Her back bowed as lightning flares of sensation radiated from her stretched netherhole, radiating through her body, pulsing in her cunt.

She was tortured, tormented by the demand of his burrowing shaft into her tight hole. She bucked against him, feeling another hot pulse of fluid as he whispered a curse, his voice tight with pleasure. Her arms trembled as weakness flooded through her, the heat of the fluid at first burning, then soothing as he forged deeper.

Finally, he sank in to the hilt, his cock throbbing, held tight and hot by her ass as she writhed against the possession. She couldn't halt the flex of her buttocks, but she reveled in Jacob's hard cry of pleasure as she did so.

"Easy, Faith." His voice was guttural, beseeching.

She couldn't fight the lust surging through her though. It was hot and demanding, controlling her body as she moved forward, feeling the tight grip of her channel along the broad length of his cock.

Jacob groaned, surging back inside those missing inches as his hands tightened on her hips.

"I can't control it—" he cried out, fighting for breath, his voice ragged.

"Fuck me, Jacob," she demanded, her voice hoarse, the agony of her near ecstasy driving her past reason. "Damn you, fuck me now."

Her muscles tightened on him again, as they did, she felt her cunt tingle, the thin separation between her anus and her vagina was no hindrance to the dual sensations attacking her. He was so thick, that even that entrance felt filled, his short strokes stimulating the muscles in her cunt, heating her.

She fought to follow his thrusts, to force a harder penetration until his palm landed with surprising heat on her buttock. She cried out, shocked at the pleasure the action brought. She wiggled against him as he pulled back until only the head remained. His palm landed on the opposite cheek a second before another pulse of fluid filled her and he surged in again in a hard stroke.

She was heated, slippery from his lubrication, from her own. Her cunt throbbed and the motion of his scrotum slapping against her only excited her further. She tensed then, fighting for the explosion she knew was coming, searching desperately for the release of fire and agonizing pleasure just out of reach. She couldn't bear it much longer. Could not retain her sanity if it didn't come soon.

His thrusts increased, his cock plunging up her ass, retreating, stretching her, making her insane with the hard bite of pleasure/pain that followed each thrust. She was close, so close. She heard him cry out behind her, felt another, harder ejaculation of his lubrication a second before his cock began to swell.

Faith couldn't stop screaming. Heat, blistering, indescribable, struck the walls of her anus, her vagina, the very depth of her womb as she began to climax. The hard knot centered in a way that pressed into the walls of her cunt, pressing those muscles together tightly as she aided in a natural clenching that further locked him inside her.

"No," she heard him cry out desperately behind her as the swelling increased, refusing him the option of pulling from her. The tight little jerks tore into her though, driving her higher as her body shook, shuddered.

Faith fell to the bed as Jacob followed her, his hips jerking spasmodically, his cock pulsing, throbbing. A strangled scream erupted from her throat as the hard jets of hot semen then shot into her ass. Deep, searing, driving her climax to yet another plateau as she could do nothing but tighten around him further, her body trembling, shaking as agonizing, brutal pleasure ripped through her repeatedly.

As the last spasms passed, she could hear him fighting for breath, gasping, his teeth locked on her shoulder as he shuddered repeatedly. Sweat dripped from them, dampening their bodies, the sheets beneath them. Faith felt her juices pooling beneath her, her swollen clit sensitized, but no longer throbbing in an agony of need.

Behind her, still buried in her ass, Jacob's cock twitched, the tight swelling slowly decreasing as his teeth lifted from her shoulder, his lips now buried in her neck as his weight covered her. He should have been too heavy for her. His massive muscles should be driving the breath from her lungs, but Faith felt only contentment, warmth as he fought to catch his breath, to allow his cock to ease from her body.

"Faith?" He whispered her name as he brushed a tendril of hair from her cheek. "God. Baby, I'm sorry. Please. Please tell me you aren't hurt, Faith."

She could hear the fear, the desperation radiating from his voice as he eased his softening flesh from her.

"Hmm," she whispered her satisfaction. "I died. Now let me rest in peace."

There was silence behind her, then he eased her over, his hands, so strong and gentle as he turned her to her back.

She looked up at him, seeing his eyes, pale and filled with concern, his face creased with worry. She smiled weakly, her body felt boneless, so completely sated she had no desire to move.

"Lay down and sleep with me, or go away." She yawned, breathing deeply as drowsiness began to fill her once again. "You can fuck me again when I wake up."

Faith felt Jacob as he moved hesitantly from the bed. She opened her eyes again, watching him as he stood over her.

"Bath." He cleared his throat rather hesitantly. "We both need to bathe. You'll relax easier."

"You go bathe—dammit, Jacob," she cursed as he picked her up.

She assured herself she would have fought him, and made plans to do just that as soon as she regained her breath and her strength.

"Let me take care of you, Faith," he said gently, staring down at her as he moved to the open bathroom door. "Stop cursing and fighting me. Just let me care for you. Just for now."

And how could she deny him? Especially when she had dreamed of nothing more.

She watched in silence as he adjusted the water as it poured into the tub, which was big enough to hold three normal sized people. She might fit in there with him, she thought with a flash of amusement.

"Are you sure you're okay?" He turned back to her, holding out his hand to help her into the steamy water that slowly rose in the porcelain tub.

"Jacob, are you okay?" She frowned as she allowed him to help her in. "Of course I'm fine. I told you I was."

He eased into the water, then drew her down between his thighs. Faith relaxed against his chest with a sigh. She was tired, ready to sleep the rest of the day away. It was rare that her body and her mind were relaxed enough for her to do so.

"You frighten me, Faith," he whispered as his hands held her to him, his body encasing hers.

Her heart jumped in her chest. She held herself still, barely breathing, afraid of breaking the tenuous air of intimacy that suddenly surrounded them.

"I'm terrified of your innocence," he said softly. "Your generosity and your emotions. You threaten everything that has kept me sane all these years. How would I live if I lost you now?"

She drew in a trembling breath. "And how would I live, Jacob, if I lost you?" she asked him, her voice just as soft.

She turned until her side rested against his chest, her head in the hollow of his shoulder. One large male thigh lifted to allow her legs room, then lay over them protectively. She was surrounded by his hard, male heat. Just as she had always longed to be.

One large palm held her head to his chest as he dropped a soft kiss to her hair. He was quiet, but his heart raced beneath her ear.

"I want to protect you," he whispered. "And I can't because I don't have the strength to send you away, the will to do without you any longer. But I fear for you, and those fears could restrict you."

She frowned, then tilted her head back to look into his face. He appeared uncertain, intense. His eyes swirled with emotions she knew he would never admit to, at least not yet, not right now.

She smiled up at him, and winked flirtatiously.

"It's the Alpha in you. Don't worry, babe, I'll keep you on the straight and narrow. No restrictions unless I can live with them."

She wanted to laugh at the shock that filled his now narrowing eyes.

"I am being serious here, mate," he bit out.

"No, my love, you are trying desperately to excuse love with a need for protection. But that's okay." She patted his thigh comfortingly. "For now, you can get away with it. Now bathe me so I can sleep. You dragged me in here, you can wash me."

She pulled a cloth from the small shelf behind him, and a small bar of soap from beside it. She slapped both in his hands and watched him expectantly.

"One day, you may not have the last word so easily," he assured her, his voice a smooth, dark warning.

She merely arched a brow in amusement and restrained her laughter. He would come around, she knew he would. He had to, or else she knew she could never survive their future.

Chapter Twenty-Two

ഇ

The alarm sounded again, just after midnight. Several of the perimeter's alarms had Jacob and Faith jumping from the bed and jerking on clothes and shoes within seconds.

"Stay close to me," he ordered her quietly as they grabbed revolvers and comm. links.

She didn't speak, but the brief glance he shot her assured him that she was following his lead efficiently. The revolver was in a readied position at her shoulder, the comm. link attached securely to her head once again.

"Expecting someone?" she asked him, barely a breath of a sound as they moved quickly downstairs then into the foyer, edging along the wall to the slender, tinted double windows that looked out to the front gate.

Jacob grunted sarcastically.

"You there, Stygian?" His voice was soft as it came through the unit.

Faith knew they were expecting another attempt to breeze the security of the house, but they hadn't been expecting it so soon. Whoever or whatever was out there was more than persistent.

"Can't see shit, Commander." Stygian's voice was disgusted, angry. "I got the alarm the minute it came through, but there's nothing out here."

But they were there. Jacob could feel it. His trouble barometer was going crazy.

"No animals, no nothing. We found the tripped unit, and it's definitely been tripped, but I'll be damned if there's anything around here," the other Enforcer continued. "And I smell Coyote. Evidently the bastards are getting smarter."

The Coyote breeds were smart enough as it was, Jacob thought furiously, they didn't need to get smarter.

"Find them," Jacob told him softly, his voice hard as he continued through the house, secure that Faith was covering his back. "Now!"

"We're on it." The link was broke when Jacob turned back to Faith.

"Cover my back. We're in a shitload of trouble if the sound of those alarms are any indication."

There wasn't just one, it seemed as though every perimeter had been breached and the shrieking protest of the electronic devices were ear-splitting as they began going through the house, looking for any sign of intrusion there.

The house was clear. There were no breached windows, no sign of trespassers. Faith moved carefully behind Jacob, her back to his, her eyes covering every inch of the rooms they moved through.

As they entered the large ballroom, a shadow of movement from the corner of a window caught Faith's attention.

"Down." Jacob swung around, taking her to the ground as a round of gunfire erupted through the room.

"Son of a bitch. Stygian, where the hell are you?" she heard him curse as they turned their guns on the window, returning fire as they scrambled to a place of safety behind the thick oaken bar unit set off to the side.

As Faith reloaded her pistol, she moved to the corner of the bar, her eyes narrowed as she stared at the new entryway into the house. Her fingers went to the comm. link, pressing at several of the buttons until she found what she wanted.

"We're fucking pinned down, Commander." A dark baritone shouted into the link. "I don't know who or what they are, but they came out of nowhere."

"Coyotes." Faith barked into the link. "You should be able to smell them. I can."

Silence greeted her words except for the sound of distant gunfire and heavy male curses. Outside the shattered windows, Faith watched several dim shapes darting about in the darkness, too quick for her to fire at, but slow enough for her to keep a careful watch on.

"We need rifles," she bit out as she felt Jacob moving around behind her. "I'm out of reloads and we'll be sitting ducks here when our ammo runs out."

"We're moving in your direction." A voice came through the link. "She's right. We have four Coyotes in the compound and a handful of soldiers. We've taken down a few and moving in for the rest."

"Watch your asses, they have night vision goggles, and have moved into a position of defense." As Jacob barked out the orders, Faith watched as the shadowy shapes shifted, merging outside. "They want in this house, and they're determined to get in. There are too many entry points to cover them all."

"Stay down, keep your eyes open." Jacob was beside her instantly, his revolver placed in her free hand. "I'm going for the rifles and ammo."

She could hear the worry in his voice, wanted to look up and reassure him but she was too frightened to take her eyes off the windows surrounding them.

"Hurry," she bit out. "I'm a hell of a shot, but there are a lot of them out there."

She fought to keep her voice from quivering, her fear from locking her up. She was a negotiator. She had to keep reminding herself of this. Why did she keep finding herself in the middle of gun battles?

"Five seconds max," he promised her as she picked up his revolver, trained both weapons on the windows and waited.

The comm. link was filled with activity. Voices were raised furiously, curses tainting the air blue with their virulence as whoever was supposed to be watching outside fought for dominance.

"Dirty bastards are moving on the back," someone yelled. "They want in that house. Kill the dirty sumabitches."

Gunfire erupted again just as those outside the ballroom decided to make their move.

"Jacob, get your ass in here," Faith yelled into the comm. link as they began firing again.

Bullets rained around her as she returned fire. She couldn't set off a barrage of killing steel as they were doing. Her only choice was to pray she was sheltered enough, that the bar was thick enough, and that each bullet hit its mark.

She watched several figures drop, but the gunfire didn't cease. Holding her weapon steady she picked off the closest target, the bastard sneaking around the side with the obvious intent of making it past one of the shattered windows. As three more took his place and her last round exploded from the chamber, Jacob burst into the room, returning the assault with a punch of machine gun fire that had the enemy scattering for safety.

He kept up the barrage of bullets as he came over the top of the bar, rolling over it and throwing himself behind the protection of the thick wood.

"Rifle, ammo." She turned at his voice, catching the heavy weapon and the shoulder pack filled with reloads.

"What the hell are they after?" she bit out, as she went back to her position, her eyes moving to sight the dim shapes once again.

"Hell if I know," Jacob bit out as he moved in beside her, covering the far windows now. "But we're in a hell of a bind. Stygian, report."

The gunfire still blazed outside, echoing in the comm. links as curses and furious orders poured through the connection.

"We're working our way around," the dark voice reported. "I have three sides covered. We're free of danger and heading your way."

"Well it seems the bastards have concentrated here," Jacob bit out. "Take at least one prisoner, I want to know what the hell is going on."

"Take prisoners?" Incredulity poured from the voice. "You ain't askin' for much are you, boss?"

"Try your best," Jacob growled. "We need to know why they're striking now."

"Do my best, boss." There was a wealth of mockery in the deep drawl.

Faith felt Jacob grunt in irritation beside her.

"You do that, Stygian," he bit out just as another round of gunfire began to sweep through the room. "Son of a bitch, Caleb is gonna be pissed over his house now."

Faith returned fire as Jacob let loose beside her. More windows shattered, spraying the ballroom with glass as the ear deafening blasts of repeated rounds assaulted her ears.

"We're comin' through. Leave off. Leave off. We have them," Stygian's voice was imperative now as he and his men cleared the side of the house and began driving the enemy away from the windows.

The bullets turned from Jacob and Faith as distant screams of fury and rushed orders echoed amid yet more firepower. Outside, fiery bursts of color exploded through the once immaculate gardens like a destructive display of miniature fireworks.

"Stay put." Jacob jumped to his feet as he reloaded and headed for the windows.

"Stay put, my ass," she bit out, following close behind him. "Sorry, babe. I'm still horny. I can't risk letting you get yourself killed on a whim, mate, until I get my BOBs. Where you go, I cover you."

There was a brief pause in the gunfire outside, a strangled chuckle over the comm. link, a gasp, a male groan and Faith's face flamed. Then need overtook shock as the battle waged once again.

"Stay behind me then," Jacob ordered, his voice strangled as he moved alongside the bar, working his way to the gaping holes where windows should have been.

"Covering your ass, babe," she promised him, doing just that as they moved towards the darkness outside.

"They're on the run," Stygian suddenly yelled. "Catch one of those bastards, dammit."

There was a fury of movement outside the windows as Faith followed Jacob at a run, well aware of the importance of catching one of the attackers. If there was no clear reason why they should attack, then they needed to know why.

"Fuckers are getting away," Stygian yelled.

"Dammit, Stygian, move on those bastards." They cleared the window frame in a running jump and were moving quickly for the tall, stone wall that surrounded the estate along the back of the gardens.

Another short, quick burst of gunfire came from several directions, and then dead silence filled the comm. links for long minutes.

"Son of a bitch," Stygian cursed again, breathing roughly. "Jacob, we just lost him. Sniper took him out."

"The sniper?" Jacob questioned as they moved through the thick foliage, coming out to where a small group of Enforcers had converged over several fallen bodies.

"Well, boss, it was kill his ass or let him kill me. And I only go so far for the sake of answers, ya know?" Deep, rough, the baritone was darker in person than over the comm. link.

Faith ignored him, despite her curiosity. She went to the fallen bodies, kneeling at their sides despite the blood and gore that littered the ground. They were definitely Coyote Breeds, but there were human soldiers as well. She knew the scent of both.

"Help me check their pockets," she told one of the Enforcers standing beside her.

The silent Breed bent and began riffling through the pockets of the other dead man. As Faith worked, she placed the few folded pieces of paper she found on the silent chest of the fallen enemy.

Behind her, Jacob was giving the others quiet orders, though she could feel his gaze on her.

"Hey, I found something." The Enforcer beside her kept his voice low as he placed several pictures on the small pile of papers Faith had accumulated. "Looks like a list of some sort, too."

"Flashlight?" she asked him, glancing over as he reached back to a thick hip pack.

Faith twisted the end of the small penlight, and was rewarded with a bright, though slender beam of light. She directed it on the bloodied pictures. There was one of her in the bar. Surprising. She couldn't recall a picture being taken of her. There were also pictures of Hope and two other women. The list gave names, locations and several small drawings that Faith assumed to be a code of some sort. She went back to the pictures. She knew Hope of course, but she knew the other two as well. All but her were full humans rather than hybrid breeds.

"Jacob, do we have any kind of Internet connection in this hellhole?" she bit out as she read over the list, and glanced back at the pictures.

"No BOBs," he bit out. "Keep your mind on the job."

Faith stilled. Beside her, she could feel the younger Enforcer holding his breath. She came carefully to her feet, staring at her irritated mate as he glanced back from the face-off he held with Stygian, and a flame-haired Enforcer that scowled dangerously.

Her eyes narrowed as she felt offended fury course over her body.

"Excuse me?" She heard the primal growl in her own voice, and would have been as shocked by it as Jacob was if she hadn't been furious.

Jacob frowned at her again. "In a minute, Faith." He turned back to Stygian.

Faith felt her body tremble with hurt. His men stood around him, watching her carefully, aware that she was the Alpha female of this pack, but his response to her had placed her in the lowest level of the hierarchy instead. So much for Alpha intelligence.

"Was he shot in the head?" She directed a look of pseudo-innocence at the Enforcer, Stygian, ignoring Jacob's narrow eyed look.

Stygian cleared his throat carefully. "Not that I can tell." His look was assessing as he watched her, wondering how she would handle her mate, and if she was strong enough to stand with them.

She didn't blame them. With one thoughtless comment born of his own anger, Jacob wiped out any initial respect they had for her.

"Is there an Internet connection available here?" Once again she directed her question to Stygian. "I will assume that the heat of battle has fried his brains, so I'm hoping you, at least, will have an intelligent response."

She ignored Jacob. It was that or shoot him.

"Well, I have a laptop—"

"Get it," she bit out. "Satellite connection?"

He glanced at Jacob.

"He didn't ask you," she reminded him. "I did."

Stygian shrugged. "He's boss. You get a laptop at his say so."

Which wasn't satisfactory. Before Jacob could reprimand him, Faith moved.

The bigger they were, the less they expected from a small, puny woman. He blocked her intended blow, so he wasn't watching her feet. Her legs tangled with his, throwing him off balance as she slid her legs expertly out of the way, pushed firmly and watched him fall. As he landed on his back, she planted her foot firmly at his crotch.

Had she been the enemy, he would have taken her then. But had he been her enemy, he would have already lost his balls, and then his throat.

Jacob cursed behind her.

"I'm smaller, and he's the asshole that left his mate for six years to play jungle tramp. He might not like it, and you might be under the impression you can follow suit. But I am still your Alpha."

Stygian shuddered, but not from fear. Deep, hard chuckles welled in his throat and shook his body as his hands reached out. He grabbed her ankle. Faith twisted in his grip, executed a flip and landed in a crouch several feet from him.

"Damn. Boss, she's a live one." He came to his feet, facing her as Faith stood to her full height. Which she admitted wasn't much when standing next to Stygian.

"That she is," Jacob growled in warning and a measure of respect she hadn't heard in his voice before this.

"I don't need your help now," she bit out, staring at him furiously.

"No, you took care of it yourself, but it was me who should have been on my ass again," he sighed wearily. "I have a laptop and satellite connection in the house. I'll show you everything you need. You're right. You proved your place tonight, I shouldn't have let my anger and worry for you get the best of me."

Shock held her still, silent.

"Damn. The boss just apologized," Stygian sniggered, his voice filled with mock incredulity.

"And you're next." Faith turned on him with a feral growl.

He stepped back in surprise.

"Damned right I am." Stygian nodded respectfully then. "It won't happen again, B.A."

Faith frowned. "B.A.?"

"Bad ass!" His head gave a sharp jerk of exclamation. "Damn, you don't just look fine, but you move like lightning. Welcome to the Pack."

Chapter Twenty-Three

ఴ

They finally ended up back in the living room, where Jacob hit the switch that closed dark shades over each window and left the interior gloomy, intimate.

"Now, we have a problem." Jacob's voice was hard, cold as he flipped the four small, glossy photos down on the coffee table. "My mission has nothing to do with these women. And I think we've just established that those Coyotes were after you, not me."

Faith sighed wearily as she collapsed on the couch, staring down at the small picture of herself. It was one that had been taken six years before, during their time in the Labs. Hope's was only slightly older. The other two she wasn't certain of.

"Why?" She shook her head in confusion. "If they wanted me, they had a better chance of it before I came here. How many Enforcers do you have? Are there enough to cover the other two women, if we can find them?"

"I have enough, if I pull in the other packs close by," he told her. "Do you think you can find the other two women? I can get started on my connections, but we'll move faster with both of us working."

She pulled the comm. link off her head, but tucked the revolver into the back of her jeans. It should have looked out of place, awkward on her, but the gesture bespoke a quiet confidence, a strength he had never thought of her having. Faith was to be protected; that she was unable to protect herself had always been his fears. Seeing differently shook him a bit, he had to admit. She shouldn't have to defend herself. Shouldn't have to live a life that required it.

"I can get started as soon as Stygian gets here with the equipment." She shrugged, though Jacob could see that nerves and weariness were tugging at her.

"We need to get some answers fast," he bit out. "Those bastards were after you tonight. A risky move, even for Coyotes. They've never attempted to steal a female back from the Pack, or target one specifically."

"Its not just the Breed females they are after," Faith reminded him. "Hope is human, and so are the other two, if memory serves me right. And they were all associated with our birth Lab."

Jacob knelt by the coffee table.

"Charity Dunmore and Honor Roberts." He frowned as he stared down at the two women. "Charity is human. She was a technician at the Lab right before it went to hell. Remember? Honor Roberts, is Honor Christine Roberts, the daughter of one of the higher members of the Council. Last we heard of her, she was still in school when all this happened. She disappeared from sight just after her father was imprisoned."

She knew this as well as he did. Her arms crossed over her chest, her hands rubbing at them as though to warm herself.

"We need to find out where she's at, and figure out what connects us. Hope and myself I understand. We're mates to two of the most powerful Wolf breeds alive. But notice the Feline Breed's Alpha mate isn't in there. Merinus, I believe. Nor her children. There are three now. None of the Felines are featured, so for at least this group of Coyotes, the focus was Wolf Breeds. I need to contact Wolfe and make him aware of the danger to Hope."

Jacob was staring down at the list and the small drawings beside each.

"Did you recognize the codes on here, Faith?" he asked her slowly, his eyes raising.

She walked over to him, staring down at the list, frowning. It took a few moments to place them.

"Fertility codes," she murmured, remembering those that had been set up at the Labs when the tests on Hope and Wolfe had occurred.

"Fertility is most possible when the female is in heat," Jacob reminded her. "According to these codes, Hope's is at the lowest mark, yours is at the highest, with the other two in between."

"But you have to be mated to go into heat." Faith shook her head in confusion. "That makes no sense, Jacob. Charity Dunmore and Honor Roberts aren't breeds and shouldn't be mated with any of our males. Why would they be on the list?"

"Unless they were, as you and Hope, slated for a mating somehow." Jacob frowned as he looked up at her. "Wasn't there some suspicion of such tests that came out during the Genetics hearings, during the days of our escape?"

There had been. Records that had been uncovered from several high level Genetics scientists that hinted at experiments delving into reversing the genetic code that would prevent the various breeds from multiplying. Nature it seemed, had only aided them in the genetic anomalies that had begun taking place in both the males and females since their first conception.

"General Roberts ordered a lot of those tests," Faith sighed. "Just from the data I've been able to gather myself, we were headed for extinction if he had his way. He thought any children we could have would be easier to control."

He considered the Breeds sub-human, that had been no secret. Assassins without conscience, without a need for warmth or life. They had been pawns in his grand schemes of power. He and Bainesmith had been a perfect pair.

"We need to contact Wolfe; he has to know about this, as well as the other Packs and the Feline Pride. We could just be looking at the tip of the iceberg here."

"Finding out why those women are targeted will be the hard part," Stygian said as he stepped into the room, followed by several other Enforcers bearing electronics.

Within minutes, a laptop was set up awaiting Faith's attention, the satellite connection showing full reception and privacy.

"How secure are we here?" Faith questioned as she sat down in a chair in front of the computer.

"Only Pack territory is safer." Jacob shrugged. "This is our base for this side of the mountains. Stygian is calling in several nearby Packs for added protection. But we won't be here long. We'll be heading back to Wolfe's territory soon."

As Alpha female of all Packs, Hope's safety and that of any babe she would conceive was of the utmost importance. They couldn't risk her life. The Enforcers would be gathering around her until the threat was eliminated.

"How soon do we move?" She clipped her headset into the cell phone at her waist. There would be a lot of work to do to get the information needed. To get any of it.

"Within days, with any luck." Jacob was already keying numbers into the cell phone he carried. "See what you can find out for now. Any information we can dig up can only help us at this point."

* * * * *

There wasn't much to find, but what did come through in the next hours was terrifying. Already, two Wolf Breed females had fallen to attackers in the past month. Thankfully, neither had died, but they weren't unscarred, either. Both females were unmated though, and had not gone into heat. Both women had been raped.

Faith trembled in fury at that knowledge. Damn the bastards, they never cared what horrors they created for others with their depravities. They had no conscience, and no sense of shame. They were merciless in their disregard of the lives they had created.

Faith put out a world wide alert to all the known Packs. She sat hunched over the computer for hours, working to alert those that she could and attempting to draw in more information. They needed to know why the Council was striking once again, and for what reason.

The Feline Pride was on heightened alert already after an attempted kidnapping of Callan and Merinus' first-born child several weeks before. Tanner, the Pride Liaison, spoke directly to Faith, and she could hear the fury in his voice. His own mate had just given birth the past year to twins, and his worry was reflected in the cold, hard edge of savagery in his voice as he spoke of the attempt.

"The Council is at it again, Faith," he said with brutal effect. "The bastards won't stop until we kill them, and Callan refuses to allow an order to take them out before they strike."

"Callan's right, Tanner," she told him wearily. "Right now, our position within world favor is too tenuous."

"Fuck world favor," he growled savagely. "These are our babes and our women we're speaking of. The world doesn't care if they survive, or if we do, or how."

There was many times that Faith agreed with him. After relaying the rest of her own information, she disconnected the call, and went back to the arduous task of contacting as many informants as possible. There had to be answers somewhere, she thought bleakly.

"What's going on?" Faith shook her head as she stared at yet another Internet transmission from an informant a long while later.

According to the report in front of her, there were no rumors, no orders, no whispered "suggestion" moving among the few Council members still in power. Due to extreme force from various law enforcement agencies, the Breeds were considered "off limits" for the time being, just as they had been for several years now. If one of them died, the repercussions that would result were more than they wanted. The kidnapping attempts of the Pride children supposedly had generated fear and worry among those Council members still free.

"How could the Council not be behind this?" Jacob was hunched down beside her chair, staring at the screen with a frown.

"I'm not saying they are not behind this at all." Faith shrugged tiredly. "But there's no information to substantiate it yet. There's definitely something going on. But either none of my informants have the information, or it's just too dangerous to leak. It could take days for me to get so much as a glimmer of information here."

"We don't have days." Jacob shook his head. "Get some rest. You haven't slept at all since the attack and not much before then. I'll keep looking."

Faith shook her head. She knew time was of the essence. Even her burning, throbbing pussy wasn't going to detract her. Damn, she needed him too much. Even in the thick of whatever new danger they faced, she wanted him. It was a sickness, she decided. A plague of Jacob.

She had been sitting there for hours, ignoring the sensual ache that throbbed through her body, the burn of the blood in her veins, the soft slide of her juices along the lips of her cunt. She tightened her thighs. Too much work to do.

"You can't ignore it forever." Jacob's voice was softer now, suggestive of the fact that he was aware, and had been all along, of her arousal.

"Too much to do." Faith felt her breath rasp in her throat, her muscles tighten in protest.

"We've done all we can today, Faith," he whispered as he pushed the heavy chair back and moved between her thighs.

Faith stared into his sun-darkened face, seeing the lazy sensuality that crossed his expression, the way his dark lashes shadowed his cheeks, his eyes glittering with lustful anticipation.

His hands spanned her hips, then pushed beneath her shirt to caress a path of destructive fire to her breasts. Faith was unable to halt the instinctive movement that pressed her nipples harder into the fingers that pinched at them lightly.

"I've smelled your heat for hours," he groaned as he stared into her eyes. "It's all I can do to function without fucking you, to think without imagining the taste of you on my tongue. How do you do this to me, Faith? Make me want you until I'm starving for you?"

"How do you do it to me?" she gasped as his lips feathered over her cheek. "Jacob, I can't think when you touch me."

"I can't think when you're anywhere around me," he retorted. "How is this fair, Faith? All I can think of is the sweet taste of your body, and the heat of your pussy gripping me. I want you, baby. I want you bad. Now."

And he did. He pulled her forward, the hard ridge of his cock pressing against the heated flesh between her thighs.

"I want you," she whispered, staring up at him. "I've always wanted you, Jacob. I've always loved you."

She watched his jaw tighten.

"You don't want to hear that, do you?" Pain tore through her chest. She had promised herself she could be content with the mating, with his desire for her, but in a flashing instant she realized how desperately she needed his love.

"Faith," he whispered huskily, his face creasing into a frown of such bitterness and pain that she wanted to scream out in denial of it.

"I don't want your pity." She shook her head, pushing him away from her. "I want your love, Jacob."

She rose from the chair, stepping away from him, fighting the shivering need that poured over her. Now wasn't the time to fuck or fight, she reminded herself.

"We have a lot of work to do," she bit out when he didn't answer but rose to his feet instead. "I have several other sources to check — "

"It doesn't work that way, Faith," he growled as he hooked his arm around her waist and pulled her to him firmly.

He was hard, hot, tense with his own need and his stubborn determination to believe no love existed. Damn him, she cursed him silently. She needed more than his cock. She needed more in a mate than a man with a ready hard-on.

"Then how does it work, Jacob?" she whispered as his hands smoothed over her back, her hips. "I'm too tired to fight with you, and too tired to deny what I need as well. I don't want to be fucked. I want to be loved."

Her chest tightened with pain, her eyes filling with tears. She hated her hormones, hated what they did to her. The incessant anger was bad enough, but this need was worse, more destroying than the six years of physical cravings she had endured.

"Don't cry, Faith." His voice was so low she could barely hear the words.

His hand rose to her head where he pressed her closer to his chest, his heart. She could feel it beating, a rough tattoo beneath her cheek. How could he not have a heart, or the love she needed so desperately?

"I don't cry." She sniffed, but she could feel the moisture on her cheeks, hear the thickness in her own voice.

"When I touch you, I want nothing more than to show you with my touch, my kiss, that you are the most important thing in my life," he sighed against her hair. "Always, Faith, you have held a part of me. A part I've never been able to hide from completely." His voice was soft, laden with pain, with his own fears. "But I won't give you an illusion. I won't lie to you and tell you something exists inside me that doesn't. I don't know love, baby. I have no idea what to compare it to, or how

222

to recognize it. All I know, is that in all my life, my only weakness has been you."

Could that be love? Faith knew it was more than Jacob had ever given another living person. His reputation, even among the Breeds, was for mercilessness against the enemy, and cold hard resolve in all matters. She knew he had backed down many times in the face of her hormonal mood shifts and her anger. Had another Enforcer, male or female, challenged him as she had, he would have reacted much differently. His men weren't wary of him for no reason.

"Will you let me love you, Jacob?" she finally asked him softly. "I need that much. At least that much, Jacob, or I can't survive."

Chapter Twenty-Four

ॐ

If he had a heart, it would have broken at that moment. Pain sliced through Jacob's soul, ripping through his body, clenching every bone and muscle in an agony of protest. Her voice was soft, so gentle and sweet it destroyed him. And in it, he heard her love. As though her soul had opened and from it the nectar of an emotional banquet poured. It washed over him. It seeped into scars and wounds he never knew he had, deep within his own soul.

His eyes grew moist as he held her to his chest, sheltering her smaller body, wanting nothing more than to protest all the innocence and belief she still held. Still. Even after the life she had been raised in. Even after all the cruelties she had seen since their escape. Still, Faith believed in love. She made him want to go to his knees and beg her to let him in on the secret of holding onto that belief. How had she stayed so soft, so delicate inside and out, when he was so hard, so bitter? What act of supreme mercy had saved her?

He didn't know. But as he held her, he thanked God with everything inside him that she had been protected. That somehow His hand had sheltered her, protected her, held her heart intact.

"You humble me, Faith." He didn't know what to say to her. He didn't understand the twisting morass of emotions tearing him apart now.

Unfamiliar emotions. Feelings and sensations he had never known in his life. Equal parts gentleness and sharp chastisement, it flooded his body and his mind as nothing else ever had.

"I don't want to humble you, Jacob. I want to love you." Her hands moved over his back, her nails scratching erotically across the material covering him.

He barely stifled his groan. The scent of her need had increased. As though her emotional storm were somehow tied to the intensity of her arousal. It beckoned him, drugged him until he could think of little else but sinking his cock deep inside her body. But there was a part of his soul that eased as well. Faith was his mate, and in her voice, in her actions, she had accepted him, even without the love that he knew she needed as well.

"You are everything to me." He fought his need to ease her, to give her whatever she desired, just because she desired it. But hell, what did he know of love, besides what she had showed him? And God knew, he had never given her the devotion, the depth of sacrifice she had given him for six years.

"It's okay, Jacob." She shook her head to give him the escape he knew he needed.

But he also knew it wasn't all right. He was failing her. He couldn't fail her, not Faith. Not again.

"If I knew love, then I know all I would have would be for you," he whispered desperately. "If my heart were intact, then it would be filled with nothing but my love for you, Faith." He held onto her, his arms tightening around her as he felt her breath hitch, felt her tears against his chest. "Dear God in Heaven, Faith, I cannot bear hurting you. Please. Please, trip me on my ass again or something. Anything. But do not cry over me."

"Not over you, you buffoon." She pushed away from him, wiping desperately at her cheeks as she stared up at him. "I'm crying for you. There's a difference, you know."

She was beautiful. Such a beautiful work of nature that she held him spellbound. Her face was flushed, her eyes so dark and wondrous sparkling with tears and emotions until they seemed filled with a thousand pinpoints of light. A frown drew her auburn brows low over her eyes, and her mouth, so perfectly formed, hinted at just the smallest pout. He had never seen a more beautiful woman. Had never wanted anything or anyone in his life as desperately as he wanted Faith right now.

"Then don't cry for me, either." He shook his head, feeling mesmerized by her. "Dammit, Faith." He raked his fingers through his hair, feeling adrift, lost in an emotional abyss he had no idea how to navigate. All he knew was that this was Faith, and that where it mattered most to her, he could feel himself failing her.

There was no way to apologize. No words that could express the wrenching emotional sensations so unfamiliar to him. He did the only thing he knew how to do. Fought to ease it the only way he knew how.

He jerked her into his arms, his lips covering hers, halting any more words, any more tears from her. His tongue pushed past her surprised lips, sweeping into her mouth with a desperation he could barely control. He needed her. Had to have her. He felt an overriding compulsion to imprint the taste and feel of his body upon her mind in a way she could never deny. In a way that would reassure her. Tempt her. Complete her.

Jacob felt her hands grip his shoulders, her nails biting into his flesh as she moaned into his kiss. She was hot and addictive. Sweetness and innocence and a sultry temptation that drove him insane.

He ate at her mouth, her lips, her tongue. The touch of her, the taste of her was burning into his soul. He needed more, needed her so hot, so desperate for him that she would never leave, never regret her love for him. Never regret that he didn't know how to love.

"Jacob." Her cry was music to his soul. Filled with hot need, dazed arousal. She made him feel like a conqueror, a rescuer. She made him feel alive. And Jacob knew that until she had walked into that dirty little bar, her arousal pulsing with each heartbeat, he hadn't lived. Not really. His life began with that night.

"I need you now," he growled as he tore his lips from hers, sweeping a path down her neck as his hands pushed beneath her shirt once more. "Right now, Faith."

Her breasts were hard, swollen, tipped with pebble hard nipples that pleaded for his attention, his caress. He tweaked the little points, glorying in her heated cry for more. She pressed closer to him, arching against him as she moaned deeply. And Jacob could do no more than give her what she needed so desperately.

He turned, his hands maneuvering her as his lips nipped at her neck, at the mark he left on her. The sensual little brand that marked her as his mate. His woman.

The door to the living room was closed, he knew none of his Enforcers would dare disturb him, but he was to the point that it wouldn't matter if they did. He couldn't stop. He had to be inside her, deep and tight, her muscles searing him as she climaxed around him.

She whimpered. A needy, breathy little sigh that made his blood pressure skyrocket and his cock jerk in response.

"Right here," he whispered, hearing the desperation in his own voice as he turned her in his arms, bending her over the back of the chair.

"The chair?" Amusement and lust vied for supremacy as she wiggled her butt at him.

Damn, that was such a fine ass. His hands cupped it, clenching on the rounded curves as an animalistic growl rumbled in his chest.

"The chair," he assured her as he reached around, his fingers quickly releasing the snap and zipper to her jeans.

Before she could do more than gasp in surprise, he had them around her ankles, as his fingers delved into the slick, wet heat of her pussy. He wanted to write a sappy poem to that particular luscious piece of flesh. An ode of reverence to the tight heat, the wet, creamy clasp of her cunt as he burrowed into it. He was a drowning man fighting for survival, and he was being done in by a soaked, needy pussy and a curvy tight ass. He wanted to howl out his arousal, his supremacy, his victory that he alone had mated this woman.

"I'm going to fuck you until you scream." He released his pounding cock just as quickly as he had stripped her of clothes. "I'm going to fuck you so hard and so deep, that you always know you belong to me. That you never doubt it, Faith. Never doubt what you are to me, and what I am to you—" He positioned the thick head at the entrance of her dripping vagina.

Ah, so hot. The frothy, bubbling brew that seeped from her seared his flesh.

"I always scream when you fuck me." She was panting now, straining back against the bulbous head of his cock, teasing him with the tight fit to come.

"So you do." Jacob realized he was panting as well. "And you scream so pretty too, baby." His hand smoothed over the rounded curves of her butt before returning to her hip.

He held her firm, nudged his cock at her entrance, his teeth gritting against the fiery heat that lapped at the head of his cock. He felt her muscles clenching, caressing the head of his cock, raining her sweet essence over it. It was fire and lightning, heated pleasure streaking through every inch of his body.

He leaned over her, his lips moving aside the collar of her shirt as his teeth scraped over the mark he had made on her. He nudged the rounded head more firmly against her entrance, hearing her whimpering cry, her husky plea for more.

"Scream now, Faith." He buried his shaft deep and hard in one long thrust that had her straightening against him, a wail of erotic pleasure/pain echoing around them.

She was shaking, trembling in his hold, her head thrown back against his chest as the muscles of her vagina quaked around him, spilling their juice along the thick stalk of his cock and dripping down along his scrotum as the small release he had triggered washed over her.

The muscles of her cunt quivered. He gritted his teeth, fighting his need to begin a hard, rapid thrusting motion inside her. He wanted to savor her now. Wanted to savor the sleek wet feel of her, the heat that damned near blistered his cock and made it harden further.

He could feel perspiration dampening his skin as he fought the need to take her hard and deep. He wanted to feel the rapid swelling, the agonizing pleasure of the knot that would lock him deep into her spasming flesh.

"Jacob," she panted as he throbbed inside her, feeling her tighten on him, milking his flesh with a fist-tight grip that made him nearly insane.

"So hot and tight," he groaned as his tongue stroked over the mark at the bottom of her neck. "So sweet and addictive. I could stay inside you forever, Faith."

"If you don't fuck me, I'm going to kick your ass," she moaned heatedly, her arm reaching back, her hand locking in his hair as she fought for release.

Her hips rotated slowly as several deep, pleasured growls came through her throat. The motion nearly sent him over the edge into oblivion. Her vagina tightened, her juices easing between his flesh and hers as she worked her inner muscles around the thick shaft.

Jacob allowed his hands to slide to her breasts as he moved tentatively inside her. Small, measured thrusts that nearly broke his control. He needed her. Needed her too badly to continue such a slow progression to orgasm.

His fingers played with her nipples as he held her close, gripping the tight little peaks, feeling her cunt spasm each time he pinched them erotically. She was damp with sweat, shaking, her hips moving against his, her body arching into him.

"Bend over." His hands moved from her breasts as he pushed her over once again, her hands bracing on the cushion of the chair as his knees bent and he drove his cock harder inside her.

"Yes," she cried out in response. "Again. Oh God, Jacob. Do it again."

Again and it might be over, he knew. But he couldn't resist. His hands clasped her hips again as he dragged the heavy length of his erection from the heated channel until only the head was still lodged inside her. He felt like screaming at the indescribable pleasure that ripped through his body as he thrust hard and deep again.

He had no control left. He couldn't stop the need, the fire that flashed up his spine, tightened his scrotum, and left him so desperate for release that he was nearly sobbing for it. Faith was already crying out in desperation. Each forceful thrust wrung a sob from her, a plea for more. Harder. Deeper. He gave her all she begged for and more until finally he felt her vagina ripple, squeeze him tightly as her orgasm began to tear through her.

She chanted his name as he thrust one last time, hard and deep before his flesh began to swell, locking him inside her. Jacob fought for breath, his body shaking in reaction as he felt the swelling, the binding that would refuse to allow even a drop of his seed to spill from her body for long, desperate minutes. It locked his cock hard inside her as his semen blasted from the tip, filling her, drowning him in pleasure.

Their gasping cries were the only sounds in the room. Sweat soaked bodies trembled, gasping whispers escaping their lips as every cell rippled with the shockwaves of pleasure.

The intensity of feeling lasted forever. Jacob's legs trembled as his hips jerked against her again, extending the pleasure, as yet another spasm caressed his distended cock. Finally, the hard tremors eased, and his cock slowly softened inside her. He pulled free of her tight grip, steadying her as he moved backward.

"What a wondrous show." The sharp voice had Jacob moving for his weapon until he saw those trained on his mate.

He jerked Faith behind him as she struggled weakly to straighten her clothes and faced a monster from the past.

Chapter Twenty-Five

✍

He had been their training master. Lieutenant Dale Marshal. Ex-Special Forces, ex-SEAL. He had been released from the military under a suspicion of cruelty to prisoners and extreme depravities. Jacob knew well that the rumors were most likely true.

Marshal had been a nightmare at the Labs. His extreme training methods and cruelties had often resulted in painful punishments. Complete obedience, no emotion, no weakness was his motto. From a young age Jacob had learned how easily an emotional attachment could be used against him by the enemy. Namely, Marshal.

As Jacob straightened his pants, zipping them casually, he noticed that the other man hadn't changed much in six years. He still stood tall, imposing. His blue eyes were cold, his blonde hair receding. He appeared as cruel as he ever had. At the moment, his gaze, as well as the two men with him, were trained on Faith as she struggled behind him to fix her clothing.

"You got past my alarms." Jacob pulled their attention back to him. "That must have taken some work."

He had known Marshal would come. As Jacob's trainer, only he had the knowledge to track him. But Jacob hadn't expected him this soon. And he had never imagined he could pass all the alarms so effectively.

Marshal sneered in response. "A few perimeter alarms? Really, Jacob. I had heard your security measures were much better than I found. I had come myself after you took out the force I sent last night. I didn't expect so few men, or alarms."

Which hopefully meant that Stygian was aware they were within the house. Jacob hadn't expected another force to move in quite so soon, but the information they needed had dictated the lack in security, which would allow them to breach the house. Always be prepared for the unexpected, he thought with a sigh. His lust had endangered Faith, his need for her had put her in the line of fire.

"My men are there." Jacob shrugged, containing his own smile of amusement.

Confidence in the face of the enemy. Never let them see you sweat. The old rules were the hardest to forget, and now he used them to his advantage. Never show weakness.

A flash of worry crossed Marshal's expression.

"Check again," he spoke into his own comm. link.

How many men were with him? Had Marshal taken any of the Enforcers out, he would be gloating over it by now. He was filled with his own self-importance, his utter confidence in his own abilities. It had been his downfall more than once.

Jacob stood firmly in front of Faith as she moved closer to his back, allowing him to shelter her for now. It would be best if the men who watched her were unaware that she was more than capable of protecting herself. Her delicate build, her air of frailty would only work in her favor. And in Jacob's.

"What are you doing here, Marshal?" Jacob asked him curiously, keeping his anger, his hatred of the man carefully controlled. "I thought the Council had given up on recapturing us. You should be more than aware of the trouble this will cause for your superiors."

Marshal frowned. "This has nothing to do with the Council," he grunted.

His gaze went to what little of Faith he could see, sheltered as she was behind Jacob's body.

"We just need your woman for a while." He smiled in lustful anticipation. The look had Jacob tensing with rage. "We promise to return her, perhaps the worse for wear, but alive, in a few days."

Jacob crossed his arms over his chest, wondering where the hell Stygian and his men were. Now would be a good time to drop in.

"You must take me for a fool, Marshal." Jacob fought to keep his voice mild, to keep his rage under control. "This is my mate you're speaking of. I think you know well I won't let her go."

A brief frown crossed Marshal's face. Jacob had been the Breed least likely to buck his orders at the Lab. Jacob had played the game well, biding his time until they could escape, careful to keep all hints of aggression contained. The perfect lapdog, Marshal had once called him. Jacob swore he would rip the man's throat out first chance he got.

"I can kill you, then take her." Marshal shrugged. "What good will you be to her dead?"

Jacob felt Faith tense behind him. He also felt her arm moving, sliding around her side. Damn, he bet that gun was still tucked into her back pocket. Keeping his actions protective, he reached back with one arm to secure her to his back. At the same time, she slid the Colt revolver into his hand. It was little enough, but it might be all that would protect them until help arrived.

"What good will she be to me if you take her?" he countered softly, his tone deadly. It was time the master learned that the pupil no longer followed his lead. "You know I won't release my mate, Marshal. So evidently you came to kill me anyway."

Marshal smiled. A baring of teeth, a cold display of cruelty.

"Emotional attachment, Jacob? Didn't we teach you better than that during training?"

And they had. Years of punishments or brutality he still remembered only in his dreams, they had taught him to never care, to never let another become important to him.

"It has little to do with emotion." Jacob shrugged, though in that moment, in that single instant, he knew better. He knew it had everything to do with a heart he thought was missing, and was only now realizing had survived, scarred, but intact. A heart that belonged only to Faith.

"No emotion?" Marshal asked him, his expression condescending. "Then you have no problem releasing her."

"She belongs to me." Jacob gripped the gun, his stomach tightening in warning as he watched the three men who faced him. "I marked her, I mated her. She's mine."

"She will never conceive." Cold calculation lit the other man's eyes. "Give her to us, Jacob. We will return her, I promise this, capable of conceiving."

What had they done to the two women they had attacked? Terror struck Jacob's heart. Had they somehow forced unmated Breed women to conceive? With what? The question sent ice spreading through his body.

"Conception isn't my concern, Marshal. Unlike the Council, I leave such things up to a higher power. I will not release my mate to you."

"You make it sound as though you have a choice, my friend," Marshal laughed in quiet amusement. A cold, hard sound that underscored the evil in his heart. "I didn't ask you to release her. I ordered you to, Jacob."

Jacob slid his finger over the trigger of the gun as he noticed the slight shadow that edged by a window behind him. He watched the wavering image from the corner of his eye in the mirrored shelves beside Marshal. So far, the soldiers with him were more concerned with Faith than any of the Enforcers that may have defeated their men outside. Help was here. The only problem left was to figure out exactly what was going on.

"I no longer follow your orders, Marshal," Jacob reminded him, now watching the men more closely for any signs of aggression. "And neither does my mate. You will not take her."

Marshal sighed heavily. "We will return her," he argued as though it would make a difference.

"After how many of your men have raped her?" Jacob asked tightly, remembering the reports of the two Breed women who had been attacked. "This woman carries my mark, my scent. She belongs to me. I will allow no other man to touch her, you know this."

"Those women were unmated." Evidently Marshal had no concept of the horrors he had brought on those women. "We merely played for a while with them. We will guard your woman with more care."

Marshal's hand moved, clasping the weapon at his side as the two soldiers brought their automatic rifles up a few inches higher, aiming them straight at Jacob's heart.

"Release her to me, Jacob," Marshal ordered again. "Or I may have to get testy. You know how unpredictable I am when I get testy."

"Unpredictable?" Jacob questioned the word. "Rabid, you mean? You are like a diseased dog, Marshal, that needs to be put down. I would never trust you with my woman."

"You are not looking at the bigger picture, you fool!" Marshal finally spat out. "She is trying to conceive. We cannot allow untested conception, Jacob. You know what it could mean to the future of civilization. The world is not ready for your kind. We must fix this problem. Only a Breed fully human can be allowed to survive."

Shock ripped through his system. Insanity glowed in Marshal's eyes. A fanatical gleam that hinted at a greater evil.

"Fully human? How could this be possible? What insane experiments are you bastards involved in now? We are not fully human, Marshal," Jacob reminded him.

"You are abominations. That must be fixed if you are going to force your seed on the world," Marshal spat out. "The Felines were bad enough. We will not allow it with your Packs as well."

Insanity. Only the insane could have conceived the plan to create the Breeds. Only the demented, true monsters could carry out their plans.

"Then perhaps your Council should not have created us," Jacob shot back. "We were to be your dogs of war, your trained pets to carry out your perverted plans. They forgot, Marshal, only humans are naturally deceptive. Naturally cruel. The breeds they chose were the most honorable, as well as the most savage. We were not meant to be your mindless puppets."

Marshal's face flushed as fury engulfed him.

"Puppets be damned. You are all animals who now think you have the right to live and multiply. The Council created you, and they will now destroy you."

Two things happened simultaneously. Jacob pushed Faith to the floor behind the dubious protection of the chair as he brought the gun to bear on the three men already pulling the triggers on their own weapons.

The glass in the windows behind him shattered as he fell to the floor, covering Faith's body, firing at the enemy that would destroy all he had ever dreamed or prayed for.

But it wasn't Stygian or the Enforcers that came through the windows, guns blazing, a war cry sounding on their lips. Jacob's attention splintered from Marshal and his men as shock tore through his body. It couldn't be possible. Even the Council in all their perversions and cruelties couldn't have actually managed to create a Breed such as this.

But they had, the proof of it rolled across the floor. Three large males in their prime, weapons blazing, rage reflecting in their cries as they focused their fury on Marshal and his men.

"Don't kill them all, dammit!" Jacob screamed as he saw a soldier fall. "Marshal, we need Marshal."

He had no idea if his words were heard above the commotion. He kept Faith covered, his heart pounding in fear as weapons blazed and bullets ricocheted around the room.

"Dammit, Jacob, get off me," Faith cursed beneath him as he held her securely to the floor, protecting her with his own body. "I'm going to kick your ass when I get up."

She jerked beneath him, her voice raised furiously.

As the last shot fired, Jacob was on his feet.

"Find out who the hell they are," he yelled as he pointed imperiously at the three winged men slowly coming back to their feet. "Dammit, we don't need any more fucking Breeds running around the world. Kill the fucking Council members I say…"

He rushed into the hall, shouting orders as he went, cursing the blood and the damage done to the house.

"Does this look like my house?" he yelled out as he passed through the doorway. "Goddammit it, Caleb is gonna kill all of us."

* * * * *

"Not if I kill you first," Faith muttered as she turned to face the three men watching her, their aristocratic expressions immediately setting her hackles up.

"Let me guess," she said roughly. "Alphas of course. Where the hell are all the betas, don't any of them survive genetic selection? Betas are good things."

Chapter Twenty-Six

သာ

Marshal didn't make it to questioning. Neither did any of the others. Faith listened to Jacob curse loudly, violently.

"One. All I ask for is one. Just don't kill one of them, so we can question them," he growled as he faced Stygian furiously. "What happened?"

"They had bigger guns, boss." Stygian shrugged. "Shoot first, worry about questions later. This ain't no place for serious wounds."

Faith watched Jacob as he wiped his hand over his face in a gesture of extreme frustration. She stood back patiently as she shared an amused look with Cian, the second in command of the Winged Breeds.

Jacob turned to Faith. "You find something amusing here, mate?" He scowled.

Faith shrugged. "Maybe."

Jacob's eyes narrowed. She could feel his lust, his aggravation, his fury, all combining in a way that made her blood pressure soar.

"Such as?" he bit out.

"Such as the fact that our new Breeds have some interesting information." She shrugged. "While you were taking care of Alpha business, I was being the good little Liaison and gathering facts."

"Like?" A thread of suspicion entered his tone.

"Like the fact that the Council has developed an intriguing little serum. One that they believe will force conception, but in doing so, will ensure that all Breed DNA is reversed in the child."

Shocked disbelief lined the expressions turned toward her.

"They believe they can fuck with nature a second time, within the same genetic code?" He growled. "Have they lost their minds?"

"Did they ever have any?" Cian asked him then as he leaned casually against the wall in the kitchen where they were gathered. "They have two human women, who they have forced into heat, similar to what the Breed females suffer. By studying these women and their physical and hormonal changes, they think this can be done."

"What else have they done to them?" Jacob asked darkly.

Cian shook his head. "There is one at our Labs, where our commander and two of the youngest of our clan is being held. Her screams…"

He went no further.

"Which one? The Dunmore woman or Roberts' get?" Stygian bit out, his voice cold, hard.

"Charity Dunmore. She was brought in several months ago. She was still there when we escaped. We do not believe she will live much longer. Whatever they have done has…affected…her.

"Call Wolfe." He turned to Faith. "I want Aiden and his men here."

"Taken care of." Faith nodded firmly. "I've also put out a call to any Packs close enough to aid us."

"Have they moved the Lab?" He turned back to Cian.

"They will not move it. It is very heavily defended though. Part of the mountain itself. It will not be easy to breach."

"None of them are," Jacob assured him. "We'll begin planning when Wolfe and Aiden arrive. Until then, we prepare. Faith." He turned to her slowly again. "Get ready, you'll be returning to the Pack compound to stay with Hope.

I'll need you there to coordinate the Packs, and to protect the home base."

Chapter Twenty-Seven

❧

Hours later, after a hot meal and a steamy bath, Faith awaited Jacob in their bedroom. She sat in one of the chairs, facing the door. Some of Jacob's plans and preparations would of course have to be revised. His latest bombshell in regards to her would be shelved, or she was going to shoot him herself.

Provide protection for the home base. She snorted rudely. As though any would be needed. Every man, woman and child was trained to protect and uphold the security of the home base. And Hope would never allow Wolfe to leave her behind, this Faith was certain of. Just as she would not be left behind either. It was time her mate learned that they were now a team, no longer separate entities. He was going to have to get over this protection issue he seemed to have problems with.

She didn't have much longer to wait for him. He entered the bedroom quietly, closing the door behind him as he took a deep breath. Faith reached over and flipped on the small lamp, catching a glimpse of his haggard, worried expression before it cleared.

"Everything ironed out?" she asked, keeping her voice carefully bland.

"Wolfe and Aiden will be here in the morning. We will hit the Labs three days from now." His voice was cold. Hard.

"And is he leaving Hope behind?" She tilted her head, watching him curiously as he cast her a fulminating glance.

"You are going to get just as stubborn as our Leader's mate, aren't you?" he bit out furiously.

And he was angry. She could see it pulsing in the air around him, glowing in his pale eyes.

"You know, Jacob, being a mate to you is becoming particularly frustrating. You cannot protect us the way you want to. You can't wrap me in wool and set me on a shelf, only to take me down when you wish to play."

She settled herself back in her chair, watching him with lazy amusement. He was snarling silently, the strong points of his canines gleaming in the dim light of the room.

"Did I say I wished to do this?" He removed his shirt with short, furious movements.

"There are some things you don't have to say, Jacob," she pointed out. "I will not return to the Pack home base. I will fight by your side, or I will leave you. And I promise you, there will be no returning when I do so."

Shock held him rigid. Faith watched his body tense, his eyes widen as he faced her.

"Why?" he whispered roughly. "Why would you do this, Faith, when you know I want only to be assured of your safety?"

She wondered if he was aware of the edge of pain, or fear that ran through his voice. She was, and though it broke her heart to see him come to terms with what he felt was a weakness within himself, she refused to back down.

"Because you can't assure my safety," she told him bleakly. "Because our lives have been a fight from the time of our creation. Because there is no protection for me or for you. I am your mate. I was created by man, but nature made me compatible to only one male. And that male is you. I will not stand alone while you risk yourself, time and again. I won't wait in silence, wondering if or when you will return. I won't do it, Jacob, because I can't bear the separation."

"So you would risk yourself?" he bit out. "Risk any child you would conceive, and my sanity by rushing into danger beside me?"

"The same as you risk yourself, and protection a child of ours would have if you died," she snapped back. "Should I conceive, then I will of course reconsider my options. But until that day arrives, if a separation occurs between us, then consider it permanent."

"I would have no other woman—"

"Do you think this has something to do with jealousy or trust?" she asked him, furious now as he stared at her with dark hunger. "Do you believe I do not trust that you would never touch another woman? I do trust you, Jacob. But my place is at your side, not locked in a compound away from you. I will not do this."

She watched as he plowed fingers through his hair in frustration. His face was lined with pain and bitterness, and his own worries for her safety. A safety he was well aware that he could never ensure.

"I stayed away from you to protect you," he finally bit out roughly. "Six years I denied everything I was, because of my fears for you. You expect me to forget these overnight. To go on, as though the danger to you does not exist."

"No, Jacob, you stayed away from me because you were a coward," she argued fiercely, ignoring his surprised anger at her claim. "Too cowardly to admit that I mattered, and that you needed me as desperately as I needed you. I am growing tired of this, I want your love, as well as your cock. I do not want one without the other."

"And you think you do not have my love?" he yelled out to her, striding to her and jerking her from the chair as he stared down at her, angrier than she had ever seen him. "Do you think I do not know now exactly what you are to me, damn you! I would die, Faith, literally put a bullet in my head were something to happen to you. Do you think for one moment you do not hold everything I am?"

He was yelling at her. Jacob, who never lost control enough to yell unless during the heat of battle, was yelling at her. His face was flushed, his eyes glowing as he snarled down at her.

"Do I have your love, Jacob?" She couldn't stop the hope that filled her, the whisper of dreams that raced through her system.

"My love?" He shook her just slightly in exasperation. "Faith, you are my love. You are my heart. When I saw those bastards so intent on taking you, knowing if they killed me they could take you, I nearly lost my sanity." His voice lowered to a whisper. "I did not even know how much a part of me you were, until I knew I could lose you. Forever, Faith. One careless move, one stray bullet, and I could lose you."

He was trembling, but so was she, Faith realized. Shaking in reaction, and emotional overload. His hand moved to touch her cheek, as though he cherished the feel of her.

"When you were thirteen, your skin began to chafe. Do you remember?" he asked her.

Faith frowned, wondering what this had to do with anything.

"I remember."

"Wolfe and I, we hoarded money that we stole on our missions, waiting for a time that we could escape and establish safety. From my stash, I bargained with a sympathetic guard for the lotion you now use. At the time, it was so expensive that Wolfe and I argued over it continually. But your skin was so soft, Faith. Even as a child, it glowed with satin and purity. I could not bear to see it irritated by our harsh conditions."

Shock held her immobile. She had thought Aiden had provided the lotion. She had never known it had been Jacob.

"The apartment you cherish so dearly," he continued. "I provided for you. The moment I would learn there was something you wanted, something you needed, I ensured you were able to purchase it, no matter the cost. Because I wanted to bring you joy. I wanted you comforted, even though I wasn't there. I did this, Faith, not knowing, never realizing I did it because I loved you past reason. I did it merely for the thought of the joy it would bring you. I would dream of your surprise, your pleasure, when you acquired what you sought. That is all that has kept me going for years. For these things I have fought for."

Faith licked her lips, pain tearing through her at the sacrifices she saw through his eyes. To others, it may seem little enough. But to Jacob and Wolfe, money was security, it was safety for the Pack, it was freedom. To know he had paid for the comforts she so cherished, showed her that Jacob had not forgotten about her as she had always feared. He had instead, been with her the only way he knew how.

"Those comforts brought me more joy than you know, Jacob," she whispered tearfully. "But they do not replace you. I will not live without you again. Not for a moment. We are mates. We fight together, or we don't fight at all. If I return to the compound, then you will return with me, or else we will never be together again."

His lips thinned. As though he had expected his announcement to sway her decision.

"You are so damned stubborn," he growled, throwing his hands up as he stalked away from her. "Why are you this way?"

"And you are trying to manipulate me with the love I feel for you, and your own emotions," she accused him. "Why can't you stop, Jacob? Why can't you admit you can't protect me as you wish? Do you think the job of Liaison is without danger? That I am not forced, on a regular basis, to protect myself?"

He stopped pacing. She watched his body still, the muscles of his back tighten in rejection of her claim.

"It is not the same," he finally growled.

"The barrel of a gun at my head, and Council soldiers hunting me down is somehow safer than being with you?"

She watched the blood drain from his face as her words hit him. His hands came up to wipe at his face, then tunnel through his hair once again. When he faced her, resignation and a strange kind of relief seemed to fill his expression.

"I love you, Faith. But you terrify me," he said deeply, his voice strained. "I will die of a heart seizure due to fear for you, before any Council soldier can get a chance to shoot me."

Faith rose from her chair then and walked to him. He stood alone in the middle of the room, watching her intently, his face drawn and tight, his eyes bright with such a maelstrom of emotions that it made her want to weep.

"All I can think about is holding you. Being wrapped in your heat. And the hell my life would be without you." He wrapped his arms around her, holding her tight, warm against his bare chest. "What would I do now, Faith? Without you."

She heard the dark loneliness, the years of pain and bitterness that he had suffered without her. The same dark years alone that she had suffered as well.

"What would I do without you, Jacob?" She held tightly to him, wanting nothing more than to melt into his skin, to be a part of him for all time, wherever he went, whatever he thought, to be a part of it.

His hands smoothed over her back, creating a heat, a longing unlike any that had come before it. His touch was firm, sure, his hands cherishing rather than possessive, though the dominance of his touch would never change, she knew. And he was dominant. He held her close, despite the lightness of his touch, as his arousal began to flame higher.

Faith tipped her head back to stare up at him, but found her lips caught in a kiss that mingled desperation, hunger and devotion instead. He licked at them, then plunged his tongue inside as she moaned in rising need.

She held onto him tightly, moving her body sensually against his, her nipples rasping against his bare chest, the friction of her cotton T-shirt creating a heat that made her desperate to remove it.

Jacob was ravenous in his demands for her kiss, as well as her touch. His hands gripped the neckline of her shirt, ripping it from her with one strong movement of his hands. Her cunt spasmed at the action, the sensuality of it ripping through her body with the strength of a hurricane.

Then his hands were on her bare back, pulling her forward, pressing her breasts firmly into his chest as he groaned with dark arousal.

"I hunger for you," he whispered as he lifted his lips from hers, his hands working at the snaps of her jeans. "My entire body, Faith, hungers for you."

Faith licked her lips and lowered her eyes.

"Then eat me," she whispered, watching his eyes widen, then narrow.

His hands pushed her jeans down her legs as he lowered his body until he was kneeling before her.

"Red Riding Hood ran from her wolf," he told her with an edge of amusement.

"Red Riding Hood didn't know what the hell she was missing," she groaned, her voice rough and filled with heated longing as his lips caressed her inner thigh, his hands lifting one leg to pull her jeans from it, then the other.

"Perhaps Red Riding Hood knew how dangerous the wolf was," he suggested as his fingers feathered over the damp lips of her cunt.

"She was a scared little wuss," Faith panted, her hands going to his hair as she shifted, opening her thighs wider. "For God's sake, Jacob, touch me before I die."

Chapter Twenty-Eight

ဆ

Faith cried out as Jacob's tongue speared into the heated slit of her pussy. She was wet, slick, primed and ready for him. An inferno of need blazed inside her, melting her, spilling its essence along her thighs to be caught by his greedy lips.

She felt him groan against her clit and nearly climaxed then. Had his hands not been holding her thighs, steadying her, then she knew she would have collapsed into a broken heap on the floor. Damn him, his tongue was like an instrument of pleasurable torture. Hot and firm, stroking her, licking over her then delving into the slick valley for more of her cream as his fingers stroked her buttocks, her thighs, soothing her even as he drove her higher.

She widened her legs, her hands in his hair, her groans pleading, urging him on. Her hips tilted as his hands gripped the flesh of her buttocks, his tongue stroking over her clit, then sucking it gently into the heat of his mouth. He was searing her. Burning her alive with her own desperate needs.

After one last, slow lick to her throbbing clit, he drew back, wafting a heated breath over the pulsing little bud.

"Lay down." He eased her back until they reached the foot of the bed.

Faith sat down, her body trembling in reaction, in arousal, as she then lay back on the firm mattress, trembling in anticipation. Jacob followed her quickly, his head lowering between her thighs as his hands forced them further apart. His tongue plunged hard and deep into her clenching vagina as her cry shattered the dim interior of the room.

Waves of sensation washed over her. They beat at her nerve endings, rushed through her veins, threw her into a whirlwind of such unbelievable heat she feared she would never survive it.

His tongue fucked her with a wet velvet slide of heat and hunger, throwing her quick and hard into a climax that had her body arching tightly, her hands gripping the blanket of the bed in desperation. There was no slow love play, no soft, devoted caresses. He was hard and hungry, and Faith could feel her own control spiraling out of reach.

She could do nothing but cry out his name as he moved over her. No preliminaries, his lips came over hers, his tongue plunging into her mouth as his cock pushed deep and hard inside her empty vagina. Her hands clutched at his back as he set up a fast, driving rhythm that sent ripples of lightning arcing through her body. It was a pleasure that destroyed her, re-created her.

She held him to her, feeling the hard, thick length of his shaft separating her, driving her to a pinnacle of pleasure that threatened to destroy her. Hard, deep thrusts that touched her cervix and triggered a chain reaction of pleasure that wrapped around her entire body.

Faith could only whimper beneath him, his tongue tangled with hers, his hands holding her close as his hips powered harder, thrusting with a strength that carried her along on a wake of such ecstasy she didn't know if she would survive it.

Finally, the need for oxygen had him tearing his lips from hers, his head lowering beside her, his hands gripping her hips as he cried out above her. She felt his cock throb, thicken as a hard jet of fluid prepared her for the coming knot. He groaned as she cried out, thrust deeper, harder, sending her shattering over a precipice of an orgasm that left her screaming breathlessly as his cock swelled thicker, harder, until he was locked deep and tight inside her.

"Faith. God help me, Faith. I love you." The words were torn from him as he shuddered, his seed searing her cunt with yet another brutal climax.

She could only gasp his name. Whisper her love for him. Her body tightened repeatedly as it followed each hard ejaculation of sperm with another, smaller climax that ripped through her body. She was gasping for air. Panting with the unbelievable pleasure that never seemed to dull. Each time he touched her, each time he took her, it seemed only to build, to grow stronger in intensity.

Finally, sweat drenched, lungs heaving for breath, they eased down from the brilliant heights of their release only to collapse weakly on the bed. Jacob fell beside her, pulling her weakly into his arms as she snuggled drowsily against him.

"Pray that the Council does not attack for a while," he whispered. "I would be little help in the battle, Faith. You have taken all my strength."

"Hm, maybe you're just getting old." She smiled against his chest as she felt a hard, male leg move over hers.

He grunted at that. It was clear he disagreed yet found the matter small enough not to argue over.

"I need coffee," she yawned. "Or I will never wake up."

"No." His voice was firm, almost alarmed. "No coffee. No more sex until I rest. You will kill me at this rate. Sleep for pity's sake, Faith. We will rise when Wolfe and Hope arrive and begin our plans. I have a feeling I will need the coffee myself to deal with your stubbornness."

"I'm not going back, Jacob." She hoped he had realized that by now.

"No, Faith," he agreed quietly. "You will not go back, baby. You are mine. And I pray it is truly what you want, because I do not think I can let you go now."

"Did anyone ask you to?" She settled herself more comfortably against him, yawning once again. "If I can't have my coffee, then let me sleep. Then you can love me some more before we go back downstairs."

But would it be possible to love her more? Jacob stared down at her as she relaxed against him. Her weight was light, her breathing deepening in sleep. He would keep her well satisfied physically, he thought in amusement. Her arousal seemed to trigger his whether he liked it or not. But her woman's heart more than confused him. How could she love so deeply, so strong, a man who had turned her away for so long?

There were no answers to his questions. A smile lit his heart. She loved him though, he knew this. And though he wasn't comfortable with the power she held over him, he knew now that it stemmed from his love for her. He, who had not believed, and yet always had loved this tiny spitfire of a woman.

Jacob pulled the sheet over their cooling bodies, wondering how they had managed to make such a mess of the blankets. He sighed deeply and closed his eyes as his arms tightened around her.

"My Faith," he whispered as he relaxed then, more at peace than he had ever been. "I love you, my Faith."

Epilogue

∽

"This is Charity Dunmore." Cian laid the picture in front of Aiden then stood back respectfully. "She has been held for months at the Labs. We aren't certain of the experiments they've been doing on her, but Keegan, our leader, could sense her weakness even before she aided in our escape. She could be dead by now."

Aiden picked up the small picture. He remembered Charity. She had been quiet, always watching, doing her job within the Labs and speaking very little. He had felt at one time, that she could have been sympathetic to the breeds. He had revised his opinion in that last month before their escape.

"How did she aid your escape?" he asked quietly.

"It was she who triggered the release mechanism on a dome that led into our training facility, at a time that we were not chained. She had warned Keegan she would do so. Had it not been for the younger ones being caught within the automatic nets, then we would have all escaped."

She was a slender woman, not frail or tiny, well-built with full breasts and big blue eyes. Her ash blonde hair was caught in a thick bun at the nape of her neck, so there was no telling how long it was. Aiden would guess though, that it came close to falling to her hips.

"What shape was she in last you saw her?" he asked Cian, trying to ignore the demon pulse of attraction that filled him.

Whether she had helped them or not, she was still the enemy. She had participated in the Lab experiments he had been in, and if her masters had turned on her, then that was too bad for her, but still no more than she deserved. He refused to feel any sympathy for her.

"She was very weak. Keegan is quite concerned for her. Whatever they have done to her is taxing her, not just physically, but mentally. He insists we rescue her first."

Aiden looked up at the proud Breed slowly.

"Have your Leader wait until he's present to issue orders," he growled. "This link you have with him is all well and good. But I do as I see fit, not what one who is still imprisoned would order me to do."

"She has aided us, Aiden," Cian argued. "For years she has done so, trying all she knows to help us escape."

"And yet she did her job, did she not?" Aiden bit out. "She ran their tests, took your blood and your semen, and pumped you full of drugs to replace it. Just as they ordered."

"She fouled readers, misread blood diagnoses, and risked her own life for us as our psychic powers began to emerge." Cian leaned closer, his hand clapping on the table in anger as he faced Aiden. "I do not know her reasons for it, and I do not care. It is my Leader's orders to me, that the girl be rescued and cared for. Do as you will, but my men and I will go for the girl."

"What is it about this girl that inspires such loyalty?" he asked them mildly, ignoring the vulnerability he glimpsed in the picture-caught blue eyes.

Soft cheekbones, pouty lips, thickly lashed, shadowed eyes.

"She has been loyal to us." Cian straightened up once again. "We will be no less to her."

"Have you fucked her?" He ignored the primitive flare of fury at the thought.

Disgust and fury warred on Cian's aristocratic features.

"None of my clan have touched her, Wolf Breed. She is not ours to mate, but another's." Fury welled in his voice, then in his expression.

Aiden saw immediately that the Winged Breed had said more than he intended to. It intrigued him, this psychic link this new Breed had established between one another. But even more importantly, it seemed their Leader's powers were even more advanced.

Aiden leaned back in his chair, ignoring the interest they were generating from the other Wolf Breeds gathered within the hacienda kitchen.

"Whose mate is she then, Cian?" he asked with mocking amusement. "What could be so important about this one female, that you would risk the rescue of your people for her?"

Cian crossed his arms over his chest, staring down at Aiden coldly.

"I had heard the Wolf Breeds had more honor and justice than the Council did. What is so unimportant about this woman, that you deem her not worthy of rescue?"

Aiden looked at the picture again. He remembered a time when he would have felt sympathy for her. When he would have found warmth in his heart for the innocence he had glimpsed in her eyes six years before.

She had been young then. New to the Labs. So quiet she was nearly a shadow within the compound. Always watching, always waiting it seemed. He had felt a measure of sympathy for her, for a while. Until she had proved her cold heart. Proved she was no more than a mindless follower of the Council who paid her.

"What I believe doesn't matter," he finally said, his voice hard as he pushed the anger back down. Down, where it no longer mattered, no longer had the power to enrage him. "You are asking me to risk damned near every Enforcer our race possesses, and several of our Packs, for a full human who is no more than a Council whore. I will know why, or I will kill her myself to save anyone else the trouble."

Cian tensed, his golden eyes icing over, fury reflected in the hard shudder of his wings.

"You wish to know why this one woman is so important, wolf." He bit out. "You wish to know why she must live, even at the sacrifice of my own Leader, and the young of our Flock. Shall I tell you why, you mongrel pup? Because this woman is a mate to one who knows only darkness, only fury. A mate to one who sees only what the Council shows him, and only his own cold soul. A monster. One who would hurt and maim and become no more than a rabid creature without her. That woman." His finger pointed harshly to the soft image displayed in the picture. "That woman is Charity. She is all that is soft, all that is giving. She is your mate, you scrappy excuse for less than a hound. A woman too soft, too kind for the likes of a bastard such as yourself."

Shock rushed over Aiden's body, though he held it carefully in check, knew no hint of his feelings shown in his expression. At once, a fist punch of sensation plowed into his loins. He remembered her hands, so silken and warm on his cock. Ignoring his harsh orders, silent in the face of his curses as she milked his seed from his body. Giving to the bastard scientists the seed they needed for yet another experiment.

Only Aiden had possessed the power to fight their drugs, their aphrodisiacs, and their threats. For years, they had believed him impotent. Until the touch of her hands. Until her soft tongue licking the flared head of his cock, sucking it into her mouth with a soft, whispered apology.

It was then he hated her. Hated her affect over him. Hated her innocent look, her blue-eyed charm, and her tempting body. And he had never forgotten that hatred. She had obeyed their orders when she could have walked away. Had volunteered, volunteered to bring him to arousal rather than allowing one of the whores they hired from nearby towns to try. She had revealed his weakness, even to himself, and he hated her for it.

"That's too bad." He finally shrugged, keeping his voice hard, unrelenting. "If she's my mate, then it's my decision…"

Cian laughed. Amusement flashed in his golden eyes, dispelling his fury in the blink of an eye.

"Fight, wolf," he said softly. "You may fight her and your own nature all you wish. But know this. The first child born of your pack will come from that woman's body. Without her, without the secret she carries, your race will slowly die out, your women will expire from their own arousals, and your men will find no hope, no recourse within their lives. Save her, or be responsible for the death and destruction of all you hold dear."

Why an electronic book?

We live in the Information Age—an exciting time in the history of human civilization, in which technology rules supreme and continues to progress in leaps and bounds every minute of every day. For a multitude of reasons, more and more avid literary fans are opting to purchase e-books instead of paper books. The question from those not yet initiated into the world of electronic reading is simply: *Why?*

1. ***Price.*** An electronic title at Ellora's Cave Publishing and Cerridwen Press runs anywhere from 40% to 75% less than the cover price of the exact same title in paperback format. Why? Basic mathematics and cost. It is less expensive to publish an e-book (no paper and printing, no warehousing and shipping) than it is to publish a paperback, so the savings are passed along to the consumer.

2. ***Space.*** Running out of room in your house for your books? That is one worry you will never have with electronic books. For a low one-time cost, you can purchase a handheld device specifically designed for e-reading. Many e-readers have large, convenient screens for viewing. Better yet, hundreds of titles can be stored within your new library—on a single microchip. There are a variety of e-readers from different manufacturers. You can also read e-books on your PC or laptop computer. (Please note that Ellora's Cave does not endorse any specific brands. You can check our websites at www.ellorascave.com or www.cerridwenpress.com for information we make available to new consumers.)

3. *Mobility.* Because your new e-library consists of only a microchip within a small, easily transportable e-reader, your entire cache of books can be taken with you wherever you go.

4. *Personal Viewing Preferences.* Are the words you are currently reading too small? Too large? Too... ANNOYING? Paperback books cannot be modified according to personal preferences, but e-books can.

5. *Instant Gratification.* Is it the middle of the night and all the bookstores near you are closed? Are you tired of waiting days, sometimes weeks, for bookstores to ship the novels you bought? Ellora's Cave Publishing sells instantaneous downloads twenty-four hours a day, seven days a week, every day of the year. Our webstore is never closed. Our e-book delivery system is 100% automated, meaning your order is filled as soon as you pay for it.

Those are a few of the top reasons why electronic books are replacing paperbacks for many avid readers.

As always, Ellora's Cave and Cerridwen Press welcome your questions and comments. We invite you to email us at Comments@ellorascave.com or write to us directly at Ellora's Cave Publishing Inc., 1056 Home Avenue, Akron, OH 44310-3502.

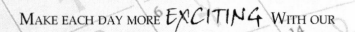

MAKE EACH DAY MORE *EXCITING* WITH OUR

ELLORA'S
CAVEMEN
CALENDAR

✞ WWW.ELLORASCAVE.COM ✞

erridwen, the Celtic Goddess of wisdom, was the muse who brought inspiration to storytellers and those in the creative arts. Cerridwen Press encompasses the best and most innovative stories in all genres of today's fiction. Visit our site and discover the newest titles by talented authors who still get inspired - much like the ancient storytellers did, once upon a time.

CERRIDWEN PRESS

www.cerridwenpress.com